FATE'S ARROW
RISING WAVE

MICHELLE DIENER

THE RISING WAVE SERIES

ABOUT FATE'S ARROW

A dark force at work

Ava and Luc are asked to head north to Skäddar, a move neces-sary to save the alliance they have created with the mountainous country. Something terrible is killing Skäddar villagers and leaving messages behind with their bodies that the deaths will continue as long as the Skäddar are in alliance with the Rising Wave. If Ava and Luc can't convince the Skäddar Collective to stand up for their new friendship in the face of the tragedy, they will lose a vital ally in the region.

A dark room to cage a prisoner

Massi is deep inside Grimwalt, successful in her mission to find Ava's incarcerated friends, Tomas and Velda. But the two are not being held alone. Massi finds many others being kept with them, as well as a prisoner kept in darkness whose power shines so bright, Massi can't imagine how the Speaker imprisoned him to begin with.

A dark cloud that needs to be dispelled

Duncan has been held far from his home on the Skäddar border, and he takes the chance of escape that Massi gives him with both hands. When he and Massi have to part ways, though—Massi to get Ava's friends to safety, him to return to the forest he was ripped away from—he can't deny his attraction to the fierce archer, or his reluctance to let her go.

But when he gets home, and finds the power of his domain is being used to commit terrible atrocities, he'll need Massi's help, and those of her friends, to rid Grimwalt of the blight that is trying to take hold.

Fate's Arrow is the third book in the Rising Wave series. The series begins with The Rising Wave, a prequel novella, and continues with The Turncoat King and The Threadbare Queen.

CHAPTER 1

Duncan lay on stone.

Damp, dead stone.

He had not managed to find a way to escape it. Yet.

Not that he'd managed to escape even before he'd been chained to a stone floor.

But he had been close, and they had known it.

They had moved him here a month ago.

Maybe.

Time had begun to lose meaning.

He brushed his fingertips over the cold, hard surface. There was nothing here for his magic to latch onto.

At least before, even if he knew it would do him no good, he could feel the spark inside him.

But the rock was dead.

There was, however, one single upside to the move.

Now he was in the middle of the prison. Surrounded by the other inmates, where before he'd been kept on his own, separate and isolated in his own hut.

The hut had been in poor condition, and had been set near the fortress wall, with the forest right up against it on the other side. It had been a sweet madness to have the keys to his escape so close, and maybe he had gone a little crazy at the end, trying ways to escape that he would never have considered had he not been desperate.

They had decided he might just manage to do it.

So now the whisper of the trees and the smell of growing things was gone, replaced by the murmurs and weeping and conversations of his fellow prisoners, deep in the heart of the prison.

He had missed the sound of human voices, he realized.

He hadn't been around people much since he had come fully into his power at seventeen, but the few encounters he had day to day had been more important to him than he'd realized, until they were taken away.

Some of those trapped with him wondered about him. About why he was chained up like a rabid wolf in the central tower.

Others saw his treatment as just more of the same cruelty that had put them in this place along with him.

Some tried to speak to him, and he welcomed the contact.

It humbled him to realize that he was the same as everyone else.

Despite what he'd told himself, he needed contact, too. Needed to find connections.

And he suspected most of those around him were like-minded citizens of Grimwalt. Some might even be as magical as he was.

This was the Speaker's way of hiding his dirty secrets.

The way more and more people had arrived in the time he'd been chained here, shocked and shaking with fear and, sometimes, anger, at their unjust imprisonment, those secrets had to be getting harder and harder to keep.

A shoe scraped against the stone of the floor, and Duncan went still.

"Dunc." Tomas kept his voice to a loud whisper.

Duncan rolled up into a crouch.

"Catch." Tomas tossed him a piece of bread, and even though the light from the torch far down the passage barely reached his cell, Duncan snatched it from the air out of instinct.

He glanced at it, then looked up at the old man on the other side of his bars, waited for an explanation.

"Velda and I don't need as much to eat. Not like you. Never seen a man so tall and broad get so thin."

Velda was around the same age as Tomas, late sixties, Duncan guessed, and of everyone here, they were his closest allies.

They knew a spell caster, he guessed. Knew and loved them.

A child, he wondered? A grandchild?

This was the first time they had given him their food, though.

There was little enough to eat here as it was. And no one cared that much about his wellbeing, even if they sympathized with him.

Even if they were spell casters themselves.

And if they were, they wouldn't out themselves if they could help it.

Admitting to magical prowess had a bad habit of making people disappear in the last few years, he gathered from the whispers.

And wasn't he the living proof of that?

Duncan studied the old man. "What they feed us here isn't enough to satisfy anyone, Tomas." He held it back out to his friend.

"That may be true," Tomas shrugged shoulders Duncan guessed had not been so boney before he arrived at this hidden compound deep in the Grimwalt forest. "But you're looking too thin. You're fading and if anyone needs their strength to get us all out of here, it's you."

Duncan picked up the chain that anchored him to the stone and moved closer, careful not to let it clink.

When he reached the furthest it would let him get to the bars that were set ceiling to floor, he sat down cross legged.

"Why do you think I'll be the one to get everyone out?"

"You know why."

"Who's there?" The guard's call had Tomas melting back into the darkness.

Duncan knew Tomas had found a way to get the door to his cell open, although that only gave him access to the tower, not to an escape route out into the yard. And even if he had been able to manage that, there were still the walls or the front gate to negotiate.

When the guard arrived at his cell, torch lifted to light the way, Duncan was back in the middle of the stone floor, curled up, eyes closed.

The light played over him for a bit, lighting orange and purple behind his eyelids.

Then he heard the guard walk away, and counted the steps back to his watch station.

Thirty six.

When darkness settled back around him, and the cold of the floor clutched at him like a bitter lover, he lifted the bread to his mouth and began to chew.

He must look bad for Tomas and Velda to give up their food for him.

It was his fault he was so thin, though. Not the guards.

He was using up too much magic trying to find a way out of the stone.

And there *was* no way out.

As he shivered himself to sleep, he decided to start saving his strength, just as Tomas said.

If there ever came a day they could escape, he would not be let down by a body too thin and starved to meet the challenge.

CHAPTER 2

Massi found the dogs in the fifth week of her mission.

She had had difficulty believing Ava's story about how she had turned them from a hunting pack for the Kassian military into her faithful companions, and even more difficulty believing she would find them after Ava had been away from them for so long.

But after she had made it through the mountains, done what business she needed to do in Grimwalt's capital, Taunen, and then headed to Ava's family's estate to pick up the trail, they were actually relatively easy to find.

People tended to notice a large pack of hunting dogs wandering around.

She had not even had to ask around about them.

Grimwalt taverns were cozy, warm, and a hotbed of gossip.

It seemed everyone on the route she had taken from Ava's grandmother's estate to the north had a story about seeing the dogs. The theories about what had happened to Tomas, the groundsman on the Yngstra estate, had been just as interesting.

Ava believed he and her grandmother's housekeeper, Velda, had been imprisoned because of their connection to Ava, and it was clear they had disappeared.

The dogs were blamed, in some versions of the story.

Ava herself was a suspect, as well.

Massi paid attention when that version came up. Looking long and hard at who might be spreading that untruth.

Anyone pointing the finger at Ava was most likely an agent of the Speaker of the Court, Grimwalt's leader. Or foolish dupes who had been fed the story by agents.

After she reached the small town of Waldrand, the dog story took on a more immediate tone.

Massi stocked up on supplies, listened carefully to people who'd seen the pack first hand, and then she walked into the woods and headed north west.

There were definite nerves in the town around the dogs.

Some of those nerves were because a pack of wild dogs could be considered dangerous, but she suspected someone was fear mongering. The dogs hadn't harmed anyone so far, but someone wanted them to be seen as a problem to be solved.

If she were to guess, it was because they were bringing attention to the area.

Someone didn't want anyone looking in that part of the forest.

Someone had something to hide.

She'd overheard many a conversation about how the mayor of Waldrand had petitioned the army to send a small unit to deal with the dogs.

She realized she had to find them first.

And so she followed the route the last person babbling about seeing them had gone, and here they were.

The first one was standing on the path in a shaft of light, its head turned toward her, a low growl coming from its throat.

Massi pulled the piece of fabric Ava had given her out of her pocket and walked slowly toward it, the scrap held out in front of her.

The dog was big, a breed with a large head and a stocky, muscular body.

The growl deepened as she approached.

She slowed even more but kept moving forward, fabric outstretched.

It suddenly charged her, lips curled back, incisors visible. She caught a glimpse from the corner of her eye of the rest of the pack moving on either side of her, through the trees.

She held her ground.

Ava hadn't been wrong yet, much though Massi hated the need for her magic.

The dog half leaped toward her, and she shoved the fabric at its nose. It dropped to the ground, took a cautious sniff and gave a yip, its whole body transforming from stalking predator to happy puppy.

It jumped up suddenly, but instead of grabbing her throat, it licked her face, and Massi found herself rubbing it behind the ear before she was surrounded by all twenty of the pack, a mixture of hunting and tracking dogs of various sizes.

They all sniffed the fabric, and one of them sat back and lifted its head to the sky, gave a sad howl.

"You wish I was Ava, don't you?" she asked it, rubbing its head.

The dogs pressed against her, some shivering in excitement.

A feeling of icy fear and awe settled on her, chilling her through.

Ava was controlling this pack, and she wasn't even here. She was hundreds of miles away, in Fernwell. And she was doing it with nothing more than a scrap of fabric with a few stitches worked into it.

Massi rubbed the collar of the shirt she wore, which had some of Ava's magic woven into it, too.

She once again fought the suspicion that Luc's love for Ava might be a manipulated thing, fought the deep-seated fear of what Ava was capable of.

She had been a victim of spell casting herself, and she still woke in the night sometimes, gasping, fearful that she was being made to do something against her will. A loss of her agency.

She had almost killed Ava. Had worked against her for weeks. All because she had been spelled.

Seeing a big pack of dogs come meekly to heel did not help alleviate her fear.

But Ava had never harmed her.

She had saved Luc, and the Rising Wave, again and again.

And yet . . .

Massi forced herself to stand, pulling her bow and arrows, her pack firmly over her shoulder.

"Why don't you show me what is so interesting in these woods?" she told the dogs.

CHAPTER 3

Well, there definitely *was* something in the forest that whoever controlled these parts wanted to keep hidden.

Massi let the dogs jostle for a place close to her as she crouched near the wall, carefully studying the set-up.

A central tower made of stone rose up above lower, thatched roofs. It was moss covered and crumbling in places——a single, tall gray edifice, perhaps a lookout, or a place for a forest warden to live long ago.

The roof was slate and the only windows were thin slits, just right for archers.

She touched her own bow in appreciation.

The wooden buildings built around it, some attached to it, others standing alone, were made from timber sourced from the trees around the tower.

Massi had seen evidence of where the old pines had been cut down and sawed all around this place.

A wall surrounded it, a circle of half-trunks, thick and impenetrable.

And surprisingly for the remoteness of the location, there seemed to be plenty going on inside.

She could hear shouting, talking.

Gartan, the diplomat who Ava had suggested Massi see first after she snuck over the border into Grimwalt, had told her, hands trembling, that there was a place people were being threatened with if you complained about the Speaker. A lonely outpost where no one would find you, and from which there was no return.

He had the vague notion it was in the north west, in the deepest part of the forest there, and it looked like he was right.

Or he had been setting a trap for her.

She had thought not, but possible betrayal was always part of her planning.

Dak was constantly urging her to be more positive, to trust a little more, but the one time she had done that recently, she had been enspelled.

Luc had had to free her, and she had fought him all the way.

She shook her head.

She was how she was. A product of years spent imprisoned in a Chosen camp. A product of the subsequent war for her and her fellow Cervantes' freedom.

Her suspicious nature had kept her alive and saved more than one friend.

She was good with it.

The dog leaning against her pressed a little closer and whined, and Massi ran a hand down her back, feeling her ribs.

The dogs were skinny. Too thin and too ragged.

"Come on." She stood, moving through the trees to lead the pack away from the walls, although from the look of the trails they'd made, they had been here many times.

Looking for Tomas and Velda?

She had a feeling the answer to that was yes.

She had spotted a small herd of deer a little way to the east, and she kept up wind, made the dogs lie down beside her, even though they were shaking with the need to hunt, and lifted an arrow from her quiver.

She leaned against a tree, sighted a young buck, and shot.

Her arrow went straight into its eye.

The rest of the herd ran, back legs kicking up in panic, and then she jogged forward, the dogs at her heels.

It was a clean kill, and she used her knife to open the deer's belly and stood back, allowing the dogs to feast.

She had not missed what she aimed for, not once, since Ava gave her the shirt.

Luc had always called her his arrow. The archer in the Wave who never missed. But since Ava worked her magic, Massi had begun to try harder and harder shots.

She had always been good.

Excellent, actually.

A true Cervantes in her ability to fight.

But now, she was a step beyond good.

Just like Luc was now a step beyond, himself.

He was close to unbeatable since Ava.

Although the stitching Ava had given him was into his very skin, not on a piece of clothing.

Massi rubbed her collar again, and sighed.

Face it, she told herself, *you'd like to be this good on your own merits.* But she would still use what Ava had given her.

She'd be a fool not to.

The new queen of Kassia had been weakened by the terrible treatment she'd suffered during her abduction by the Speaker, and she had not had much time to work magic into Massi's clothes before they parted ways near the Grimwalt border.

She and Luc had been needed back in Fernwell before her absence was used against them by their enemies, but even so, with her power diminished and in a hurry, Ava had managed to make Massi's aim extraordinary.

She had given Massi what help she could, and while she'd apologized more than once for her weakness, Massi had yet to see evidence of it.

It was late afternoon by the time she brought the deer down, and she let the dogs eat their fill and then sleep it off, making a small fire and roasting strips of meat over it for herself.

The dogs had obeyed her before, but now a few flopped beside her, adoration in their eyes, and she found herself rubbing ears and scratching chins.

She had never had a pet, or even a working dog, before. She was ill-equipped to lead a pack such as this, but again, Ava had eased the way for her.

She had thought Ava's worry about the pack strange when they had spoken the last time, just before Massi had left for Grimwalt and Ava and Luc had raced at full speed for Fernwell.

Ava had been almost as worried about the dogs as she was about Velda and Tomas, feeling guilty for taking them away from their kennels and thrusting them into danger.

Now she had met the dogs, Ava's worry made Massi like her more.

When the sun had just set, she roused herself from a light doze and stood.

Some of the dogs got sleepily to their feet, but she shushed them back down. Ordered them to stay and rest.

Then she moved back toward the strange fortress.

Better to go without the dogs, and in the twilight.

She stopped when she was in sight of the wall, moving carefully in the deeper shadows thrown by massive trees.

She approached the wall cautiously, moving carefully around it, looking for a way in.

The wooden barricade was unbroken, solid, but there was a tree growing close to it on one end, and the thatch of a small hut built up against it on the other side.

She climbed the tree, looking for a way over.

When she reached the branch closest to the wall, she blinked, trying to work out if her eyes were seeing properly in the tricky light of sunset.

It looked as if two slender branches below the thick branch she was perched on had grown parallel to each other, arching up and then over the fence, and smaller branches had grown between the two, forming the steps of a ladder.

She ran a cautious hand over the top of it, tugged experimentally on the uppermost step.

It held, firm and sturdy.

Someone cleared their throat just below her, and she stilled.

The faint whiff of smoke floated over on the breeze.

"Turned this into a guard hut, have you?" Someone spoke in a rasping voice.

"No one else is using it since they moved the freak out. And we needed a place to boil the kettle."

There was silence at that.

"Anyone else also get called in to talk to the Boss Man today?" a new voice spoke up. "Anyone ever seen him before this morning?"

So there were at least three of them.

"It wasn't just you," the Kettle Boiler said. "And aye, I've seen him before. Little over two months back, he came to check up on us."

"Do you think we'll die here?" Number Three asked.

"What?" Raspy Voice sounded shocked.

"He threatened me with death if I tell anyone about this place, because he heard I'm the one who usually goes into Waldrand to get the supplies."

"What of it? He wants to keep this place secret."

"What of it?" Number Three gave a dry laugh. "Did you not hear me say he threatened to kill me?"

"That's just talk, isn't it?" Kettle Boiler asked.

"Didn't sound like talk to me. He has those eyes, you know . . .?"

"It's simple. Just don't talk about what happens here, and you're safe." Raspy Voice sounded impatient.

"But what happens if we want to leave? I was planning to go

before midwinter, because my mother fell ill before I came here and I need to check on her. The moment we're in Waldrand or beyond, he and the warden lose control of us." Number Three clearly didn't care to let this go.

"People leave," Kettle Boiler scoffed.

"Who?" Number Three asked. "Not since I've got here, they haven't."

"Careful what you say," Raspy Voice said, his own voice very low. "Not saying I don't agree you have a point, but caution is advised."

"Given who I've seen dragged in here, that goes without saying." Kettle Boiler sounded quieter, too.

"We'll be here until we go out in a box. Mark my words." Number Three sounded like he was scuffing his boots on fallen leaves.

The sound of a kettle boiling reached her, and then the pouring of water, the slurp of drinking. Conversation had stopped and when the men moved off, they were just as silent.

Massi waited a few minutes and then moved forward on the branch, trying to work out how the tree ladder had gone unnoticed.

She looked over the wall and saw two other ladders lying on the ground, the top sawed off of both of them.

It looked as if they were growing shoots where they had fallen, as if they had rooted where they had been tossed down.

A chill ran through her.

This was spell work.

Someone had come before her, and tried to gain entry.

And the guards below had seen and cut the ladder down. Twice.

And yet, here was one again.

She turned, surveying the forest behind her, and wondered who else was out there, like her, looking for a way in.

She felt no eyes on her, and eventually she turned back, looking critically at the ladder again.

Whoever was working this enchantment had gotten sneakier the third time around.

She could see now where the first two ladders had grown out of the trunk, the stubs where they had been hacked off were obvious when you knew what to look for.

This third ladder had grown directly behind the hut, pushing through the thatch eaves, hugging the prison wall closely.

Massi leaned over, parting the dry silver-gray of the grasses covering the roof. The thatch extended beyond the hut's back wall to the outer wall, creating a protected, covered space between the two structures, open on the sides, but shadowed and gloomy within.

The ladder would be difficult to see, even during the day.

It hadn't finished growing, now she could see the rest of it, but it was close enough to the ground that she could still use it.

She decided to wait a little, see if there was a pattern to the guard duty she could pick up, and then, use this magic to gain access.

She rubbed her collar.

She was already using Ava's. What did a little more hurt?

CHAPTER 4

"The Boss Man wants to talk to you."

Duncan finally looked up at the guard who had been leaning against the bars of his cell for a few minutes in silence.

It was a petty game they played, staring at him like he was a caged beast, but they had never told him someone wanted to speak to him before.

"The Boss Man?" It was a ludicrous name, and he made no effort to hide his amusement.

"We don't know his name," the guard shrugged, "so that's what we call him."

"To his face?" Duncan asked.

The guard gave a sneer. "No."

"And he wants to speak to me?"

"That's right. Go sit in the middle of the cell." The guard took out a key from his pocket and waited while Duncan complied.

He had not been allowed to leave his cell since he'd been moved here, and he was almost desperate to feel a fresh breeze on his face, to smell the forest.

He caused no trouble as the guard unchained him from the

metal eye set into the floor and looped a shorter chain around his wrists, through a ring and down to wrap around his ankles, giving him just enough length to shuffle forward.

A second guard stepped up when he was out of the cell, and he was sandwiched between them as he was led out of the tower, down the narrow, wood-walled passage, and into the prison warden's office.

Duncan's gaoler, Warden Farnt, stood in a deferential pose beside his own desk, which was currently occupied by a tall stranger with a dark beard. He was dressed in traveling clothes, hardwearing but well-made, and his eyes glittered in the waning light of the day.

Duncan had to turn his head away from the brightness of it, his eyes watering, unused to even this mild light after three weeks in the gloom of his cell.

"Duncan Erdo." The man's voice was raspy but polite. "Warden Farnt says you arrived here just under two months ago, and have caused some trouble in that time."

Duncan said nothing to that. It was illogical to capture someone and then expect them to accept it without struggle.

One look at the man behind the desk and Duncan could tell he would fight until there was no breath left in his body if he were the one taken.

The chiding tone from him on this point was ridiculous.

The man's lips twisted, and Duncan couldn't work out if it was in irritation or humor.

Warden Farnt made a movement. Duncan caught it out of the corner of his eye, but the stranger shook his head sharply and the big gaoler subsided in place.

"You don't look good, Duncan." The man's voice sharpened, as if he was displeased. "I have to say, I wasn't consulted on your capture, and I didn't realize you were here until recently.

Duncan finally risked looking back at the window. The light still hurt a little, but less than it had.

He could see the roofs of the outer buildings and the pink of an early dusk sky, but no trees. He must be close to the very center of the fortress because he knew the trees were there. He could feel them.

"What are you doing to him, to have him this ill?" The Boss Man asked Farnt.

"Nothing." Farnt sounded put upon. "We keep him inside. And while maybe it would be better for him to see the sun occasionally, I can't risk it. If we let him outside, he starts his nonsense again. We can't promise he won't escape any other way than keeping him locked in the stone tower." He waved a hand. "Stone is the only thing that's worked. That's how they brought him to us, in a stone-lined cart, and it gave us an idea of how to hold him when he nearly escaped."

The Boss Man sighed. Got to his feet. "I'll be blunt, Duncan. Apparently, there is some plan for you to be useful. Your deterioration is not beneficial. You clearly need some exercise, some light."

Farnt made a noise of protest, but the Boss Man ignored him.

"That sounds good to me." Duncan's comment was automatic, an unthinking response, while his brain was stuck on the word *useful*. Useful to whom, he wondered?

"We can't do it." Farnt was shaking his head. "The guards can't trust him. Can't hold him."

"Is that so?" the Boss Man asked. "They're afraid of him, too, from the looks of it."

The guards drew themselves up in offense, but Duncan knew he spoke the truth.

The guards were terrified of him.

"I've watched them since they brought him in. They're afraid enough that I'm concerned they might just kill him if he so much as looks at them wrong."

There was a moment of silence, and Duncan realized he no longer cared about what the guards might do.

Had he given up?

He didn't think so, but he also could only be afraid of the consequences for so long. Perpetual fear was not possible, and it had been replaced with a sense of fatalism.

What would be, would be.

"You say the escape attempts all stopped when you put him in the stone tower?" The Boss Man spoke eventually.

Farnt nodded. "But as I said in my report, he's been . . . deteriorating . . . since we moved him."

Duncan wondered with a jolt what he must look like, that even the sick asshole who ran this place had a note of pity in his voice at Duncan's condition. Tomas and Velda giving him their food was one thing, this was another.

He looked down at his hands, really looked at them, and realized they were almost skeletal.

The Boss Man sank back down behind the desk. "Your report's why I'm here. The Speaker needs him in at least useable shape, and . . ." He tilted his head, shook it a little. "He does not look useable right now."

Duncan kept his face blank, but beneath it he felt the stirrings of fear again. He thought he was done with it, but this was a specific threat.

They had captured him, taken him out of his forest and held him prisoner, but until now, they hadn't seemed to have any real interest in him beyond making sure he was in their power.

Now fear rose up again as he realized he was mistaken. They did want him for something.

And whatever it was they wanted was something he was not prepared to do.

He would never help them.

"What can we do about it?" Farnt sounded nervous, likely unsure if the Boss Man appreciated the trouble Duncan could——and had——caused.

The Boss Man bent down, lifted a bag that had obviously been set at his feet, and put it on the table.

"Lucky for you, the reason I haven't been able to visit for a while is because I was retrieving this." He handled the bag carefully, as if he was afraid of what was in it.

"What is it?" Farnt may be mendacious and cruel, but he was no fool, Duncan noted. He had taken a big step back.

"I had to chase someone almost to the Cattha border to get this back." The man nudged the bag. "It took me way too long. I only just got back to Taunen four days ago, and saw your report. I decided it might as well be put to good use, given the trouble I had retrieving it."

"Someone stole something from you?" Farnt's voice was slightly breathless, as if he couldn't believe it.

The Boss Man sent him a sour look. "A freelance agent failed in her mission, and rather than face up to it, decided to head home instead, along with the tools I'd given her and her partner to do the job." He stood up. "Let's see if it'll solve our problem here, shall we?"

He set a second pack on the table and drew out a pair of thick leather gloves from it, slid them on.

He then carefully pulled a rope out of the first bag, holding it away from him with arms outstretched to keep it from touching his body. Then he moved around the desk, toward Duncan, who turned to face him.

"Stay still! Face forward."

The Boss Man's words chilled him. There was actual fear in his tone.

Whatever he was holding was dangerous.

Duncan turned back to face the desk, holding very still as he tried to remember any legend he'd ever heard about ropes.

That this was a spell-worked rope was clear.

The Boss Man wouldn't be wearing gloves, wouldn't be so afraid of what he was holding, if it wasn't.

Arms came around him and his rough cotton shirt was lifted up, the rope looped around his waist. It went around twice, and the Boss Man made a sound, as if he was surprised.

"I thought it was longer," he said under his breath. "If that Sirna cut a piece off . . ."

There was a rage there that Duncan considered with interest. It was always good to understand the strong emotions of your enemies.

"What does it do?" Farnt asked, and Duncan could hear the nerves in his voice.

"You need to listen to me now," the Boss Man said. "Because some have misused this item in the past, and that has made me very, very unhappy, do you understand?"

"Yes, sir."

Farnt called him sir with no hesitation. This was Farnt's boss, no question.

"This is a rope that saps energy and strength from whoever touches it."

As he spoke, he tightened the rope and tied it off. Duncan could feel the bumps of the braid pressing against his skin.

And he felt . . . good.

But he was supposed to feel bad, he realized.

So he flinched away from the Boss Man.

"You can put it on Duncan here and let him out into the yard for some exercise and sun, and he will not be able to use his magic, he will not have the strength to run. But too much exposure to the rope and it will sap everything out of him. Someone once kept it on a prisoner too long, and I could see through her. As if she was a pane of glass."

The Boss Man breathed in through his nose, as if remembering the incident. "She became useless for what I wanted of her. That cannot be allowed to happen to Duncan, am I clear?"

"Yes, sir. So just when he's out in the yard? For how long?"

"Start with an hour. See how it goes."

Duncan focused back on the rope. It was as if the magic woven into it was bolstering him——giving, not taking.

It made him nervous that the Boss Man was so sure it was harmful. This was not someone who made mistakes, but for now, Duncan was happy to play along.

He bowed his head.

"So we're not to touch it?" one of the guards who'd brought him in asked.

"I'd recommend against it. Touch it and it'll take from you. It's not picky." The Boss Man stepped back. "Lead him outside and see how it works."

Duncan could feel the Boss Man's eyes on him, assessing, and he shuffled just a little slower as he was led out of the room.

The route out of the office to the courtyard was short, and Duncan was the only prisoner outside.

This time of the day, the others would be eating in the narrow mess hall on the opposite side of the open area.

He had never been inside the mess, but he'd seen it through the window when he'd been held in the hut and the guards had brought his food from there each day.

The ground was grassy, with clear trails walked into it——paths of frustration and habit that the prisoners had created.

Duncan ignored them, walking to where the grass was green and springy and dropped to his knees. He put his hands out, so he could feel the scratch and tickle of the blades under his palms.

He closed his eyes, head bowed.

"What if this does more harm than good?" Farnt sounded jumpy, like he knew exactly who would be in trouble if that happened.

"Like I said, keep an eye on it. I have to return to Taunen at dawn tomorrow, and I'm spending the night in Waldrand. I'll have to trust you to work it out for yourself. He has to be in good condition for when the Speaker needs him, but I understand you can't have him trying to escape. This will let him outside, which I think he needs, but it hobbles him, too. If he's no good to us, the Speaker will be very displeased. Very."

"And the rope? Where do I keep it?"

"Somewhere safe." The Boss Man's voice went down a pitch. "I would not like to have to chase it down again. So you put it back in the bag, using the gloves, and you keep it locked up when it's not around his waist. And it had better be here when I come back."

Duncan allowed himself to fall over to the side and then roll onto his back, face raised to the darkening sky.

The sound and smell of the forest washed over him, and he considered reaching for it.

He forced the reaction down, conserving his strength while he was under the Boss Man's eye.

No sense showing any sign of power now.

The Boss Man was going tomorrow, and Duncan had battered himself to almost nothing, trying to reach for the forest in the stone cell.

The magic in the rope felt gentle, helpful, but it was not very strong. It may be fading, or had been worked by someone who only had a touch of spell casting in their blood.

Why the Boss Man thought it would harm him, suck his power and energy, was a mystery.

Maybe someone had switched the ropes, and because it was considered dangerous, those who used it as a means of control had not touched it since it had been replaced, and did not realize what had been done.

Duncan liked that idea. Liked it a lot.

He closed his eyes and felt the prick of grass against his neck, felt the wind ruffle his hair.

The Boss Man was right. This was what he needed.

And now he finally had a way to escape.

CHAPTER 5

Massi saw the men walk out into the open space between the hut, where she was hiding, and the cluster of buildings around the stone tower.

They had a prisoner with them.

She could hear the chains around his wrists and ankles clinking as he walked.

He looked weighed down, too thin, and he stumbled and fell to his knees, and then slumped onto the ground.

A rope was wound around his waist.

She caught a brief glimpse of it before he lay on the ground, and thought she'd seen its like before.

Ava had told her and Luc about the rope her kidnappers had used on her for the first part of her abduction, until she had destroyed it and created another one.

Massi remembered the one like it that they had taken off some Grimwaldian spies on the way to the Kassian capital. It was stored in the palace now, and Ava had told her that as soon as she returned, she was going to destroy it.

Burn it, just like she had the other one.

She had said that even if it could be useful to them, there was something evil in it, and Ava would not tolerate its existence any more.

Could this be a third rope?

It looked as if it was having the same effect on the man as Ava described it had had on her.

Weakening her, sucking her magic away.

The Speaker of Grimwalt obviously had access to a powerful spell caster, one who had no qualms about what he was asked to create.

Of the four men that had brought the prisoner out, and who stood watching his collapse, one looked like he was on the road often, his beard and sharp face reminded her of long journeys with little time to stop for food.

He was talking in low tones to a large man who wore the clothing of an innkeeper or prosperous farmer, rather than the ill-fitting uniform of the two guards who hovered near the prisoner as if they were afraid he was going to leap up and bite them.

All he seemed to do, though, was stare up at the sky, as if he hadn't seen it in weeks.

A rustle close to her made her glance back and down, and she saw a thin vine extend from the bottom of the ladder she had used, and snake its way through the grass toward the men.

No.

Toward the prisoner.

Could this be him, she wondered? The 'freak' as the guards had called him, that they had moved from the hut.

Maybe he was the one making the ladders. Trying to escape.

And now he was calling the tree to help him again.

The rope would make sense, then. They would need something powerful to contain a strong spell caster.

She had never been more shocked than when she'd seen Ava for the first time since her abduction.

She had been gaunt. A shadow of her former self.

This man looked equally thin, although she could tell he was taller than the guards.

The snaking vine stopped, then curled up on itself, drawing back past Massi until it disappeared into the shadows behind the hut.

Interesting.

He had decided not to make a move yet.

Massi thought it would be very funny if the Speaker had taken the rope Ava had made to replace the one that had harmed her, and was using it on this prisoner. Because knowing Ava, she would have woven what magic she could into it to help her recover.

Maybe he was being healed, rather than sapped of his strength.

Maybe he was playing along.

The two guards bent down and hauled the prisoner to his feet, and while he was being lifted up, he glanced back toward the hut.

Toward his vine. His ladder.

Massi stared at him.

He was bearded, like the man who was clearly in charge, so it was hard to see his face, but his eyes seemed to find her in the shadows.

Was that surprise that flashed across his face?

He was dragged away, and she couldn't decide if she had been seen or not.

Minutes after they disappeared, a stream of people began to emerge from a long building to her left.

The prisoners returning to their cells after a meal, she guessed.

She had only the vaguest description from Ava of what Velda and Tomas looked like, but now that she was here, she wanted to raze the place, not just rescue two people.

It didn't matter who they were, she would get everyone out.

This fortress reminded her of the Chosen camps of her childhood. A pall of fear, hunger and rage hung over it like a noxious vapor.

Guards walked, strung out on either side of the snaking line, four on each side of it. They didn't seem particularly nervous or attentive, watching the prisoners with bored expressions.

They had been here a while, Massi thought. They were in a rut.

That was good for her.

The prisoners were a mix of men and women, ranging from around her own age to much older. The guards were all on the young side, untrained, she could see from the way they moved. They had swords and they had clubs attached to their belts, and they had prisoners worn down by a lack of food and poor living conditions.

She could take this whole place on her own.

It was what the Kassians had trained her to do.

CHAPTER 6

Ava nodded to another stall holder as she made her way through the market.

Luc shadowed her, unseen by anyone but herself, the scarf she had spelled with invisibility wrapped around his neck.

She had thought she might be annoyed at his watchful presence, but she found she was not.

He needed to do it, needed to keep her safe, and she found she could not deny him.

She was still too thin, too brittle after her abduction.

She could see it in the shocked looks of the citizens of Fernwell as she tried to interact with them more, spend more time in public.

When she had first returned, she'd made up a story about no supplies for a few days on her way back to Fernwell after a trip to the border with Jatan, but as she was the only one who was thinner, that story had been disregarded.

Since then she had not explained again, but she was aware that the gossip was that she had been ill.

Rumor had it that Grimwalt might have had something to do with her illness.

A magical blight. An attempted assassination.

No one made any attempt to stifle the stories, and since they'd taken hold, Ava noticed a little more sympathy in the looks she was getting. It was better than the shock and horror she'd seen at first.

She had never considered herself vain, but she realized she had some sense of pride in her appearance, because those first looks had cut.

Luc had never looked at her with anything other than love, but even he treated her as if she might break.

As someone who was used to being strong, it was hard to accept.

It helped that she was recovering, gaining weight and strength, every day.

All she needed now was word from Massi, and she could feel that things were truly going well.

The headache of her negotiations with the nobles and town councilors from all over Kassia were a necessary part of the plan she, Luc and General Ru had come up with when they had taken Fernwell, but her attention constantly wandered back to Grimwalt, and to Massi, who was doing what Ava felt she should be doing herself.

Saving Velda and Tomas. Taking down the Speaker.

Finding out how deep the rot in Grimwalt went.

Massi had been gone over four weeks now, and had only sent back one missive, to let them know it had taken her two weeks of dodging border patrols to sneak her way over the mountains into Grimwalt.

Since then, there had been nothing.

If Ava were to give the word, Luc would assemble an army and march, the rage at the damage she had sustained in the Speaker's attempt to abduct her still burned in his eyes, especially when she caught him looking at her when he thought she was unaware.

A hand brushed her shoulder, and she closed her eyes and smiled, even though the contact was fleeting.

Luc just letting her know he was right there.

She had taken a road that led back to the palace, and she could feel him relax the closer they got to the gates. To safety.

"Ava!" Rafe waved to her, standing just inside the gates. A young boy was standing beside him, and Ava approached with a smile.

"This must be Theo, here at last." She studied Rafe's nephew. He looked like his uncle, the broad shoulders apparent even though he wasn't yet twelve, his hands and feet looking too big for him.

"Your majesty." A little wide-eyed, the boy seemed unsure whether to bow or put his hands together in a Cervantes greeting.

"It's Ava." Ava tucked an elbow through Rafe's. "You are very welcome here."

Rafe grinned at her, face beaming with delight. "They arrived this afternoon. My sister and her husband are unpacking in tent city, and I've been giving Theo the tour."

"I'll leave you to it." Ava could feel Luc behind her, and she stepped back. "I hope we will see you and your parents with Rafe at dinner tonight, Theo."

"I'll be sure to bring them." Rafe ruffled Theo's hair and Ava gave a wave as she walked away.

"He looks just like Rafe, doesn't he?" she asked softly.

Luc slid a hand along her back. "He does. He'll make a good soldier."

The guards at the palace doors opened them for her and Ava nodded in thanks as she walked inside.

For the moment, she and Luc were alone in the large foyer, and she stepped in close to him, lifting her hands and slowly pulling the scarf from his neck.

"Thank you for seeing me safely around the streets of Fernwell," she murmured, her face lifted up to his.

"There is nothing I would have rather been doing." He took the scarf from her and slid it into his pocket, holding her gaze as he did it.

"Luc. Ava." General Ru leaned out of her office. "I've been waiting for you to get back."

Luc ignored Ru for a beat, bending his head and brushing his lips over hers.

Ava smiled against the kiss, eyes closed.

"It's a message from Massi," the general called, voice sing song.

Ava's eyes snapped open, and she saw relief in Luc's eyes.

Massi was like a sister to him. The thought of her alone, behind enemy lines, was hard on him.

"Thought that would get your attention." General Ru's lips quirked. She waved a tiny roll of parchment at them.

"Did this come through the messengers we left at the border for her to use?" Luc asked, walking over to the office and stepping inside.

Ava was right behind him.

"Yes, but one of the two messengers apparently fell ill, so the one who brought this took it as far as Bartolo and left it with Heival, then headed straight back."

"Should we send a third person?" Ava asked. "So they have more flexibility?" She knew it was her own selfish interests talking, because tying up three soldiers to act as messengers was wasteful.

But it was Massi they were talking about. And Tomas and Velda. And she would do whatever she had to to protect them.

General Ru hesitated. "Your call. It'll have to come from your side of the Rising Wave."

"I'll authorize it," Luc said. "Who delivered the note to the messengers? Not Massi herself?" He cracked the seal and began to unroll the message.

"No," General Ru crowded close, as curious as Ava to know what it said. "It was handed over by a merchant who was a friend of your family's, Ava."

"I gave Massi some names, I'm glad she was able to get something to us through one of them." Ava had been afraid that no one was going to help Massi. It eased something in her that that wasn't the case.

Luc was reading the parchment. From his face, Ava couldn't tell whether it was good or bad news.

"What does it say?" General Ru asked. "I don't know how to

read Cervantes code."

"All it says is she's caused some trouble for the Speaker in Taunen and that she thinks she's narrowed down where Velda and Tomas are being held. She'll send another message when she's investigated."

Ava couldn't help the churn of worry that Velda and Tomas were still unaccounted for, but at least Massi was alive and well, and hadn't given up hope of finding her friends.

"And the Speaker?" she asked. "What trouble did she make for him?"

Luc shook his head. "She doesn't go into detail, but that would have required a longer message, is my guess. We'll hear more when she has something concrete."

"Now that you're back from your walk, I have to tell you we received another message this morning, from the Skäddar." General Ru walked to the door, which Ava had left open, and spoke to a guard before stepping back inside.

A moment later, Pilar and Helmi, the two Skäddard warriors who'd accompanied them back to Fernwell after they'd helped the Rising Wave against the Jatan, appeared in the doorway.

General Ru waved them to the couches she had set around a low table on one side of her office.

"Bad news?" Ava asked, as neither Skäddar looked happy.

"Bad news," Helmi confirmed. She was wearing Skäddar warrior dress, and the green and blue patterns on her face were faded almost to nothing, indicating that she'd been in Fernwell for at least a month.

"Tell us." Luc sat on the couch opposite them, and Ava joined him, with General Ru taking the armchair set at the end of the table.

"Skäddar is made up mostly of mountains and forests, and some of the communities are very isolated." Pilar leaned forward, and Ava noticed his hands were clasped together, as if he didn't know what to do with them. "One village, which is a week's journey from the next settlement, is tucked into the corner where Skäddar joins with both Jatan and Grimwalt. For all that it is isolated in terms of distance, it's a trading hub, the perfect marketplace for goods from Jatan, Grimwalt and Skäddar to be bought and sold." He twisted his fingers around each other, then looked up, face grim. "It has been wiped out."

"Wiped out?" General Ru frowned.

"Over a month ago, some merchants from another village traveled up there to trade, and found everyone dead or disappeared. Some of the missing were later found in the forest, dead in the same way as those in the village. They may have tried to run away, but whatever was doing the killing chased them and brought them down." Helmi's voice was soft with the horror of it.

"Whatever was doing the killing?" Luc asked. "What does that mean?"

"They were killed by the trees." Pilar's hands were white-knuckled now.

"The trees?" Ava gentled her voice.

"Their bodies were pierced and they were pinned to the ground and bled out. Roots, branches, even grass. As if the ground itself had risen up and murdered them all." Helmi leaned back in her seat, as if trying to relax, and then gave up, leaning forward again.

"Has anything like this ever happened before?" General Ru asked.

"Only in our folktales," Pilar said, voice almost a whisper.

"Folktales?" Ava tried to remember of any she had heard of that involved trees and death.

"The garanda." Helmi cleared her throat. "But it is just a tale to be told around the winter fire."

"What does the garanda do?" Ava asked.

"It controls the forest. The trees answer to it. And when it thinks someone has disrespected the forest, it punishes them by feeding their life force to the woods." Pilar finally released his hands, flexing his fingers on his thighs.

"This happened over a month ago?" General Ru asked. "And it has something to do with us?"

Of course. In the horror of what Pilar and Helmi had told them, Ava had forgotten that there had been a message from the Skäddar Collective for them.

"There was a message left in the village, written in the blood of the villagers." Helmi swallowed. "It said that if we continued our alliance with the Rising Wave, more villagers would pay the price."

"A threat," Luc said, voice thoughtful. "I'm assuming a garanda is not usually interested in political alliances?"

"No." Pilar almost laughed. His lips quirked. "And you're right, some of the Collective see this as a diabolical attack on the alliance by either the Jatan or the Grimwaldians, or even a small, disaffected tribe of Skäddar who had applied numerous times for the village that was attacked to be included in their area. They have also been one of the few groups who were against the alliance with the Rising Wave."

"But?" General Ru asked.

Helmi sighed. "But most Skäddar don't want to believe it could have been one of us who killed so many innocents."

"So they prefer to take the warning seriously?" General Ru said. "They want to withdraw on the urging of a message left in blood?"

Helmi gave a nod. "Some do. Some prefer to believe in the garanda than accept the alternative. Enough that it's become an issue for the Collective."

"Could someone have killed these villagers by normal means, and then set it up to look like they had been attacked by the forest?" Ava asked.

Pilar hesitated, then gave a nod. "By the time the merchants found the bodies, they were severely decomposed. It was possible for someone to have done what you suggest."

"That is what some of the Skäddar Collective leaders have suggested, as well," Helmi said. "It's considered the most logical explanation."

"But others are still unconvinced?" General Ru crossed her arms.

"Unfortunately. And now, the whole agreement is in jeopardy."

Ava forced herself to consider their alliance with cold logic.

It would be a massive blow to lose the Skäddar.

They had solid agreements with the Venyatux, the Funabi, and those would not easily be broken, but their new alliance with the Jatan and the Skäddar created a whole new dynamic in the area. It made Grimwalt isolated, surrounded on all sides by Rising Wave allies.

If they lost the Skäddar, it would be an outsized loss, weakening the whole agreement, and giving Grimwalt more options.

More ways to cause trouble.

"Grimwalt is the only country who benefits from Skäddar's withdrawal," Luc said.

"That's what I was thinking." General Ru gave a nod.

"Could Grimwalt have someone amongst them who could kill a person with a root or branch?" Pilar asked.

Ava hesitated. "I haven't heard of magic like that. The only magic I know from Grimwalt requires weaving spells into items. I suppose someone could weave a spell into a tree, but then they would have to hope whoever they wanted to harm would walk past that exact tree."

"So it's possible, but unlikely?" Luc said.

She shrugged. "That's my guess, but maybe there's magic that we don't know about."

There was a moment of silence.

"What does the Collective want us to do?" Luc asked eventually.

Pilar lifted his head. "Come and talk to the Collective at the Gathering. Persuade the leaders who are wavering of the benefits of our alliance."

"The Gathering?"

"Once a year, all the leaders of the Patchwork come together to discuss the issues affecting the whole country. That meeting is called the Gathering, and it happens less than two weeks from now." Even just speaking of it, Helmi's eyes lit up, as if she loved this event.

"You call the areas of Skäddar that elect a leader the Patch-work?" Ava asked, thrilled at the thought.

Pilar nodded. "Because from the top of the mountains, it looks like a patchwork quilt, the fields and stretches of forest all laid out."

"Who do the Collective want to talk to at this Gathering?" General Ru asked, as always focusing on the practicalities.

"The Queen." Helmi nodded to Ava. "And the Commander and yourself, General Ru."

"That would leave us without any leadership in Kassia," Luc protested.

Pilar nodded. "I think if only two of you came, that would satisfy them. They understand the need for strong leadership."

"If I go, Ava goes with me. And if I'm the one to stay, Ava stays with me." Luc turned to General Ru. "Although I know that it's unfair to you to leave you behind again, if they want two of us, it has to be me and Ava."

General Ru sighed. "You will owe me, Luc Franck."

"I will."

"There will be Grimwaldian spies watching near the northern border. They might see a unit of Rising Wave troops moving close to Grimwalt as an aggressive act." Ava didn't care if they did, but it might be strategically wise to keep the fact that they were going up to Skäddar secret.

General Ru nodded. "Probable. But if we pretend it's just some Venyatux troops going home, that might muddy the waters. We already have some troops moving through Kassia to get home to Venyatu on leave."

"That's a good idea." Ava knew at least a third of the Venyatux army had already returned home, but there was no reason why another group leaving Kassia would be seen as suspicious.

"My people can pretend to be Venyatux," Luc agreed. "Ava did, after all." He sent her a quick, amused grin. "It's practically a tradition among the Rising Wave."

General Ru chuckled. "That's true enough. There are a number of my people who actually are due to return home. I can add them to your unit and they can continue on when the rest of the unit carries on up to access the Skäddar border in Venyatu's north."

"And what will you tell the people of Fernwell?" Helmi asked.

"We can tell them I've gone to Venyatu to deal directly with the High Commissioner on a trade deal." Ava knew that would delight the traders and business owners who were part of the group negotiating for a new form of government.

General Ru's lips twisted in amusement. "At least I won't have to pretend you're still here."

"Exactly. Maybe everyone needs some breathing room after the intense negotiations we've had the last few weeks."

Luc had said nothing while she was talking, but she could feel the tension in him slowly ease as she made her point.

"Happy?" she asked.

"Yes."

He had been feeling caged here in Fernwell, she knew. This was a chance to get back out on the road. To do something more than guard her and grit his teeth at the slow grind of consensus among the stakeholders of Kassia on a new way forward.

"When do we need to leave by?" Ava asked Pilar.

"The Collective have decided to hold the Gathering in the Dallir Valley this year, on the border between Skäddar and Grimwalt, which will make the location as close as possible for you, but even so, given the distance, we will need to leave as soon as possible."

"And if it turns out Grimwalt is responsible for what happened to your village?" General Ru asked. "What then?"

"It will be difficult to prove, especially after so much time has elapsed, but if they are responsible, then we will be at war with Grimwalt," Pilar said, tone implacable.

"As we are your allies, then we will be at war with them, too." Luc didn't sound unhappy about that. Ava glanced at him and saw he was thinking dark, bloody thoughts.

For what he had done to her, Luc wanted to find the Speaker of Grimwalt, and cut out his still-beating heart.

A war would suit him perfectly.

CHAPTER 7

There had been someone in the shadows behind the hut where he'd spent the first month of his imprisonment.

Duncan couldn't quite make them out, but he knew they were there.

His power had surged, and as he forced it back down, it had brushed past the figure.

Was it someone following the Boss Man? Looking to get back the rope he had retrieved, perhaps?

The Boss Man had spoken of having to chase someone down for it, but the way he'd spoken, Duncan had the sense he had not left that person alive.

Just as they reached the entrance to the fortress, a dog howled in the distance, a long, melancholy sound, and the guard on his left stiffened slightly.

"Those fucking dogs."

The other guard spat on the ground. "They'll be dealt with soon enough. There's an army unit coming up from Taunen to deal with them. They'll be here soon."

"What did you say?" The Boss Man and Farnt had been following behind them, and the Boss Man put a heavy hand on the guard's shoulder. He turned to the warden. "What's he talking about?"

"There's a pack of hunting dogs. Rumor has it they belong to one of the prisoners in here. They keep coming back, nosing around the walls. Drawing attention. So I persuaded the mayor of Waldrand to call for a military unit to deal with them."

There was a moment of silence, and Duncan sensed the guards' nerves as they continued on into Farnt's office.

The Boss Man followed behind, moving past them to pick up the gloves he'd left on the desk and put them on.

"A pack of dogs?" He untied the rope around Duncan's waist carefully and put it back in its bag.

Duncan felt the faint buzz of healing magic cut off, and could not help the shiver that ran through him.

The Boss Man glanced up, gaze piercing, but there was nothing suspicious in his eyes.

He still thought this was a punishment, not a boon.

"I was worried some of the villagers would try to hunt the pack down themselves. I thought if they knew someone else was coming to do it . . ." Farnt sounded nervous as he trailed off.

Duncan hadn't heard the dogs before, but then, if they'd arrived since he'd been in the tower, he wouldn't have.

He wondered who they belonged to.

A pack of hunting hounds was an expensive thing to have and to keep.

Most likely, there were people here who had the means, but had run afoul of the Speaker.

Duncan wasn't part of the Taunen Council, so he didn't recognize anyone here. Didn't know who was who.

He had never set foot in the capital, had never spoken to anyone in office.

It made him hard to find.

It made him easy to keep locked up, as well.

No one of any importance knew he was missing, because no one in Taunen knew he existed. As for the villagers near his forest, his own community, he wondered what they had done about his disappearance.

"You're right." The Boss Man rubbed the bridge of his nose. "It *is* better if people believe someone else will take care of it. I'll find out who the mayor sent his request to before I leave tomorrow morning and when I get to Taunen I'll let them know the issue has been dealt with, that they don't need to come."

"You don't want the Speaker to send an army unit?" Farnt asked.

"No."

Duncan could guess why that was.

What he'd worked out since he'd been here was that the Speaker could not count on large-scale support. He wouldn't be locking up respected citizens if he could.

Those who understood what was happening, objected to it, and had some power, ended up a prisoner here. Those who understood and approved were a small minority.

The rest of Grimwalt seemed to be living in ignorance.

The Speaker had to make sure those who didn't understand what was going on stayed ignorant. The army as a whole couldn't be under his control, and if a unit was sent here and they saw the fortress . . . it might just alert those not under the Speaker's thumb that something was amiss.

Some generals had to be in his confidence, but Duncan didn't think it could be too many, especially as he'd heard mutterings from some of the prisoners around him that spell casting was involved in his hold on power. The Speaker was using magic to control those he couldn't persuade.

But magic didn't last forever.

"What'll I do about the dogs, then?" Farnt asked.

"Send out a couple of guards to kill them," the Boss Man said. "Even if they only get a few at a time."

Farnt made a sharp sound, and the Boss Man turned to him.

"Problem?"

"I only have ten guards. We were supposed to have thirty prisoners, maximum, and now we have forty. I don't have enough people."

The Boss Man lifted his shoulders. "The more guards, the more chance of this place being discovered. And the Speaker has encountered more resistance than he anticipated." He clapped a hand on the warden's shoulder. "Do what you can."

Farnt looked like he wanted to protest, but instead he glanced at Duncan, thinned his lips, and waved his hands at the guards to get him back to his cell.

As Duncan was led away, he heard the sound of the other prisoners, back from their meal and settling in for the night.

He thought about the person in the shadows, and wondered if they would venture closer inside.

After weeks of nothing, things were starting to happen.

The guards shoved him back into the cold stone of his cell, and he wanted to throw back his head and howl like one of those dogs out of pure, unadulterated sadness as the cold stone blocked his link to the forest.

He forced himself to shrug off the feeling of loss and remember he now had a way out.

His time in this place was coming to an end.

MASSI WAITED.

She had heard one of the dogs howl in the distance, and she hoped they stayed where she'd left them.

Their presence would rouse the guards, and she wanted them dull and bored.

Eventually full darkness settled in, and the bearded man who seemed to be in charge left via the front gates, heading toward Waldrand.

The warden walked him out, then turned to make his way behind one of the wooden buildings.

Things got very quiet, but it was a relaxed, sleepy silence.

That was good.

She counted two guards inside, another six had walked over to what seemed to be their barracks, and only two guarded the gate.

Clouds obscured what little light there was from the moon, and while she had the chance, she crossed the open ground between the hut and the main prison quickly, moving as if she belonged.

Better to be striding confidently than creeping across.

She reached the door and pulled it, unsure whether she would find it locked or not.

It opened with a creak under her hand.

She slipped through, pleased to find there was only one lantern on the wall, and the rest of the area was in shadow.

There was a closed door to her left, with a passage stretching in front of her. From up ahead she could hear the murmur of many people corralled together.

The smell of too many bodies forced together took her right back to the Chosen camps, and she realized she was holding her breath.

She tried to get a grip, leaning against the wall in a show of weakness that distressed her almost as much as the smell and the sense of entrapment.

When she'd managed to take a full, steadying breath, she straightened and pulled her knife, holding it close to her thigh as she began to move forward again.

She had a fleeting thought that she had not intended to do more than reconnaissance tonight, but here she was, right in the belly of the beast.

Retreat was still an option, but as the passage curved, she passed locked rooms to her left, the wooden additions to the stone tower. She could hear the sound of women talking softly within, and something in her burned a little hotter.

The three doors after that contained the low rumble of men.

Finally, she encountered a guard station, set up in front of the entrance to the stone tower itself.

Massi crouched down in the shadows to watch.

Two guards sat across from each other at a table, playing cards to pass the time, and Massi kept her gaze soft as she observed them, having been alerted to eyes on her more often than she could count. She knew the power of a focused gaze, and the tension and awareness it could create.

One of the guards threw down his hand of cards and stood, moving up a sloped passage behind him, deeper into the stone tower.

The other guard was sitting with his back to her, and deciding to take her chance while she could, Massi moved up behind him, hitting his neck with the blade of her hand at just the right spot to render him limp for a moment.

Then she got her arm around his neck, and cut off his air.

When he slumped, unconscious, she dragged him back down the way she'd come, patting him down for restraints, but finding none.

With no other choice, she took his baton and hit him again, hard. With luck, he'd wake up sooner or later.

She moved back up the passage cautiously, but the other guard wasn't back yet.

She passed the table quickly, aware she was fully lit in the small antechamber, but then she was back in gloomy shadows, with the light behind her, so she would be difficult to make out to anyone looking toward her.

She could hear the guard up ahead of her by the jangle of his keys, and his off-pitch whistle.

She wondered how many more people were being held up ahead. She could hear quiet voices, but the guard was closer, just up ahead.

She moved slowly, pressed up against the wall, following the curve of it.

The guard was standing in front of a cell created with metal bars set a hand width apart.

The guard had taken a torch with him, and she could see the light of it playing over the prisoner she'd seen in the courtyard. He was sitting in the middle of the cell, and she just caught the glint of a chain attached to his ankle.

The guard seemed to just be staring at him.

She couldn't work out why he would do that, until he turned away with a chuckle.

He was taunting him.

Rage flashed over her, and as it did, the prisoner suddenly lifted his head, and she saw a gleam of interest in his eyes as he stared at her.

She lifted a finger to her lips and ran at the guard, leaping as she swung the baton at the base of his skull.

He collapsed without a sound. The torch he was holding fell and rolled up against the wall where it continued to burn, throwing wild shadows over the room.

She crouched beside the fallen man, found the keys she'd heard jingling, and rose up with them in her hand.

"You were hiding behind the hut." The prisoner stood close to the bars.

"Yes."

She moved over and unlocked the cell.

The prisoner didn't come any closer, but then she saw he couldn't. There was a shackle on his ankle.

Power hummed off him.

She could feel it brush against her skin.

This was Ava's doing again.

Since she'd given Massi the shirt that protected her and improved her aim, she had had feelings about some people. Felt a strange buzz off them.

Her protections locking into place.

She kept her distance as she worked through the keys, looking for a smaller one that would fit the shackle, and then glanced up when she had it.

"I don't bite." There was a faint thread of humor in his voice.

She smiled. "I do."

She moved forward and he crouched down, his leg extended, so it was easy for her to unlock it.

"You know two prisoners called Tomas and Velda, and where I can find them?"

He was already out of the cell, grabbing the guard's feet, when she asked, and he stared back at her. "Yes."

She helped him drag the guard inside the cell, gave a snort of humor when he took the few moments to clamp the shackle around the guard's ankle.

"What did you do with the other one?" he asked, flicking his gaze down the passage.

"Same," she said. "But he's closer to one of the other cells. No sense dragging him here."

He gave a grunt of agreement and put his hand out for the keys.

"I'll keep them, thanks." She wasn't handing over control to anyone, especially not someone who exuded such focus, such intensity. He was dangerous. "Tomas? Velda?"

"Tomas is further up this way," he said, eyes still a little amused. "Velda is back the way you came." He waved his hand, as if inviting her to go first. "Who are you?"

Massi hesitated. "My name is Massi Joure. You?"

"Duncan Erdo. At your service." His eyes were dark brown under straight, severe brows, his face too gaunt, his beard shaggy. He was taller than her by at least a head, and though he was thin, he moved like he had once been muscular and broad.

This place had not been good for him.

The faint sound of a shuffle from up ahead had her hand tightening on the baton she'd taken.

A man stepped out of the darkness and came to a shocked halt at the sight of the torch, still burning against the wall.

"Duncan?"

"This is Tomas," the prisoner told her.

The man's gaze flicked from Duncan to her, face slack with surprise.

Could it really be Tomas?

She wondered for a moment at the chances of the very person she'd come to rescue escaping from his cell just as she arrived to rescue him, but he looked like the man Ava had described to her; white-haired and a little grizzled.

His eyes were kind and he looked too thin. Like everyone here.

"Ava sent me," Massi said.

Tomas gasped, and then he stepped toward her, hand reaching out. "She's alive?"

"She's the new queen of Kassia," Massi told him.

"The old queen is dead? And that bastard of a cousin?"

"They killed each other," Massi said, then lifted a shoulder, "with a little help from Ava, I think."

He reached her, clasped her close, and while she had a sudden spike of fear that this was a trap, a way to get close to attack her, she could sense the relief in him.

He drew back, and she was none the worse for it.

"You count the queen of Kassia as your friend, Tomas?" Duncan's tone was dry.

"She wasn't the queen when I was brought in here. But her father was related to Kassian royalty, that I did know." Tomas shuffled back a bit. "Our association with her is why Velda and I are in here, Duncan. We were making too much noise about the Speaker trying to grab her a few months back. They needed to keep us quiet."

"Ava wanted to come and find you herself." Massi kept her voice as low as she could. "But the Speaker abducted her off the streets of Fernwell just over a month ago. It took a while for her to get free, and by then, the citizens of Fernwell were getting restless. Everything the Rising Wave had sacrificed to win was in jeopardy, so she was forced to return to the capital, and I offered to come for you in her stead."

"And the young man? The one in the Rising Wave she was going to find?" Tomas asked. "Did she meet up with him?"

Massi almost coughed out a laugh. "Luc?"

"I don't know his name. She was imprisoned by the Kassian with him——"

"Luc." Massi sent him a wide smile. "The Commander of the Rising Wave. The Turncoat King himself."

"It sounds as if you have more than one story to tell me about Ava." Tomas's gaze flicked beyond her, to the guard station.

Massi turned to keep an eye on the passage, then glanced at Tomas. "How are you out of your cell?"

"The lock on my cell is easy to open, so I come most nights to keep Duncan company."

Massi had seen the narrow slice of bread in his hand.

He'd come to share his food, too, if she were to make a guess.

"Then let's get everyone ready to run. Can you get the men in your cell moving?"

He nodded and she glanced at Duncan as Tomas disappeared back down the passage. "Any suggestions on how to get everyone out?" she asked.

He stepped closer, and she had the sense of a force of nature coming toward her. "We can't leave the guards able to get help for at least a few days to give everyone the best chance."

"Lock them up?" She had known Velda and Tomas were elderly, that it would be better to get away without being noticed. They may well not have the stamina for a hard chase. "Will someone from Waldrand come and check on the guards if they don't come into town?"

Duncan shrugged. "I don't know."

He did not seem particularly concerned, but she would prefer not to leave the guards and the warden to die of thirst and hunger.

Tomas appeared from the passage again, this time with five other men in tow. Their gazes went to the cell first, then flicked to Duncan when they realized he was not inside; that one of the guards was, instead.

They were wary of him, Massi noticed. Some deliberately didn't meet his gaze, and she wondered if they were spell casters themselves, careful not to be as obviously magical as he was.

A strange reaction, if she read it right. This was Grimwalt, after all. Where spell casters were supposedly safe and accepted.

Except, of course, they weren't.

The Speaker had tried numerous times to abduct Ava, and Ava thought the reason for it was he was co-opting or forcing spell casters with useful magic to help him hold onto power.

Massi would have to ask Duncan how he'd ended up here.

He had an edge to him, an almost feral glint in his eye that appealed to her.

She had the sense that he had walked part of his life in darkness.

Like recognized like.

"Ready?"

"Very." He gave a smile that shot a hot arrow of excitement through her.

It promised mayhem, and mayhem was something she was fond of herself.

One of the prisoners, a man in ragged robes that looked as if they were something a councilor or palace advisor would wear, put a hand on her arm.

"What's the plan?"

Massi flashed him a look and he dropped his hold, took a step back.

"The plan was to rescue Tomas and Velda, but having seen the accommodations here, I thought the rest of you might like to leave, as well."

A few of the other men chuckled.

"We might be able to free the women and get out into the courtyard, but after that . . ."

"Duncan here has already taken care of an escape route," she said. "How do you think I got inside?"

Duncan gave her a sharp look at that.

"Who are you?" one of the men asked, eyes suddenly narrowed.

"I'm Massi Joure of the Cervantes. Part of the Rising Wave."

"What is a Cervantes doing here in Grimwalt, interfering in our struggles?"

Massi stared at him for a beat. Turned to the rest of the group. "Is this man an enemy plant? Do you trust him?"

For a moment, the man stared at her, open-mouthed.

"She's getting us out of here, and you're complaining about where she's from, Gregoire?"

The man who spoke was the one in the robes.

"I'm suspicious, that's all."

"You're welcome to go back to your cell, then." Tomas waved a hand back toward the darkened passage.

Gregoire hesitated, and Massi actually thought he considered it, then he gave a tiny shake of his head.

No one was quite ready to accept him back on the same footing, though. She could see it in the way most did not meet his eyes.

"Any more questions?" she asked.

Duncan caught her eye, and she saw the flash of amusement on his face at the snark in her voice.

No one responded.

"Then let's go."

CHAPTER 8

Massi Joure was something.

Beautiful. Sleekly muscled. And the way she moved . . . he could tell she had trained as a warrior.

She said she was Cervantes. Duncan didn't know much about them, other than for years they had been under the cruel thumb of the Kassian queen, syphoned off into camps to be trained as soldiers to carry out the dream of Kassian expansion.

They were fodder on the battlefield, but useful fodder, because the Cervantes were known to be fierce and skillful warriors. Natural fighters.

He had always taken that generalization as nonsense.

No group was more naturally skilled at fighting than any other. It was culture and training that determined those things.

But now he was looking at Massi Joure, at the way she slid through the shadows, and he could just catch a shimmer of magic around her.

Maybe the Cervantes did have a magical edge. One that made them faster, stronger, more coordinated than others.

It would explain a lot.

Massi opened the last door, freeing the last of the women prisoners, and everyone began moving quietly toward the door.

Tomas was right behind him, his arm around Velda.

They had dragged the other guard into one of the cells and locked him in.

The warden's office was to the right, but it was closed, and there was no light under the door.

The barracks where the guards slept were close to the food hall, and Duncan knew from when he'd been kept in the hut that after dinner, five of the guards went on duty, five went to sleep. All ten were on guard during breakfast, and then the night guards went to bed and the day guards took over.

The warden must have his own suite of rooms, but Duncan didn't know where they were.

"Any of you here able to work a sleeping spell?" Massi whispered when they'd all gathered at the door leading to the courtyard.

"What did you have in mind?" a woman asked from amongst the crowd.

"Anything that will make the guards who are sleeping in the barracks keep sleeping for a long time. The longer it takes for them to raise the alarm, the more time we have to disappear."

"I can make sure the guards can't easily leave their barracks," Duncan said. "I can do the same for the warden's sleeping quarters, but I don't know where they are."

"I do." A man, Duncan remembered his name was Lars, edged out of the crowd to make himself known. "I've had to clean it a few times."

"I can make them sleep while our Forest Man does his working," the woman admitted. "But I'll need a little time."

Duncan glanced at her, amused at the nickname she had for him.

It was better than some he'd heard.

"That's fine. I can work with you."

"What guards will be on duty?" Massi asked.

"Beside the two we've locked up, there are two at the gate, one on patrol. They take turns with patrol duty. They switch every hour." Duncan had had a long time to learn the rhythms of the fortress when he'd been kept in the hut.

"I'll deal with them." Massi put her hand on the door handle. "Tomas, keep everyone else safe here, until I come get you."

Duncan had no doubt she would deal with them. It would take her no time at all to kill them with her arrows, but so far she had not spilled blood.

It seemed that she wasn't planning to, if she didn't have to.

He wasn't feeling quite so generous, but he would follow her lead.

She had certainly helped him escape far sooner than he would have been able to do himself.

She slipped out, and Duncan followed, with Lars and the woman who could spell cast sleep right behind him.

Tomas clapped a friendly hand on his shoulder as he passed him, and Duncan gave the old man a quick smile.

Massi was already gone when he stepped out, but his gaze was drawn to the gates, and he guessed she had gone that way to deal with the guards watching the entrance.

He moved across the courtyard with the spell caster—who had introduced herself as Camille—and Lars, making for the barracks.

"What do you need to do?" he whispered to Camille.

She knelt on the ground, feeling around for something, and came up with a small stone. She crouched in front of the door and began to scratch something into the wood, trying to make as little noise as possible while she did it.

Behind him, toward the gate, Duncan thought he heard someone make a sound, but only for a moment and then the night was silent again.

He focused back on the barracks, and while the woman scratched out her working, Duncan put his hand against the planks of the wall and felt the wood tremble.

Thin branches burst out of them, a chaotic tangle that crossed and twined around each other, covering the two windows on either side of the door in a thick latticework.

Camille gave a final scratch and moved back, and as soon as she did, the branches wove over it, sealing everyone inside.

The guards would have to hack their way out with an ax.

"The warden?" Duncan asked.

Lars was staring at what had become of the barracks, and he jerked at Duncan's question.

"This way." He glanced covertly at Duncan and Camille as they followed him around the back of the building to another about half the size.

Smoke was coming out of a chimney and there was a lantern light on in the front room.

This would require more care.

"It doesn't seem like he's asleep. I'll need a different spell." Camille stared at the lighted window thoughtfully.

"What do you suggest?"

She tapped her lip. "Maybe a fear of opening the doors? That could last for a few days."

Duncan liked it. A lot. He gave a grunt of approval.

Lars looked less enthusiastic, but he kept quiet and didn't get in the way, which was all Duncan required of him.

"I can mark the back door. It'll work just as well," Camille said.

They moved around the house.

The woman started scratching at the back door, but Duncan couldn't work the same magic he had on the walls of the barracks. This building was mainly stone, some old outhouse that had been part of the original tower, he guessed.

He crouched down, putting his hands on the ground beside a climbing rose that was only just clinging to life. Someone had tried to train it in an arch over the back door, but no one had cared for it in a long time, by the look of it.

Duncan cared for it now.

It began to grow, and he told it what he wanted and then stepped back as it covered windows, curled around the house to the front door, and then back again to enclose the back just as Camille finished her spell.

"Ready to go?" Massi appeared out of the darkness, her gaze flicking to the house and then back to him.

He nodded.

"We need to make sure the guards I've dealt with can't raise the alarm." She strode away.

When Duncan caught up to her, he saw she'd fetched Tomas, Velda and the others, and everyone stood near the gates.

Dogs howled in the trees beyond the wall.

All three guards had been laid down on the floor of the small wooden hut beside the massive gates, and Duncan could see they were unconscious.

No arrows had been needed.

"I can spell them to sleep, same as the others." Camille held up her stone.

While some of the prisoners opened the gates, he and Camille went back to work, spelling the guards and binding the hut.

When they were done, and everyone stood outside, there was a moment of silence.

"Waldrand is that way," Massi said, pointing. "It's an hour's walk."

"Waldrand?" one of the prisoners asked. "Will it be safe to walk there?"

"I would wait until mid-morning before you arrive," Duncan said. "The man who oversees this place was here this afternoon, and he's spending the night in Waldrand and only leaving tomorrow morning."

"You could even spend the night here," Massi said. "No one will stop you leaving tomorrow morning."

That idea didn't sit well with any of them, Duncan could see. He felt the same way.

He did not want to go back inside now that he was finally out.

"I'd rather sleep in the woods," Camille said.

Massi looked torn.

Duncan thought she'd anticipated the prisoners would go their separate ways, and she could take care of Tomas and Velda, but they were all still milling around, looking to her for direction.

He felt the ground beneath his feet tremble a little, and then a pack of dogs burst through the trees.

Tomas made a sound of delight, even as most of the prisoners drew back in fear, and he dropped to the ground as the dogs leaped on him, licking and nosing him, tails wagging in delight.

"That's how I knew where to find you," Massi said. "Stories of the dogs led me here."

At the sound of her voice, some of the dogs ran to her, then back to Tomas, then back to her, as if they couldn't decide who they were happier to see.

"You've made friends," Velda said, patting the head on one of the dogs that had come to sit at her feet. The old woman seemed to have been introduced to Massi while he'd been dealing with the barracks and the warden's cottage, because there was a lot of warmth in Velda's voice.

"Thanks to Ava," Massi said. "She . . . eased my way."

"Ava Yngstra?" One of the men in the group stepped forward. Duncan remembered he was the one who'd berated the suspicious Gregoire when Massi had come to rescue them. "She sent you here?"

"Yes." Massi eyed him. "How do you know her?"

"I'm Ranulf Harkonan. A friend of her parents." He looked over at Tomas and Velda. "I heard the Speaker had banished her. I tried to ask questions about why, and was shut down."

"I didn't know that." Velda turned to him, her face full of warmth. "Is that why you were sent here?"

Ranulf shook his head. "It may have been part of it, but I think it was because my job as High Commissioner in parliament was to oversee the artifacts vault. When I discovered things were missing, and began to investigate, that's when I was taken."

"Missing artifacts." Massi knew Ava had wondered where the Speaker had been getting the many rare and powerful items he'd used in his pursuit of her. An artifacts vault in Grimwalt's parliament sounded like a good place to find such things.

"Massi says Ava is the queen of Kassia now," Tomas said. "The Rising Wave has taken Fernwell."

A large number of the crowd drew in audible breaths.

"Your Speaker tried to abduct her when she escaped from Kassia and returned home to Grimwalt, and then he tried to abduct her again, after she was crowned queen. She escaped, but he harmed her. There are those in Kassia who understandably see the attack on their monarch as an act of war." Massi kept her voice neutral as she spoke.

She was looking for reactions, Duncan saw. She was trying to see how this news would be taken.

"He's only Speaker because he's used spell craft to keep himself in power. Otherwise he would have been removed." The woman in the crowd who spoke up sounded bitter. "Whatever he's done to the queen of Kassia, it was not in our name."

"How does Ava Yngstra have claim to the Kassian crown anyway?" someone else asked.

"Her father was the old queen's half-brother." Ranulf spoke slowly. "He renounced his sister, and she exiled him, so it wasn't much mentioned, but I knew of the connection."

"But you say the Rising Wave took Fernwell?" Another man asked. "Why would the rebels replace one queen with another?"

"Because Ava rode with them, to revenge her parents' murders." Massi was still watching the crowd, gauging responses. "And she is heart-bound to the leader of the Rising Wave, Luc Franck."

There was silence at that, as everyone absorbed the implications.

Duncan knew he didn't understand the politics of Grimwalt, had deliberately kept clear of Taunen and the machinations of the parliament, but now he wished he knew more.

Most of these prisoners were citizens who had stood up to the Speaker and risked their safety in order to protest or push back against him. They obviously understood the ramifications of what Massi was saying far better than he did.

A few others, like himself, were here not because of their politics but because they were spell casters. There was Camille, the woman who'd set the sleep spells, as well as a few others he got a buzz from, a pull that made him think they were more than they seemed.

Only Camille had had the courage to help, though. The courage to reveal herself to her fellow prisoners.

"So, what will Kassia do? What will Ava Yngstra do?" Another man posed the question Duncan guessed most of them were thinking.

"Kassia has already had a missive delivered," Massi said. "Demanding an explanation."

Ranulf snorted. "The Speaker will deny it."

"Maybe," she shrugged. "But the accusation is now out there."

"He won't make it known," someone called out. "He'll keep it to himself."

"That would be difficult for him." Massi gave a sharp smile. "The missive was put up in front of the parliament gates for everyone to see."

Something told Duncan that Massi herself had done that. He was sure of it.

"Well, that's something. It will certainly start people asking some questions."

"And I will make sure more are asked, when I get back to Taunen," Ranulf said.

"You're going back?" Camille asked, shocked.

"I'll be safer in Taunen than back at my estate, where I can be more easily abducted, out of sight of prying eyes like I was this last time. The more noise I make, the more I surround myself with others, the harder it is for him to make me disappear without even more questions being asked." Ranulf looked around at the others. "And the more of you who join me, who sing the chorus of where we were taken and why, the less likely the Speaker is to be a danger to us and to our families."

"You have a point." Lars nodded his head. "The more of us making a noise, the safer all of us will be."

"What is the Speaker's spell craft?" Massi asked. "He must have some, or he would never have got as far as he has."

"He can persuade. I'm not sure how he does it, but he can convince people to do as he says. Even people who would never think to obey him." Ranulf sounded bitter, as if someone he knew had been persuaded to betray him.

"All well and good, but what do we do *now?*" One of the women in the group rubbed at her face, as if she was exhausted.

Massi looked as if she wanted to gather those she'd come for and walk away, but when she glanced at Velda, her face smoothed to neutral. She turned to him.

"Can you use your magic to make a shelter for everyone? I can light a fire and we can catch what sleep we can in the forest, and wait for the Speaker's man to leave Waldrand."

There was silence as everyone turned to look at him.

Duncan had spent a long time working his spells alone, but since he'd been imprisoned he'd used his magic in flamboyant displays as he tried everything he could to escape.

He couldn't blame these people if they expected him to use it again, this time to help them all.

"I can," he said.

"Then let's move deeper into the woods, and settle in." Massi hitched her quiver of arrows on her shoulder, turned, and started walking away.

The dogs bounded to her heels and Duncan stood for a moment watching her stride away, a goddess on the hunt.

CHAPTER 9

L uc liked being on a mission again.

Especially as this time, Ava was with him.

It reminded him of their time together in the Rising Wave, moving toward Fernwell, gearing up for battle. Things hadn't been simple——with Ava, that was impossible——but there had been less pressure on them, less in the way of expectations.

The palace was a different story.

Since they'd returned to Fernwell a second time, Ava had thrown herself into untangling the snarled threads of power and demands that had accumulated in her absence.

She was less concerned with causing offense than she had been before, though. It was as if the rope that had drained so much from her had taken her patience, as well.

The nobles kept forgetting that Ava had demoted them, and the councilors, realizing they now held more power, had stepped into the void, demanding time and concessions that never seemed to end.

On the road, with a team made up of thirty Venyatux on their way home, and fifty Rising Wave warriors who would come with them to Skäddar, the weight of that tangle lifted with every mile they traveled away from Fernwell.

They had passed Bartolo by midday and had made good time traveling north, keeping to the Bartolo River. As the sun set, there was an air of camaraderie and happiness among the riders. They found a good, flat area beside the river to set up camp, and Luc could hear good-natured laughter between the two groups.

Everyone sounded relaxed.

Maybe Fernwell had weighed on more than just him.

Some were clearly as pleased to be out of the stone-walled city and in the open air as he was.

"Fernwell isn't terrible," he said.

Ava, helping him set up their tent, looked up with amusement in her eyes. "You sound like you're trying to convince yourself of that, not state a fact."

He grinned at her. "Maybe I am."

She laughed. "It's not terrible. But it's not what either of us are used to. I can't believe how stoic General Ru is about staying behind yet again."

"We can thank Talika for that, I think." That one of his soldiers had captured the heart of the Venyatux general was still slightly surreal to him. And yet, it would only help seal the bond between the Cervantes and the Venyatux even more.

Ava had done her share to help the bond, too. She'd traveled with the Venyatux, pretended to be one of them, and she was wholly accepted by them all.

Luc wondered if the Venyatux back home would be able to get their heads around the fact that their army was so fond of the new Kassian queen.

Before, the very thought of the queen would have caused them to spit on the ground in disgust.

"Travelers approaching." The call went up from the watchers facing east, and Luc strode to the outrider who had returned with the news. Before he reached them, there was a cry of welcome from Pilar.

When Luc reached the two newcomers who had ridden into the camp, they were already out of the saddle, in Pilar's embrace.

Luc didn't speak Skäddar, but it was clearly a warm and happy reunion.

"Luc." Pilar turned to him. "This is Britta and Dragir. They are friends from home."

They had been riding hard, Luc could see it in the way their horses were breathing, and in the sweat in the riders' hair.

Which meant bad news.

Luc had yet to find someone who rode through the night to bring good news.

"Trouble?" he asked.

"More strange than immediately dangerous," Britta said.

"Then see to your horses, set up camp, and wash and eat. When you're feeling rested, come and find me, and we can talk."

Both riders gave a nod of thanks at that, and Pilar led them away to help settle them in.

Luc could hear Helmi and Britta laughing together in delight at seeing each other as they moved away.

"Trouble?" Ava asked, when he rejoined her.

She had finished putting the tent up, and he gave a chuckle at how exactly her thoughts followed his own.

He rubbed a hand through his hair. "Probably. Two Skäddar warriors have come with a message. I told them to rest and eat first."

She nodded, pulling out clothes from the saddle bags she had carried over to their tent. "I'm going to wash off in the river, change, and then eat."

She took out a needle and thread and a scarf, and bit her lip in concentration as she stitched the corner.

"What does that do?" he asked, always amazed at how effort-lessly she seemed to create something beautiful.

The design she'd stitched into the scarf looked like a leaf.

"This should let me wash up in the river without anyone seeing me strip down." She raised her head. "I won't have to worry about prying eyes."

"You could order everyone to look the other way," he said, and as he knew she would, she scoffed at that.

"I should really just wash with everyone else, but . . ." She looked down at herself.

She was still self-conscious about how much muscle and weight she had lost since she'd been abducted. He knew it, but sometimes, he realized, he didn't understand how deep it went.

Telling her she was beautiful as she was wasn't going to help—— he had tried that already.

Time would slowly bring her back to how she had been before, but until then, he was prepared to indulge her as much as she needed to be indulged.

"Have you got another scarf for me?" he asked.

She shoved her hand into her pack, rummaging around before she pulled out a second scarf. "You don't really need it."

"I quite like the idea of being invisible in the water with you."

Her head jerked in surprise, as if she'd expected him to push back against her, say exactly what he'd just managed to stop himself from saying. Then she gave a slow smile. "Well, put like that . . ."

She bent her head to stitch a leaf into his scarf. When she lifted her gaze to hand it to him, her eyes were serious. "Thank you."

"Why are you thanking me?" he asked, lunging forward to scoop her up, shocked as always by the strange lightness in her bones. He let the happy sound of her laughter against his chest lift his spirits as he strode to the river with her tucked close to his heart. "Naked swimming with my queen? It's me who should be thanking you."

DINNER HAD BEEN MADE BY THE TIME THEY WERE DRESSED AND presentable again.

Ava sat close to Luc in a spot they found by the fire.

There was some banter from Dak——who had successfully

argued that as he had been left behind last time it was Revek's turn to remain at Fernwell——about how long it had taken them to wash and dress, but it was done with lighthearted approval.

Luc's warriors liked seeing him happy, and over the last few weeks Ava had also worked out that his romance with the new queen of Kassia was a point of pride among them.

Their commander hadn't just conquered Kassia, he had replaced the old queen with a woman who loved him.

Ava had worried that the warriors of the Rising Wave would dislike her for keeping her link to the crown secret, but because neither she, Luc, nor General Ru had addressed the matter, the rumor that had risen up and was quickly accepted as fact was that Luc had known of her claim to the throne all along, and it had been part of the plan.

She was happy to let that explanation stand.

While they ate, the Skäddar joined them, everyone shuffling over to give them room to sit. Luc didn't press for information, waiting for the newcomers to be handed bowls of food.

They ate as if they hadn't had a good meal in a while.

When they were done, both riders put their bowls aside slightly shamed-faced, as if they just remembered they were sitting with the Commander of the Rising Wave himself.

"You met Luc earlier," Pilar said to them. "And this is Ava, Queen of Kassia."

Britta choked, coughing hard until Pilar slapped her back.

"Queen . . ?" she asked, weakly.

Dragmir eyed his friend, and Ava guessed he was seriously weighing up whether Pilar was teasing them.

"It is my pleasure to meet you," she said, to save any embarrassing accusations. "I count Kikir as a good friend, and I'm pleased to meet some of his fellow warriors."

"Your Majesty." Britta began to rise, and Pilar pulled her back down.

"Ava doesn't expect or want any ceremony." Pilar sent her a

quick smile. "Better for any possible watching eyes to think she's just one of us, eh?"

"Of course." Dragmir nodded. "Well, it is both of our honor to meet the queen that Kikir has told us so much about. It was you who presented him with the scarf containing the pattern reserved for our best warrior?"

"I made it for him, yes."

Britta gasped. "You made it for him? I thought you had it commissioned as a gift, not that you had sewn it with your own hands."

"Ava here is always sewing something," Dak said, his voice teasing and warm.

He had come a long way in his opinion of her, Ava was glad to see.

There had been a time when he had thought her a dangerous distraction from Luc's mission.

"So, you have news?" Luc asked, pulling her a little closer to him.

He was steeling himself for something bad, she realized. She curled her arm around his waist and gave a gentle squeeze.

"Britta and I were originally sent to wait for you on the border between Skäddar and Venyatu, to take you to the Gathering, but then strange happenings were reported by the border guards patrolling where the Gathering is set to take place, and we decided to come down and escort you personally." Dragmir leaned forward, elbows on knees, expression serious.

"Strange how?" Dak asked.

"I don't know if you're familiar with it, but the border runs through the Mirror Mountains range. The mountains are divided by a long valley that splits the range in two, with the Dallir River running through it. On either side of the river is thick forest growth, but our border guards started to notice that the Grimwalt side has grown unusually thick in places." Britta gave a slightly sheepish shrug. "We have wardens that breach the river occasionally, to thin back growth on the Grimwalt side so we can move across easily, if we need to. Suddenly, almost overnight, some thickets have become impenetrable."

"It's not just that." Dragmir had been scraping the last out of his bowl while Britta had been talking, and he set it back down. "In other places, the trees are dead. Not just slowly dying, but dead already. Old trees that would usually die slowly, if they die at all. These have gone from healthy to dead in a week or less."

"Is there a pattern to this?" Ava asked.

"No. We can't see any logic to what's happening. But something isn't right. None of it is normal or easily explained." Britta lifted her hands.

"And that's not all." Dragmir straightened up, glanced over at Britta.

For a beat they were silent, and Ava felt the tension rise.

"What else?" Pilar asked.

"Some have seen a gilla." Britta spoke hesitantly.

"A gilla?" Pilar's tone was scoffing. "What kind of gilla?"

"One moment, there is a man, then a stoat." Dragmir said. "Or sometimes a fox, or an owl. And you know what that means."

"What does it mean?" Luc asked.

Pilar gave a sigh. "A gilla is a spirit that can shift between person and beast. And if you see one . . ." He glanced over at his friends.

Helmi was sitting on their other side, and when they didn't answer, she leaned forward herself. "If you see one, it spells your impending death."

"Has anyone seen the person actually change into an animal?" Ava asked. She did not discount talk about strange things coming out of Grimwalt. It was the land that had made a home for spell casters, after all.

"No." Britta looked over at her, relaxing a little when she heard no skepticism in Ava's voice. "But it's happened enough times it seems it can't be coincidence. And what is someone doing, haunting the forest at the edge of the border in a robe with a hood, taunting our guards, anyway?"

"They're trying to seed panic and superstition," Pilar said.

"Make us wary before the Gathering. Add to the conviction in some minds that we need to walk away from the alliance with the Rising Wave."

Dragmir nodded. "I agree, but this is happening on the Grimwalt side, not our side."

"This could connect to the reason we're on our way to Skäddar." Luc spoke slowly. "If the Grimwaldians are responsible for the deaths in the village, then it makes sense they're causing trouble on the border, but are staying on their side, in relative safety."

"*If* they are responsible," Helmi said, but she didn't sound like she thought Luc's idea was outlandish. "Or it could be two separate things."

"When did whatever is happening in the Dallir Valley start up?" Ava asked.

"A few weeks ago," Britta said. "So that would have been after the village was destroyed."

"If the Speaker is behind this, he's playing games with you, using your myths against you."

It almost sounded too complicated for the Speaker, who'd used bribery and abduction to achieve his aims so far. He was a blunt instrument, whereas this seemed to be more subtle.

"Is this going to change where and how you conduct your Gathering?" Luc asked.

Dragmir shook his head. "It'll take far more than a few dead trees and men in hooded cloaks to make the Skäddar Collective blink."

"What magic could they be using?" Pilar asked. "If this is magic, and not trickery?"

More than a few eyes turned Ava's way. Maybe it was just because she was from Grimwalt, she thought. Maybe they didn't suspect her of being a spell caster herself.

"There are so many types of magic, and so many don't want to admit they have the ability, that it's impossible to say," she said at last. "The gilla might not be real, it could well be a trick."

"Even in Grimwalt, people don't want to admit to being spell casters?" Britta asked, surprised.

"Think of it this way." Ava gave a wry smile. "When you have an ability that is rare and useful, others sometimes look at you with envy, and wonder whether they can use that ability for their own benefit. So it becomes safer to pretend you have no ability at all, even if the place you are living claims to be accepting of your gifts."

Everyone around the fire seemed various levels of shocked or surprised by her explanation.

"I had never thought of it that way." Dak leaned back, and the glance he flicked her way told her he suspected what she was. "That is a hard way to live."

He really had no idea.

CHAPTER 10

Duncan seemed to be inhaling deep breaths of air as they walked, as if he had been suffocating in the prison.

As he walked past trees and bushes, he touched each one.

"Here," he said, coming to a stop. "We camp here."

She would have preferred a place which had access to water, but as she thought it, a small spring began bubbling up from beneath the rock Duncan was standing beside.

It pooled and then began to run in a tiny stream away from them.

"Stand back," he called to his fellow prisoners.

They hadn't walked for much more than thirty minutes, but Massi could see the exhaustion in some of the faces.

Everyone seemed to stop with a sigh of relief.

The Forest Man crouched, his hands flexing in the pine needles and dirt, and then the trees around them shot out branches just higher than head height, twining around each other where they crossed over, forming a canopy in the clearing where they stood. A hole was left in the very center of the ceiling.

Once the overhead covering was complete, plants began

growing out of the forest floor, tiny-leafed ground cover that smelled sweet when Massi stepped on it, and bushes that sprung up around three sides, forming a rough shelter.

"We need firewood," Duncan said, and Massi joined him, and the few prisoners who still had the energy, in search of dry branches and sticks.

"Clever," Massi told him when Tomas had built a fire in the middle, below the hole in the roof, and they had warmth and light. It looked cozy and welcoming. "I know who I'd like to have as a companion if I ever have to move through a forest."

Everyone settled down, with the dogs seemingly appointing themselves as guardians, snuggling up to the prisoners.

"I know who I want coming for me, if I'm ever made prisoner again," Duncan glanced at her. "Although today was the first time I thought I might be able to escape on my own."

"Why's that?"

His lips quirked. "You saw. They let me outside for the first time in weeks. They thought some rope that the Boss Man brought with him was going to stop me doing anything with my power, and they needed me in better health than I was."

She noticed that he already looked better. He had lost some of the paleness, some of the hollowness around his eyes.

"The rope wasn't going to stop you, though?" She thought again of Ava, of what she'd done to a rope like that.

"What do you know of it?" He had picked up something in her voice, the way he turned to look at her made that clear.

"My friend was bound with a rope like that. She was able to destroy it, although she was so weak from its effects she couldn't run away from her captors, but she made another one to replace it, and wove as much healing into it as she was able, given her weakened state."

He stared at her. "How did she destroy it?"

"She threw it in the fire. Then she used the hair from horse tails to weave another."

"And they didn't notice?" he asked.

"They were too afraid to touch it. So, no."

He gave the first real smile she'd seen on him. "I think the rope she made was the one I wore today."

"I wondered," Massi admitted.

"What happened to your friend?"

"She managed to escape in the end." She had to be careful here, Massi realized. Duncan knew the rope he'd worn was spelled. If she mentioned Ava's name he would know she was a spell caster. And that was not Massi's secret to share.

Just then Velda called a soft good night to her, and she waved back.

Duncan gave a wave, too. "It's good you came to free them. Where will you take them?"

Massi didn't know. "I was going to take them back to Fernwell, but they don't look as if it would be an easy journey for them."

None of the prisoners looked as if they would easily make a long journey.

"Our guards didn't have enough supplies and they were running a skeleton crew," Duncan said. "The Speaker is probably trying to hide the funds he needs to run the prison from other members of the council."

"The mayor of Waldrand is definitely in the know," Massi said. "It makes me nervous about letting any of them go there tomorrow. I hung around the town for a few days, picking up information about where the dogs might be, as well as where Tomas and Velda might be being held, and there's a definite bias for the Speaker there."

She thought about the mayor of Bartolo, who had been enspelled to cooperate with Ava's cousin, the Queen's Herald, in a plan that would have put the people of Bartolo in danger.

Thought of her own enspellment.

"Either that, or the mayor of Waldrand is under the influence of a magical item."

Duncan gave a grunt at that, stepped back from her. "I need to walk in the forest. Sleep. No one can come close without my knowing about it."

She turned to face him fully. "How did they get you?" She still couldn't fathom it.

He gave a sharp shake of his head. "Sleep. No harm will come to anyone tonight."

He turned and disappeared into the darkness, and even with her keen Cervantes senses, she could no longer see or hear him.

She moved closer to the group, found a spot in front of the shelter's opening, putting herself between the prisoners and the entrance, and lay down.

A cold nose touched her neck, and then two of the dogs, bodies wriggling in joy, settled on either side of her.

With a sigh of relief, she closed her eyes, sure she wouldn't sleep, but happy to rest.

And then was sucked into the darkness.

CHAPTER 11

These woods were not his own, but they rejoiced in his presence, all the same.

Duncan waded into the stream to the north of the camp he'd created, and when he found a deep enough pool, immersed himself in the water. He scooped soft sand from the bottom and scrubbed the dirt of months from his skin, came up for air to snap leaves that he knew released soapy foam when rubbed, and worked the sap through his hair.

When he climbed back onto the bank, he felt more himself than he had in a long time.

With the sense of relief, though, came anger.

He had tamped it down in the prison, had concentrated all his energy on escape, but now . . .

The massive oak he was leaning against groaned and shuddered against his palm, and he drew back, ran a calmer, soothing hand down its trunk in apology.

He circled the camp, touching the trees as he went, so that by the time he had come full circle, no one could cross the route he'd taken without him knowing about it.

Massi lay at the entrance to the shelter, two dogs curled up with her. She was a beautiful woman, younger and softer in sleep than she seemed when awake. And smaller than he realized. Her personality made her bigger than she was.

He studied her.

Dark haired, long-limbed and sleek.

She would be a deadly foe, a valuable ally.

He found a spot close to her.

One of the dogs pressed up against her looked up, studied him, and then dropped its head back on her arm with a sigh.

He settled onto the ground, not intending to do more than doze, but his whole body relaxed at the smell of green around him, the feel of the cool ground cover beneath him, the whisper of the branches above.

Free. At last.

He woke with a start, to the sound of low murmurs.

He was no longer on the ground, but instead cradled in an intricate hammock, built from slim, flexible branches that had grown from the forest floor.

The trees had built him a bed.

He smiled. Just like home.

A throat cleared behind him and he glanced over at Massi, found she was studying him.

"You look surprised to find yourself there," she said.

He gave a neutral shake of his head and swung out of his comfortable resting place.

He felt better than he could remember.

Even as he thought that, burning, white hot rage rose inside him, and he closed his eyes, concentrated on bringing it under control.

"It wasn't just lack of food, was it?" When he opened his eyes again, Massi was still watching him. "Something else was making you so thin, because you're already looking better."

The lack of food hadn't helped but he knew why he'd looked so gaunt. He had tried to use too much power, to no avail.

Out in the forests, even ones like this that were not his own, every time he worked magic he got something back.

He had never worked out exactly what the formula was, but when he expended magical energy on things that grew, there was always a net gain to him.

Not a lot, but more than he had when he started.

He had often felt this was somehow wrong. That he should pay a price for using his magic.

But nature was generous with its power and it always rewarded him, no matter what he asked of it.

In the prison, he had used up too much energy and got nothing in return.

"What are your plans?" he asked, ignoring her question.

She narrowed her eyes at his attempt to change the subject, then gave a shrug. "I'll have to talk to Velda and Tomas first, then decide."

She turned away and walked toward the prisoners, most of whom were up already, taking turns to scoop water from the spring he'd allowed to bubble up to the surface.

He followed her, taking note of who was moving slowly, who seemed to be fit.

"They won't all be able to walk to Waldrand." He kept his voice low, standing close to her.

She smelled of the spicy perfume of the ground cover, and he could see dampness on her hairline, so she must have washed already.

"You're right." She sounded calm, but her fingers were flicking against her thighs as she watched their charges. She gave a sigh. "I had planned to run with two people. Now I have forty." She tilted her neck from side to side, as if it were stiff. "I brought this on myself when I acted in the moment last night. I hadn't planned to rescue anyone until I'd come up with an escape route, but then opportunity presented itself." She shrugged, and he didn't sense that she was sorry about it, just slightly annoyed that things weren't going as smoothly as she'd like.

He felt a sudden need to change that. To smooth the way for her.

He hadn't felt that way in some time.

Helping her, helping his fellow prisoners, was also a way to thwart the Speaker, he reasoned. A way to assuage some of the fury inside him.

"We need carts. There are some back at the prison." Even as he spoke, something he was uncomfortably aware was fear clutched at his throat.

Until he had been taken by the Speaker's agents, he had never really known fear.

They were intimate friends now.

And he did not want to return to the prison.

And yet, he knew he would.

He had assumed he would be gone the moment he was free, but he felt an odd sense of aimlessness. A need to do something, strike a blow against his enemy——their enemy——that was both immediate and that would really hurt.

He also wanted to stay around to see what Massi did next.

Something about her, the way she smoothly switched from reconnaissance to action last night, the wildness he had a feeling was just below the surface, called to him.

"How many carts?" She turned to look at him, speculation in her eyes.

"I only saw two."

At his words, she turned sharply to face the direction of the fortress.

"I remember smelling horses." She glanced up at him, and he could see she was annoyed with herself. "I forgot about them while we were getting everyone out. I should get them anyway, whether there are carts to pull, or not. They'll be better off with us rather than back there, with no one to water and feed them until the soldiers are found."

She walked back to where she'd spent the night, lifting her quiver of arrows and her bow over her shoulder.

Of course she would see it as her duty to go. He found he didn't want her to, and also, that he wanted no one else to come with him.

He was strangely unsure of himself, and he never felt that way.

Perhaps it was just that he couldn't bear the thought of anyone being caught up in that place.

Going back meant a chance of recapture.

But they did need the horses. And the carts.

And she was right about the animals being better off out of their stables, as there was no one to care for them now.

He forced himself to nod.

She had come on a mission that would seem to be a personal favor, and yet she had the bearing of a commander of troops.

"Duncan and I will be going back to the prison to get carts and the horses to pull them."

Some of the faces that stared back at her were pictures of horror. Duncan could see he wasn't alone in his fear of returning to that place.

"It's too dangerous," Velda said.

Massi shook her head. "We'll be careful. It's more dangerous for us to move too slowly now in our escape. This is the safer option."

There was a moment of silence as everyone absorbed the implication of her words. That she wasn't going to abandon them to their own devices.

"You'll be taking a risk for those of us who are too old or ill to walk out of here." One of the more frail women slowly got to her feet.

"Everyone leaves together." Massi's gaze swept the bedraggled prisoners. "That is the way we do things in the Rising Wave."

"We are not the Rising Wave," the old man who questioned who Massi was last night muttered.

"Maybe not, but I am." Massi flicked a look at him. "And this is how I work. How some of your own do things, too, as Duncan's the one who told me about the carts."

Duncan kept a stoic expression in the face of the surprise from some of the group.

"Let's go, Forest Man." She strode away, moving silently, and he followed her as she disappeared amongst the trees.

The dogs, realizing she was leaving, streamed after her without so much as a bark among them.

He lost his line of sight on her a few times as she moved between the thick trunks, but he could sense her journey over the root systems of the trees he'd touched the night before and he eventually caught up to her.

"Worried?" she asked when he fell into step with her.

"I worry for whoever tries to stop us," Duncan said, and realized he believed it.

She would not be deterred. And he would bring down his rage on any who got in their way.

He seemed to have a bottomless well of it.

CHAPTER 12

I t was strange walking openly up to the gates of the fortress.

Just yesterday, she had been sliding around the walls, keeping to the shadows.

She glanced over at Duncan as they came to a stop at the entrance, listening. The dogs whined, eager to get in, and she took that as a sign there was no danger.

Duncan crouched down and put both hands on the ground, closed his eyes and then slowly rose to his feet again.

"They are all still asleep. Nothing is moving in there."

Someone had closed the heavy wooden gates on their way out last night, and he opened one side. The dogs surged in and Massi opened the other gate to make it easier to get the carts through later.

Duncan moved ahead of her and she notched her bow as she followed him, just in case, but as he said, it was still and there was no movement other than her, Duncan and the dogs.

He moved around the barracks and she followed him, found the stables. It turned out there were four horses, as well as the two carts Duncan had told her about.

They were old and rickety, the wood a little splintered and pale silver with age, but they would make all the difference.

"This was a good idea," she told him as she greeted the horses.

They had put their big heads over their stalls and nickered at her.

He nodded, then walked out, and knowing the feeling of being back in the prison that held you, even if you were no longer a prisoner, she let him be.

She remembered returning to the Chosen camps after they had turned on the Kassian army. They had been set to fight the Venyatu for the Kassian queen, but Luc had made a deal with General Ru, the commander for the other side, and the Venyatu had withdrawn in the night, giving the Cervantes soldiers the freedom to turn on their masters and wipe out the Kassian troops the queen had allocated to support them in the fight.

Then they had raced back to the camps before word of their victory could spread, to rescue the children still held there.

Those children had been used to control them, to keep them compliant, just as they had been used on those older than them in the years before.

But Luc had smashed that cycle, and they had ridden like lunatics to the camps, and even though she was there to liberate, Massi still recalled the sick feeling of dread she felt as she rode through the camp gates.

So she would let Duncan go, do what he needed to do.

She gave the horses water, then harnessed them up. She hauled out bags of horse feed to take along, feeling the pleasant strain on her muscles as she tossed them into the back of the carts.

She stopped to listen a few times as she worked. Duncan was still nowhere to be seen and the dogs were gone, too.

The quiet made her twitchy.

She led the horses harnessed to the first cart out, around the side of the barracks. The filigree of branches that encased the building seemed denser than they had been last night, and some of them had grown leaves and tiny flower buds.

Duncan was standing in front of the barracks, studying it. There was still no sound from within.

He started when she came around the corner.

"Sorry. I'll get the other one." He strode toward the stables, and she led the cart to the dining hall.

If the horses needed feed, she and the others needed supplies, too.

It would help if they had at least some food of their own. Especially if they wanted to avoid Waldrand, which definitely contained spies for the Speaker.

The door to the dining hall was open.

She wasn't sure if it had been left like that or not, and she drew a knife as she stepped inside.

A dog darted out from the shadows on the far side of the room and gave a yip.

She was more on edge than was usual for her, because she started, then relaxed as the dog came, tail wagging, for a pat.

There was no danger here.

She moved through to the kitchen. It did not smell good, like sour milk and rancid fat, but she found a few bags of apples, some dried biscuits, and a bag of oatmeal that could be cooked over a fire.

She put everything in an old flour bag and tied it off.

It wasn't much, given there were forty of them, but it would help.

She dragged it out of the hall and saw Duncan had brought the other cart up alongside her own.

He walked over to her and took the bag, putting it in the back of his cart as if it weighed nothing.

The muscles in his arms bunched, and she thought they looked a lot more substantial than they had the day before.

He turned, looking at the tower where he'd been held.

The wise thing to do would be to go now, but that might be the jumpiness talking.

"What are you thinking?"

He glanced over at her. "The warden's office is there." He pointed to the door they had come out of last night.

"You think we should search it?" She could see a few good reasons for that. "We could use some funds. It won't be easy to feed everyone and while I have some money, I was expecting two escapees. Not the horde we have."

"Yes." That's all he said, but she felt the tension coming off him.

"I'll go. You can hold the carts." This place did not hold the same power over her as it did him.

"No." He patted the flank of one of the horses. "I need to understand why." He began walking across the open courtyard.

"Why they brought you here?" she asked as she followed him.

Halfway across, he stopped.

Most of the dogs had emerged from wherever in the compound they'd been, and were nosing around a strange patch in the grass.

She altered her path to see what it was and Duncan followed her.

Tiny flowers and mushrooms grew in a roughly human shape.

She stared at it for a long moment before she remembered.

This is where Duncan had lain yesterday.

She thought of the intricate cradle that had grown up around him last night, and wondered what kind of spell caster he was.

"You make an impression."

His lips quirked a little at that, his gaze still on the ground. "These aren't my woods, but they welcome me all the same."

She wondered if these weren't his woods, what his power might be like when he was in his element.

She wondered again how anyone could have taken him prisoner.

Duncan crouched beside the strange bed, brushed it with his fingertips, and then rose. "Time is wasting."

True enough.

She headed for the door and he joined her. All the dogs were at her heels by the time they reached it.

One gave a yip of disquiet when she opened it, and she smelled it, too, as the air escaped from within.

Despair, hunger, and pain.

She glanced at Duncan, but his face was unreadable.

She ran a soothing hand over the dog's head, and thought Duncan could probably use a friendly pat as well, although she didn't touch him.

She stepped through and found the warden's office directly to her left.

Duncan reached around her and tried the door. It wasn't locked.

She stepped inside, with him close enough behind her she felt the heat of his body.

The room was laid out like a study, the desk large but roughly made, as if it had been put together from wood chopped from the forest around the prison.

There were papers piled to one side, and she ran a quick eye over them.

Records of who had been held here.

She took them, folding them into the pack she always carried.

If the Speaker was ever brought to trial, these might be useful.

Duncan was opening drawers, and he pulled out a large tin box.

He shook it gently, and they both heard the rattle of coins.

He set it on the desk and began looking for the key.

Massi handed him a paper knife and he took it with a smile, levering the lid open.

They stood shoulder to shoulder, looking inside.

There was money, although not as much as she would have thought the warden would have needed to run this place. As it was clearly operating on starvation rations, she shouldn't really be surprised.

But the coins were not what was holding Duncan's interest.

There were two small pine cones lying in the box, as well.

He made a sound as he took them out, holding them cradled in his palm.

"What is it?"

He gave a sharp shake of his head and slid them into a pocket.

When he turned to her, she almost took a step back at the darkness in his brown eyes.

Instead, she forced herself to move forward, lifting the tin and dumping the money into her pack.

"Let's go." His voice was hoarse, as if he were holding in a scream. He strode out before she could even nod in agreement, and as she walked back to the horses, the dogs coalesced around her, as eager to leave as Duncan.

There was still no sound from the barracks or the guard hut. She guessed the sleeping spell was at work there.

She left the gates open. It would be easier for someone to find them that way.

All she cared about was having enough time to make a clean escape.

They had food, money, transport.

It was time to go.

CHAPTER 13

Duncan could feel the two cones in his pocket, resonating with him.

He knew them.

Knew where they had come from.

He wondered why they were in the tin box.

Of everything he'd expected, two pieces of his forest were the last.

Finding them had thrown him.

But it was more shocking than that.

Someone hadn't just been in his forest, these pine cones had been taken from the very center of it.

The need to return was almost overwhelming.

Besides, he wasn't really needed here any more.

They had made it back to camp and Massi had gathered up her chicks, putting all who couldn't walk fast enough in the carts.

He had never seen himself as brooding, but he was definitely brooding now, taking up the rear as they headed east, wondering whether he should peel off to the north straight away, or stay with the group a little longer.

The only thing holding him here was the sight of Massi, striding up ahead, the dogs with her.

The light that filtered through the trees illuminated her dark hair, the elegant curve of her cheek, and he found it hard to look away.

She stopped suddenly, turning to face south, and he felt it coming through the ground as a vibration before he heard it——the thunder of hooves.

Massi held up a hand, and Tomas stopped the front cart, forcing the back one to stop, as well.

They couldn't outrun a fit person on foot, let alone a unit of riders. No point trying.

Duncan crouched down, put his hands on the ground.

"Five minutes away," he said to Massi, who was jogging back to him.

"Soldiers," Tomas said. "Coming for the dogs."

Massi pursed her lips, gave a nod. "Probably. They may not be on the Speaker's side."

"Be a bit difficult to know until we talk to them," Ranulf Harkonen said.

"You need to hide," Duncan told her.

She turned to him, eyes wide with surprise.

"Yes." Velda hopped down from the cart. "Take the dogs with you."

"You hide with me," she said. "Better we're both out of sight, able to give help, depending on which way it goes."

He hesitated. He wanted to vent his rage against his enemies, to stand facing them while he did it, but she was right. Being out of sight would give them the advantage of surprise.

Ranulf Harkonan was looking through the trees. The sound of hooves was clear now. "Hurry. It would be better if news of the presence of a Cervantes warrior from the Rising Wave didn't become common knowledge."

Massi nodded, whistled to the dogs, and disappeared off the path.

Duncan followed her, found her stopped at a screen of ferns where they could crouch down out of sight, but still have a good view of the clearing.

The dogs jostled around her and she motioned them to lie down.

Duncan followed suit and Massi landed beside him just as the first rider appeared.

A woman in a Grimwaldian Guard uniform pulled her horse up and let it dance beneath her while the rest of her unit crowded around her.

"Greetings," Ranulf called from between the carts.

"Greetings." The officer's gaze took them all in.

"Can we help you?" Ranulf's tone was polite.

"We were told there was a pack of wild dogs in these woods that needed dealing with."

"The dogs aren't wild," Tomas said. "But as you can see, they are not here."

Duncan sensed the tension in every person, whether they were on foot or sitting in the carts.

If fear had a smell it would be swirling in the air.

"Where are you headed?" The officer had picked up on the tension, on the feeling of balancing on a knife's edge.

"May we ask who you are, first?" Ranulf had clearly decided to step up as the leader.

The officer blinked, and her surprise seemed to affect her horse, who moved restlessly beneath her.

"I am Lieutenant Chart, of the Grimwalt Fourth Division." She glanced across at the man Duncan guessed was her second-in-command. "Who are you?"

"Ranulf Harkonan," Ranulf stated. "High Commissioner to the Council of Grimwalt."

Duncan almost heard the quick intake of breath the officer made.

"I had heard you were missing," she said.

"Not missing. Incarcerated in the stinking prison down the road." Ranulf pointed the way.

"What has this got to do with wild dogs?" Chart's second-in-command asked.

"All of us were held in the prison," Tomas said. "The dogs you were told about are mine and they followed me here after I was taken."

"The problem was the dogs were drawing unwanted attention to the prison," Ranulf broke in, "so you were sent up here to make them go away. To help the Speaker hide his illegal activity."

There was a long moment of silence.

"Who sent the request?" Chart asked. "That wasn't mentioned in my orders."

"The prison warden asked the mayor of Waldrand, who's sympathetic to the Speaker," Camille spoke up.

"If you claim you were in this prison, how are you here now? Did you escape?"

"Clearly," Ranulf answered. "We are on our way back to Taunen."

"I would like to see this prison you're talking about." Lieutenant Chart spoke slowly. "Will one of you show me the way?"

"No." Velda shook her head. "We won't return there. If you want to go look, go look. We will continue on our way."

"I'll ask you to wait here, then," Chart said. "I'll leave some of my unit with you."

In other words, she wanted to be able to round them up later, if necessary.

Chart's second-in-command moved forward. "Why were you all held prisoner in this secret prison? For what reason?" He sounded skeptical.

"For very good reason." Ranulf gave a dry chuckle. "We asked inconvenient questions. Like why the Speaker has made enemies of our neighbors. Or how it is that the Speaker has managed to accumulate more power than his position allows."

"Why don't you come with us?" Velda asked. "Help us get to Taunen safely."

"Those are not my orders." Chart looked like she wished she had never stumbled upon them. Duncan guessed this was not something she wanted to write a report on. At all. "Lieutenant Ventnor will stay with you until I get back."

"If you must go to the prison, don't free the guards. Leave them as they are. They'll get free in a few days, and by then, we'll be out of their reach." Tomas's voice was soft.

Chart said nothing to that.

She was unwilling to agree to anything she didn't understand.

Duncan could respect that, even if the outcome wouldn't suit him.

Beside him, Massi shifted. "She will free them," she whispered.

Duncan agreed. There was no way a military unit would leave the guards and warden imprisoned.

Which meant the time they had to get away was now much less.

Chart bent her head close to her second-in-command and murmured something to him.

Duncan had a bad feeling about it.

"How far is this prison from here?" Chart asked.

"For you, an hour's ride, most likely," Ranulf told her. "Just be aware, while we cannot stop you leaving some of your unit behind, they will have to follow us, because we will not stop. Especially if you plan to free our abductors."

Chart shook her head. "You will stay put with Ventnor until I work out what is going on."

She wheeled her horse to the west and rode away with her team, leaving her second-in-command and three others behind.

Massi slowly drew an arrow out of her quiver.

Duncan put a hand on her arm.

Shooting soldiers would not be good for future relations with the military, and he could see now that they would need to make as many allies as they could.

She went still, her head turned to look at him, gaze steady, her expression telling him she was prepared to wait if he had a better plan.

He put a hand on the ground, reaching down to the tree roots, and sent a shiver through the earth.

The soldiers' horses began to shy.

So did the horses attached to the carts, but Duncan couldn't help that.

He could feel the location of an underground spring, and used the roots to rip the hollow created by the water asunder.

A horse reared in panic as the ground beneath its feet began to collapse and it took off. The other three followed, with the soldiers hanging on, shouting and trying desperately to control them.

The carts were still in place, but the horses were skittish.

"Get going," Duncan called to Tomas as he straightened up.

"Wait." Massi ran forward, handing Ranulf the money they'd taken from the tin box. "Here's money for food along the way. I took it from the warden's office."

"Ha." Ranulf gave a bark of approval.

"Come with us," Velda called from the front cart.

"We'll catch up. We need to make sure they can't follow you." Massi waved to her, and the horses began to move. "Protect," she ordered the dogs, pointing to the carts, and the dogs did her bidding, flowing in a silent stream toward Tomas.

As they vanished between the trees, Duncan bent again, closing the ground so no one would fall into the hole he'd made.

He turned in the direction the soldiers had taken, trying to see if they had managed to get their horses under control.

"That was clever," Massi said, staring in the same direction. "They won't even be sure it wasn't a natural phenomenon."

"Maybe." Duncan touched the pine cones in his pocket. It helped to ward off some of the desperation in him to head home, and run until he reached it. "But they know where the carts are headed, and they will release the guards."

"Yes." She sounded resigned to it.

"What do you want to do?" he asked.

"I have to follow them back to the prison. Find out what they plan to do."

She was right, it was better to know if the unit was going to hunt them down or help them.

It was also the last thing he wanted to do.

His forest called him, he could almost hear it.

"First, let me make this path disappear." It would be near impossible to follow the carts if they couldn't see where they'd gone.

The lieutenant may know the prisoners were headed for Taunen, but there were many ways to reach the capital, and he would make it as hard as possible for anyone to follow them.

Duncan moved in an arc, touching small saplings, young bushes, and, where the ground was bare of growth, touching the soil with his fingers.

When he was done, it didn't look like a path had ever been here.

He felt a spark of green pulse in his chest.

Everything he did here would come at a cost. There would be a longing when he left, like he had lost a piece of himself. And without him, everything he'd caused to grow here would wither in time.

He wondered, with actual pain, how his own forest fared, with him gone for nearly two months.

He did not want to imagine.

When he looked up, he saw Massi watching him carefully, as if he were an injured animal she wasn't sure wouldn't bite.

He didn't know how to read her. "You're not troubled by my casting?"

She lifted her shoulders. "That would make me a hypocrite."

"You have power yourself?" He thought he'd felt it, thought he'd seen it, but he hadn't been sure.

She shook her head. "I use the power of others, though."

He wondered what she meant by that, but the sound of the four soldiers trying to make their way back to where the carts had been suddenly broke into their conversation.

"Time to go." She paused, tilted her head. "You don't have to come with me. You have just as much right to escape as the others."

He looked at her for a long beat, the sound of the horses getting closer and closer. "This isn't even your country, let alone your fight. No one has more right to walk away than you do."

She shook her head. "I told Ava I would help Tomas and Velda, get them home. I need to make sure they have a clear window of time to escape."

She didn't explain further, but he sensed there was more to it than that.

He should leave.

But the thought of walking away now was suddenly abhorrent.

He didn't want to slink away.

He wanted to inflict some damage.

"I'll come," he said. He closed his hand over the pine cones again, pressing hard enough for the edges to dig into his palm.

She gave a tiny nod, then began walking back the way they'd come.

The soldiers were still blundering toward them, but having difficulty in the thick undergrowth.

He moved in place behind her and found that the longing to leave had eased a little.

CHAPTER 14

Massi kept behind the trees as they approached the fortress, Duncan a solid presence behind her.

It was a comforting feeling, knowing he was there, protecting her back.

She could see Chart and her three soldiers had secured their mounts outside the prison. They'd tied them to an old post just outside the gates.

The lieutenant had obviously decided on a cautious approach, leaving the horses outside for a quick getaway.

"Those horses might come in handy," Duncan said softly in her ear.

Massi tried not to flinch in surprise at the puff of warm air on her skin as he was suddenly beside her.

"They might," she agreed.

She moved forward toward them, and he came with her, absolutely silent as he moved across the ground.

They took all four horses, led them a short way into the forest, and after a moment's hesitation, Duncan enclosed the small grassy clearing they'd found to hide them in with bushes, corralling them in.

"Nice," she told him.

He glanced over at her in surprise, and then grinned.

The way he manipulated growing things seemed to be effortless. There was surely a cost, but right now he seemed willing to pay it.

So far he had hardly broken a sweat.

She slid through the late-morning shadows, back toward the prison entrance, and then went very still.

A tall man, standing with his back to them, was studying the open gates. His horse was tied to the same post as the horses they'd just stolen.

"The Boss Man." Duncan's soft murmur was more interested than fearful, his body a big, solid wall behind her.

It was a good thing they hadn't driven the carts toward Waldrand. They would have ridden right into him.

"I thought he was leaving first thing," Massi murmured.

"Yes. I wonder what changed his mind."

"Who's there?"

The voice that called out from within the fortress was Chart's.

"The Speaker's Aide." There was a tightness in the Boss Man's voice. "And you are?"

Chart appeared, walking toward the gate to stand in front of him, her three soldiers ranged behind her, just within the fortress.

The Boss Man's demeanor changed.

He relaxed, as if he were relieved to see her.

"I was worried when the guards at the gate didn't hail me," he said. "What's happened to them?"

"I'd like to know that myself." Chart sounded just a little upset. "The Speaker's Aide, you say? I haven't heard of that position."

"It's not commonly known. You're obviously Grimwalt military. What unit are you from?"

"Fourth Division. Lieutenant Chart. What's your name?"

The Boss Man paused.

"Here it is," Massi murmured, half turning back to Duncan. "I don't know how he can refuse to answer."

"He'll lie." Duncan shifted behind her, and she suddenly felt a frisson of awareness——of how close they stood, of how comfortable she was with him.

"My name isn't important," the Boss Man said.

That was interesting. He could have lied and Chart wouldn't have known any different. Now she was suspicious.

"Yes, it is." Chart stared at him in surprise.

"We'll have to agree to disagree." He stepped to the side, looking through the open gate to the right, and froze. "Again I'll ask you, what's happened here?"

He must have seen what Duncan had done to the guard hut.

"According to some people we met along the road, they were held here. They escaped, leaving the guards unable to go after them for a few days." Chart waved a hand. "Looks like spell casting was involved."

"You encountered the prisoners and didn't force them back?" The Boss Man's voice went low.

"I'm not a gaoler. I didn't know there was a prison here. And given one of the prisoners was the missing High Commissioner, Ranulf Harkonan, someone I have been asked to look for in case he was the victim of a crime, my question to you is what do you know of this place?"

"Oh, dear." The Boss Man lifted his hands and although she couldn't see his face, Massi could see his demeanor change again.

Now he was playing the oops-you-caught-me card.

"Maybe the Speaker has been indulging in a bit too much paranoia." He shrugged. "He shouldn't have taken Harkonan, or any of them, really, but he was worried they were a danger to the government, and he wanted to stash them somewhere secure while he investigated if they were a threat or not."

There was a long, stretched-out silence at that.

It was an absurd argument.

"Do you think I'm an idiot, Speaker's Aide?" Chart asked.

"No." The Boss Man turned away slightly, and then struck out at her, shouting something as he did it.

Chart staggered back, a hand going to her neck, and Massi

stepped forward without thought as she saw the blood running between Chart's fingers.

Duncan gripped her shoulder, holding her back, and she settled, aware there was no saving the woman now, anyway.

Of the three soldiers behind the lieutenant, one stepped forward to help and then fell, crying out in surprise and pain. As he toppled over, Massi saw a fellow soldier stood behind him, a long blade in his hand, dripping with blood.

"Both of you?" the Boss Man asked, looking between the two left standing.

They nodded.

"What did he shout?" Duncan wondered, voice almost inaudible.

"I didn't hear it properly. Some word to activate his allies?" Massi guessed.

The Boss Man hadn't known if any of them were on his side, she realized. He'd been prepared to kill them all.

And he probably could have, she admitted.

He was fast. Accurate. And merciless.

The two soldiers who remained looked less than thrilled at what had happened.

It was one thing to agree to a course of action in theory. Actually cutting down your companions was something else entirely.

"You going to hold it together?" the Boss Man barked at them.

He'd seen it, too——the dawning horror in their faces.

"What was this for?" one of them asked.

"I can't have word of this prison getting out and she didn't seem like someone who would let it go." The Boss Man stepped over her body, his focus back on what lay beyond the gate. "Or am I wrong?"

"No. She had a lot of integrity," the other soldier said, voice tinged with bitterness. "She wouldn't have let it go."

Both the Boss Man and the other soldier turned to look at him.

"Well, how was this right?" he demanded of them.

"Depends on what your version of right is." The Boss Man moved away, deeper into the courtyard.

"Not this," the soldier muttered under his breath.

The Boss Man turned, a quick twist of his body, and a knife bloomed in the soldier's throat. He grabbed it by the hilt, staggered back, tripped over the body of the soldier who'd been killed with Chart, and fell.

Massi could hear the rattle of his breath as he tried to breathe.

She already had an arrow notched on her bow, she realized. It had been a completely unconscious action.

"Yes," Duncan told her, in full agreement.

She shot.

She couldn't miss, and yet, between the moment she released the string and when the arrow should have met its target, the Boss Man moved.

Not quite fast enough, because the arrow lodged into his right shoulder, and his cry of pain and rage was clear, but she shouldn't have missed, and she'd been aiming for his eye.

Magic.

She could explain it no other way.

"Good shot," Duncan said.

She shook her head. "He's warded. Either he's a spell caster himself, or he's wearing something that protects him. He should be dead."

The Boss Man screamed to the other soldier, who ran forward, grabbed him, and dragged him out of sight.

What now?

The soldier with the knife in his throat was still breathing, but Massi could see that he wouldn't last much longer.

She eyed the gate. They could close it, Duncan could do his trick and bind it, but there was still the ladder behind the hut, which she was sure the Boss Man would find sooner or later. It was an easy way out.

Breaking cover to close the gate wasn't without risk, either.

Right now, the Boss Man didn't know she existed.

It was probably better to keep it that way.

The sound of horses hooves became clear, and suddenly the four soldiers in Chart's unit who they'd cut off from the carts galloped in from the left.

The sight of Chart, lying dead on the ground, caused the lieutenant's second-in-command, Ventnor, to rein in so hard, his horse almost threw him.

"What——?" He leaped down and ran to Chart's side, kneeling beside her. He suddenly turned his head sharply and scrambled around her body to crouch beside the soldier with the knife in his neck.

Massi saw the soldier's hand flutter.

Ventnor bent closer. It looked like the soldier whispered in his ear.

Ventnor's head came up, his whole body tense, and Massi saw the soldier who'd dragged the Boss Man to safety was peering around the guard hut, using it as a shield.

"We were attacked," he called out to Ventnor, keeping his voice low and urgent. "Come in, quickly."

But Ventnor drew a sword instead, calling a short command that had the other three each turning their horses to face a different direction, looking for danger.

"Come in, Ventnor!" The order was sharp, as if the soldier in the fortress was in command.

"I don't take orders from you, Renard," Ventnor said. "Is that blood on your knife?"

Ventnor rose up, standing over his friend, knuckles white against the hilt of his sword, his gaze steady.

Renard looked down, then across at the group again, and finally seemed to notice that his former friend was still alive, that Ventnor knew of his duplicity.

The look on his face, a sudden dropping of all pretense, was astonishing to see.

He called out a word, the same one the Boss Man had used to activate the soldiers before, and which once again Massi found she couldn't quite hear properly, but nothing happened.

He slowly eyed the four soldiers and then swore, popping back behind the hut.

There were no more allies to call on for the Boss Man in Chart's group, and they were surrounded by four well-armed, trained soldiers.

As soon as Renard disappeared, Ventnor crouched back down and then turned to his group, shook his head.

"Dead?" one of them asked.

Ventnor nodded.

He kept his eyes on the hut as he moved back to his horse, but his gaze kept flicking to the three lying dead on the ground, and Massi could see he was reluctant to leave them.

Duncan made a small sound of annoyance beside her, and was suddenly gone, melting back into the forest.

She let him go. She guessed what he might be up to, and left him to it.

"Wait." The Boss Man limped out, pressing a cloth to his shoulder to stem the blood around the arrow that he hadn't yet removed. His face had lost all color, and he was shivering.

He would do anything to keep Ventnor from talking about what he'd witnessed. About the fortress, the death of the lieutenant, the disloyalty of some of the troops.

But it looked like he was too injured to use force to do it.

"Who are you?" Ventnor asked.

"Not someone you want to cross. I want you to forget about this place and what happened here." The Boss Man leaned against the gate as if his legs needed help. His voice was not steady. "I want to know what you need me to give you or promise you in order for you to agree to do that for me."

"You're trying to bribe me?" Ventnor sounded astonished. "With my lieutenant lying dead?"

"I'm trying to keep the stability of Grimwalt intact," the Boss Man said. "I'm asking you what you need to see things my way."

"Ranulf Harkonen was telling the truth, this is a prison."

Ventnor stood beside his horse, his voice slow. "The Speaker is acting outside of his powers."

The Boss Man shook his head. "To think, I was supposed to leave Waldrand early this morning. I have to be back in Taunen urgently, but I spoke to someone last night who keeps an eye on things for me in town, and he told me there was a woman poking around, an archer, listening quietly in the inns, and I decided to warn the warden to look out for her before I left." He gave a short laugh. "I could be well on my way by now, completely unaware any of this was happening."

Massi thought he sounded wistful, as if he would have preferred to be in ignorance of the prison escape, the discovery of it by the military. One extra worry he wouldn't have on his shoulders.

That was interesting.

"That isn't a possibility for either of us," Ventnor said. "But I'm guessing you found the archer."

The Boss Man looked down at the arrow in his shoulder and grimaced. "I think so."

Well, it seemed he did know she existed.

Pity.

Ventnor had reached his horse, but he hadn't swung back up into the saddle yet, his gaze still going to his fallen friends.

"Again, what can I offer you to not go back to Taunen with this story?" the Boss Man asked.

Just then, three of the horses they had enclosed in the clearing trotted out of the forest.

A moment later, Duncan was crouched beside her again.

She gave a hum of approval.

The horses might have been useful, but Ventnor needed them more, and they still had one left.

The moment he saw them, Ventnor whistled them over.

He walked to Chart, lifting her body over his shoulder and then strapping her to the saddle. The other soldiers leaped down and did the same with the other two.

"It will be a hard job to bring what you've seen here to the right people's attention," the Boss Man commented, looking on as they worked in quick, silent cooperation. "It'll ruin your career. No one will want to go against the Speaker, and they won't want to hear any really bad accusations against him."

Ventnor studied him. "I don't know enough about what's going on to apprehend you now, but I'll know you again. You won't be able to hide from me." He swung into his saddle, holding the reins of Chart's horse, and he and his little group rode away without another word.

Massi was impressed.

"Shit." The Boss Man slowly slid down the gate and sat on the ground, his face slick with sweat and tight with pain.

Should she try to kill him again, Massi wondered? He wasn't attacking anyone right now, and he was probably still warded.

She had a feeling she would regret not doing it later, but it still felt wrong.

"Ventnor's mother is head of the Second Division," the soldier who'd betrayed his friends said as he stepped out into the open. "He won't find it as hard to get people to listen as you think."

The Boss Man dropped his head back and banged it against the wooden planks. "It would have been nice to have had that information earlier, Renard."

"Why? What difference would it have made?" Renard leaned against the wall.

"I have a small dagger in my boot, I might have risked throwing it at him, even though I can barely aim with my left hand." He got clumsily to his feet. "Now you'll have to chase him down and kill him on the way to Taunen."

"Me?" Renard gave a laugh, like he thought the Boss Man was joking. "What do we do with the guards locked behind the vines?"

"Leave them. They can hack their way out. I'm already behind because of this."

"My horse is still missing." There was a slight whine to Renard's voice.

The Boss Man moved slowly toward his own mount. His whole

right side from his shoulder down was dark with blood. "You'll have to make your way on foot to Taunen. I don't care what you do after that. I've got somewhere I need to be."

"Hey. I risked my whole career to answer your call. What am I supposed to do now?"

"When you reach Taunen, speak to someone called Carvellis, tell him I sent you. He'll find something for you to do." The Boss Man slowly pulled himself into the saddle. "But first, find a way to stop Ventnor from talking."

He turned the horse toward the gate, as if he were going to go back inside. He was just urging his horse forward when a rider emerged from the narrow track to Waldrand.

Massi recognized him. He was a heavy-set man she had seen in the taverns and inns of Waldrand.

This was likely the Boss Man's spy, who'd noticed her hanging around town.

"Who were the other group I passed on the way in?" he asked as he drew his horse up. "They were unfriendly and in a rush."

The rider suddenly noticed the arrow in the Boss Man's shoulder and his jaw dropped. "I assume the three bodies they had with them were your doing, were they?"

The Boss Man gave a grunt. "Why are you here, Gunter?"

"Message from the Skäddar border came in for you." He held out a roll of parchment.

The Boss Man reached out to take it, and then paused. "It's been unsealed."

"The mayor opened it in error." Gunter shrugged. "Forgot it was on his desk until this morning."

There was a moment of silence.

Massi had a feeling the Boss Man didn't believe that.

"You've read it?" the Boss Man asked quietly.

"Sure." Gunter gave another shrug. "I'm nosy. And you wouldn't believe me if I said no, anyway."

The Boss Man lifted his face skyward for a moment.

"It's a report from Skäddar. From some spy, maybe?" Gunter

looked completely relaxed about his transgression. "Something about a massacre a month or so back."

The Boss Man said nothing for a beat, then gave a shake of his head. "What's the bastard been up to while I was away?"

He pointed to Renard with an angry jab of his finger. "Take this one back to town, Gunter. Get him a horse." The Boss Man pulled out a bag of coins and tossed it to Renard. It missed, going wide, and landed a short distance from him. "Do what I told you to do."

Renard trudged over to the bag and picked it up. "How long will you be, because if I do as you say, questions will be asked. Ventnor isn't a nobody. Neither is Chart. I'll have to go into hiding."

"I told you, go to Carvellis. He'll fix it for you." The Boss Man's smile was all teeth. He paused. "I didn't ask you, how did you find the fortress to begin with? Why were you here?"

"We were ordered to find some wild dogs and deal with them," Renard said. "Instead, we found two cart-loads of people who told us they'd been held prisoner here. Chart wanted to see if there was any truth to their claims."

"That's why she mentioned the High Commissioner, Ranulf Harkonan?"

"He was one of them, yes."

"And was there a big man with a beard?" The Boss Man's voice was suddenly urgent.

"There were lots of men with beards. None stood out as particularly big, but some were sitting down." Renard shrugged.

"He would have gone straight home." The Boss Man gave a slow nod. "Despite what I said earlier, it looks like it's a very good thing I *did* come back here." He pulled a missive out of his bag, opened it clumsily with one hand, and used his elbow to keep the paper from curling up as he scribbled on it. He was breathing as if he'd run a mile when he eventually held it out to Gunter. "Send this to Illoa. It's urgent."

Gunter took it, and as soon as he did, the Boss Man turned his horse back to the gates and rode into the fortress.

"Where's he going?" Massi kept her voice soft. "To get the rope?"

Duncan lifted his shoulders, but the way he was so focused on the gate, it seemed he was very curious himself.

"What happened here?" Gunter asked Renard.

"Prisoners escaped using spell work, looks like." Renard pointed inside, and Gunter slid off his horse and came to stand beside him. He gave a low whistle of astonishment.

"The guard hut is completely covered in vines."

"So's the barracks and a couple of other buildings," Renard said.

"And the guards?"

"I think they're inside."

Gunter blew out a breath. "I'm fine with leaving. Right now."

"Should we wait for——?"

The Boss Man emerged, and he looked like a gathering storm. He held two bags in one hand.

"Got what you needed?" Renard asked.

The Boss Man gave him a look, one that balanced on the sharp edge of violence, and then rode away.

Massi guessed he was going to take the main route out of town toward the Skäddar border. It was the fastest way.

Whatever the Boss Man had been looking for, it hadn't just been the rope. And it looked like he hadn't found it.

She would bet her enchanted shirt he had been looking for those pine cones Duncan had taken.

She glanced at Duncan and saw his lips were twisted in a smug look of triumph.

CHAPTER 15

Ava leaned forward on her horse and narrowed her eyes against the blast of an icy wind.

They had reached their destination for the day, a flat area where the Kassian, Grimwalt and Venyatu borders intersected.

The place where the Rising Wave messengers had set up camp in order to intercept and send messages to Massi.

The Venyatux escarpment rose from the plains in the east, the mountains that stretched across Grimwalt's southern border stood tall to the north, and the open grasslands that formed part of what had once been the independent lands of the Cervantes lay south and to the west.

There were two lonely tents pitched on the side of the road, the only sign of the messengers.

A woman had come up from the river when she'd heard them arrive and was now laughing with the other Rising Wave soldiers in delight. The other messenger, Ava heard, was in Illoa, getting supplies.

Luc had gone over to the soldier he'd stationed here to talk, but Ava was too far away to hear what they were discussing.

There was no village or any sign of life.

They had passed a small settlement yesterday, but had seen no other sign of habitation since.

No travelers were in sight either, the road in all three directions was empty.

Soldiers began setting up camp all around her, and Ava forced herself to get off her horse.

Luc had the tent buckled to his horse, and he had moved on from the messenger and was now talking to their Skäddar contingent.

Usually, she'd be up there with him, participating, but she was tired.

She was much better than she had been, but hard riding and uncomfortable nights were taxing even at full strength, and she was far from that yet.

She found a rock to sit on, pulled out some knitting, and began to work on it, feeling the repetitive motion begin to soothe her.

"What are you humming?" Luc asked, surprising her from behind, his hands sliding onto her shoulders.

"Was I humming?" She did that sometimes without knowing it. More time had passed than she'd realized, the sun almost set, the sky in the west a vibrant mix of red and orange.

Luc kissed the top of her head, then bent to study the wool in her hands.

"What are you making?"

"Something to help me heal quicker," she said.

She hadn't had a clear idea of what she wanted to make when she'd started, but her thoughts kept going to the fear she felt at being weak and helpless again, and she knew that whether she planned it or not, she was weaving strength and healing into the simple tunic.

"Good." He was still watching her, she could feel his gaze on her, so she twisted and looked up at him.

"What is it?"

He shook his head. "Nothing. I'll set up the tent."

She worried him, she forced herself to admit as she watched him unbuckle the tent and set it up in quick, efficient movements.

He'd been frightened by her abduction, and even more frightened by the state of her health when she'd managed to escape.

She had to admit that in his shoes, she would feel the same.

But it was hard on a woman's ego to be seen as fragile, when she'd once been considered the unbeatable champion ring fighter in the Venyatux army.

At least he hadn't seen her when she had been so insubstantial she'd literally been translucent. She hadn't told him about that, and had decided she never would.

She put away her knitting, stood, and began to pull their bedding out of the saddle bags.

They worked in companionable silence, making the tent cozy, and when they were done, the sun had almost completely faded and the warm light of fires flickered across the camp. The scent of cooking wafted across on air that was cold enough to hurt a little when she breathed it in.

She shivered and hunched deeper into her cloak as she and Luc found a place to sit.

She let the conversation swirl around her as she ate, forcing herself to finish her bowl, even though she didn't feel like it.

She needed the energy.

"What's life like in Grimwalt?" someone asked her, and she raised her head when she realized the chatter had fallen off.

She had started her journey in the Rising Wave with a lie that she was Venyatux. Then that lie had had to change, and she'd pretended she was a spy for General Ru. And then finally, when they'd reached Fernwell, she'd had to admit to being the niece of the Kassian queen.

She'd never worked out what her fellow soldiers thought about that, but most seemed to have accepted it without too much difficulty.

Now that she was the queen, people had remembered that her father, the old queen's half-brother, had been exiled in Grimwalt, had married into a Grimwaldian family, and it was no doubt just one of the stories that seemed to sustain the troops as much as food and water.

"I didn't live in Grimwalt for long periods of time," she admitted. "I traveled with my parents, who were trade envoys, and then I was held prisoner in Kassia, but the time I did spend there was good. Dark, thick forests. High mountains. Very good cakes."

Someone groaned at that. "Cake. Why don't we have any cake?"

"Maybe we could nip across the border and get some," someone called, and there was joking about how to accomplish that.

The closest town from here was Illoa.

Her abductors had been taking her there when she'd escaped, and she had spent a night in the town. It straddled the border, with the bridge over the river serving as the check-point between the two countries.

"Illoa has Grimwaldian cakes on the Kassian side," she said, interrupting the fanciful plans of how to sneak across the river and raid a bakery. "It's no more than an hour's ride from here."

There was a sudden, thoughtful silence from the group.

"That's where Vindar, the other messenger, has gone to check for messages from Massi and to get supplies," someone said.

"Some of the unit will have to go in tomorrow," Luc said. "We need supplies ourselves."

Ava looked at him in surprise. "Wouldn't that risk drawing Grimwaldian attention?"

"Not if those who go keep up the fiction that we're on our way to Venyatu."

"You think we might learn something?" Ava asked.

It wasn't likely the Illoans would know what was going on at Grimwalt's northern-most border, but it wasn't impossible.

Whether anyone who did know something would freely discuss it with strangers was another story.

Of course, if she went, she could make them talk.

But going there herself would probably not be wise.

Luc could go for her.

He knew what she could do, could take some of her spell work and try his luck in Illoa.

But he wouldn't leave her.

She knew that without any hint of a doubt.

So no one would be forced to spill their secrets——if they had any. They'd have to take a chance that a passing trader had loose lips.

The thought of a day in town seemed to really buoy the unit.

As word of a trip to Illoa worked through the camp, she could hear a lift in the voices, an excitement in the air.

Even the Venyatux, who were set to continue on home once they crossed the border into Venyatu, seemed interested in participating in the plan.

"They're bored," Luc told her when she brought it up.

They were crouched together on the banks of the Malin River, the border line between Kassia and Grimwalt. It ran parallel to the road in to Illoa, and Ava forced herself to scoop its icy water onto her face and brush her teeth, hunching against the cold.

"Bored?"

"The war is won, and they've had many weeks of peace. They're itching for something new to do." There was acceptance of it in Luc's voice.

Maybe it was because she was not quite herself still, but to Ava, a bit of peace and quiet sounded wonderful.

"Are you also bored?" she asked, straightening.

"No." His arm came around her shoulders, drawing her close to his warmth, and she snuggled in as they walked slowly back to their tent. "But when you've spent years thinking of taking down an enemy, it's hard to switch that part of your brain off when your plans have succeeded."

"*Especially* if they've succeeded," Ava guessed.

She had done the same, she admitted. Spent years working out how to punish her cousin and aunt for her parents' deaths and her own imprisonment, but now that she had achieved her aims, she felt nothing but relief.

All she needed to do now was negotiate a system of government in Kassia that was fair and equitable, and she would be free.

To do what? a little voice whispered in her ear.

She let the thought go.

She would wait until she was actually free of the Kassian throne to worry about it.

"Commander?" Helmi stepped out of the darkness near their tent, obviously waiting for them. Pilar rose up from where he'd been sitting at her feet.

"You want to go to Illoa, as well?" Luc guessed.

Helmi grinned. "Yes. We might hear something useful about Grimwalt's relationship with Skäddar, if we're lucky."

"That's fine with me. Will Britta and Dragir go, too?"

Pilar tilted his head. "They want to see it, so yes. They never expected to get the opportunity to see something of Kassia."

"Things have definitely changed," Helmi said. "We're a bit dizzy with the idea of being allowed to have a look around Kassia, with the permission of the rulers of Kassia itself."

That was true.

Carila, Ava's childhood fight instructor, had grown up on the border between Skäddar and Venyatu, and had told her many tales of the suspicion most of the southern lands had for the Skäddar. Until recently they had been considered isolated, secretive and unfriendly.

The Rising Wave alliances had changed more than just the control of Kassia. It had created a new power structure in the region.

"Are you going?" Pilar asked.

Luc shook his head. "Ava will be in danger there, and so we'll be staying here."

There was no hint of disappointment in his voice.

"You think someone is still watching for you there?" Helmi frowned at Ava.

"The Grimwalt border is directly across the bridge over the

Malin River," Ava said with a shrug. "The quieter I am on my travels, the safer."

The two Skäddar nodded and then melted back into the darkness.

"We are building a strong core of allies," Luc said with satisfaction, looking after them. "Nothing makes us safer than friends who will not hesitate to help us."

She knew the security of the Cervantes had been his driving ambition since he'd been taken to the Chosen camps as a young teenager. He didn't just want to free his people, he wanted them to thrive. He understood that the better the whole region did, the better the Cervantes would do.

What was her driving ambition, she wondered?

Now she had avenged her parents, and had ended the system that allowed her to be imprisoned with impunity, she had a world of choices ahead of her.

And now was not the time to worry about it.

There were immediate issues that needed her attention.

After that, well, anything was possible.

Luc had gone silent, and she glanced up at him, found him looking at her intently.

"What?"

"Can't I look at my heart's choice?" he asked.

"As long as it's with desire, and not pity," she told him.

"Pity?" he shook his head. "The only people I pity are those who think to cross you." There was a faint thread of humor in his voice. "And I am not that stupid."

"Good." She felt a surge of lightness, of relief that they were slipping back into the teasing that had been part of their relationship since they'd taken Fernwell. "I wouldn't have chosen a stupid heart's choice, anyway."

She was suddenly swept up into his arms.

"Let's see how clever I can be."

CHAPTER 16

A va sat at the fire, knitting.

Luc watched her, head bent over her work, and wondered if she knew she was humming again.

He had a feeling she didn't.

There was a sense of growing tension around the camp. The soldiers who'd gone to Illoa weren't back yet, and they were already a few hours late.

Something had definitely gone wrong.

He rose to his feet, his gaze on the road to Illoa. It was time to stop hoping they'd appear, and go looking for them.

This shouldn't have been a dangerous mission.

The Rising Wave controlled Kassia, and Illoa was in Kassia, even if on its very edge.

While the population of the town weren't members of the Rising Wave, they would be attuned enough to what was happening, being a border town and a center for trade, that they would know the way the wind blew in Kassia.

They would not court trouble.

However, the Grimwaldians had easy access to the town, and so there was some risk.

Still, Dak was with the group. He had the skill to see trouble coming and cut it off before it could grow into anything serious.

The whole group had gone as Venyatux soldiers, whether they were Venyatux or not, under the pretext of spending their last Kassian coins before they moved across the border and went home, as well as buying supplies.

The bulk of the unit had stayed behind, swimming in the river and relaxing, repairing clothing, saddles, and tending to their mounts.

If there were spies watching, they would see a Venyatux unit resting for a few days before heading home.

"Are you going to go looking for them yourself?" Ava looked up from her knitting, her expression serious.

Luc knew what she was asking.

He didn't want to leave her, but he was beginning to get the stomach-dropping feeling of a need for urgency.

Going himself was something he wouldn't have hesitated to do before she was so badly damaged by her abductors.

He looked around at the men and women around the fire who were watching him intently. "Go get kitted up, we're leaving in five minutes." He counted them as they stood. "Find four more," he told Lucilla, one of the more senior soldiers. That would give him ten.

Everyone jumped to their feet and raced off, eager to be included.

He leaned close to Ava, lowered his voice. "Can you come with me? Using the scarf?"

"Invisible?" she asked, softly. She sounded as if she was considering whether to be insulted by his request or not.

"Always good to have a hidden advantage."

She tilted her head. Gave a slow nod. "The others can't know. That makes the hidden advantage a little more tricky."

"Still . . ." He pulled her to her feet. "It's much better than nothing."

"It'll look strange if my horse is coming along without a rider."

"My horse can take us both."

She smiled suddenly, and he realized she'd decided to accept the balance he was trying to keep.

Having her with him, but invisible and much less likely to come to harm. Especially if they had to go all the way into Illoa, where Grimwaldians had been waiting to take her across the border mere months before.

He had come to understand that he needed to loosen the grip of fear that overcame him every time he felt the delicate bones beneath her skin. She was not as fragile as she appeared, and he was going to damage something between them if he didn't stop trying to shield her.

He needed to remember that she had saved herself from her abductors, and from the magic they'd used on her.

He'd nothing to do with it. And then she'd come to save him.

She slipped past him, back to their tent, and he moved through the camp, keeping his voice low as he found his senior officers and let them know what was happening.

"It may be something's happened to them in Illoa itself, but just in case whatever is wrong finds its way to us out here, we need to be ready. I know we already have a watch set up, but double it."

Yarlun, the most senior officer after Dak, gave a nod. "You want us to pretend to be relaxed and unsuspecting?"

"Yes. Someone might already have eyes on us."

"So they'll know you're going off toward Illoa."

Luc lifted his shoulders. "Can't be helped. We can do a bit of joking about hauling them out of the inn."

"And Ava?" Yarlun asked.

"She's coming with me. I've asked her to hang back and shadow us, in case we need someone to go for help." The lie was another balance, keeping people from knowing about her magic, but still letting Yarlun know she wouldn't be in camp. If he couldn't find her, he'd spend precious resources searching for her for no good reason.

Yarlun blinked at that, which told Luc just how obvious he'd been in his overprotective handling of her, but eventually gave a nod. "Good luck."

"Keep on your toes," Luc warned him. Because the feeling of dread had only grown heavier.

He found his horse already saddled, and when he stepped up to it, an invisible Ava touched his back.

He mounted, then reached down, hand out to empty air, and felt her warm fingers close around his wrist.

When he lifted her up behind him he decided she was lighter than she had been before, but not the insubstantial weight that would have driven him into an icy rage a month ago.

She *was* getting better.

The ten soldiers he'd assembled were waiting for him on the road, and he moved his horse into the middle of the pack.

"We're going to pretend we think they're drunk and sleeping it off in Illoa, that we're leaving early tomorrow so we have to get them back." He kept his voice soft.

"You think someone is watching and listening?" Lucilla asked, voice almost a whisper.

"Don't know, but it isn't worth taking a chance on. Be ready for anything."

They all nodded.

He took the lead, letting his horse settle into a smooth canter on the well-kept road. Ava's weight was warm against his back, and he could feel she was resting her cheek against his shoulder.

They had gone almost all the way to Illoa when a shout off to the left, from behind a stand of trees, had Ava's arms tightening around his waist.

They slowed to a stop, listening.

Whoever was behind the trees was clearly doing the same, because there was sudden silence there, as well.

Now that Luc was looking, he could see the faint glow of firelight.

"Hello!" Luc called. It was ridiculous to pretend they didn't know the group was there. "Dak, is that you? You bastard, making me come out in the night to drag your drunken ass back to camp."

He hoped his half-joking, half-pissed off tone struck the right note as he moved his horse forward, his gaze flicking to the others in the group.

Everyone knew there was no way any of their group would be camped forty minutes from their base for no good reason.

Something was going on.

Lucilla glanced at him, gave a nod. "Eliza, you there, too? We've got riding to do tomorrow, and you're lying on the side of the road? What the heck?"

Luc saw movement, the shadow of someone slipping into the trees. He tapped Ava's thigh.

"I saw them," she murmured in his ear.

His horse stepped through the trees lining the road and he found himself in a long, open clearing that had likely been cleared by traders, a place to park their carts, end to end.

Dak had risen to his feet, his eyes gleaming as the flames of a small campfire danced in front of him.

"Luc." He gave a lopsided grin, as if he was thrilled to see an old friend, but Luc saw him close his hand into a fist and then flick his fingers out and hold them stiffly apart.

Their old signal.

Danger.

Enemies.

Ambush.

"How much did you have to drink?" he asked, keeping his tone amused.

"This much." Dak held his hands out, then adjusted them wider. He gave another smile. "And we made friends!" With an over-exaggerated flourish, he pointed to three men who were already on their feet.

They were dressed in the plain, dark clothes of seasoned travelers, but Luc could see they were most certainly not drunk, nor very friendly.

"Where're you from?" he asked them.

They didn't like his tone, he could tell.

"Illoa," one said.

"Oh, why stop so close to home?" Luc asked.

"They're going to Venyatu," Dak said, his voice too loud. "They wanted to come with us."

"I'm afraid we don't travel with merchants, we're a military unit." Luc flicked his gaze around the makeshift camp. His team had spread out behind him, murmuring softly to the others who were picking themselves up, rolling up blankets, as if chastened.

"Saddle up, we're leaving now." He leaned forward in his saddle, looking at Dak. "Can you ride?"

"Maybe, maybe not." Dak chuckled as he spoke. "Had to stop here on the way home, and then we were too tired to leave."

Dak hadn't wanted to bring these three, and whoever it was that had snuck off into the trees, to the camp, Luc realized. He must have decided it was better to find an excuse to stop traveling than to try shake them off and risk them following.

Which of course they would do right now as soon as everyone set off.

They had said nothing after the one word answer to his question on where they were from, and that was obviously a lie.

These were Grimwaldians.

They stood, watching everyone pack up and get in the saddle. There was something wrong with the way they stood so still in the midst of all the hurried action.

"Loop back around," Ava murmured in his ear. "I'll stay behind, hear what gets said."

That was logical, but he was reluctant.

She didn't give him the option of a reply, though. He felt her swing her leg over and then slide off the horse.

He had no idea where she'd gone after that.

Sometimes he could see her, even when she was invisible, just a faint outline because of his connection to her, but in the darkness it was much harder.

Dak played the fool the whole time the group was packing up, making funny jokes and stumbling about.

Luc guessed he had had to play the buffoon for a good reason, because he was sticking to the cover he'd woven for himself with no deviation.

When everyone was up on their horses, saddle bags bulging with supplies and purchases, Dak drew his horse up beside Luc, and gave a wave to the three dark figures, still standing beside the fire.

"See you in Venyatu one day, Harvey," he said, then gave a delicate burp.

"Sure." The man Dak addressed lifted a hand. "We'll be right behind you on the road."

It came out as a threat, not the light-hearted comment Luc guessed Harvey had been going for.

"That everyone?" Luc looked around, saw that all his people were on their horses, and gave the three men a cool nod of his head before he turned his horse and made his way through the trees.

"Didn't know how else to play it," Dak murmured as soon as they were on the road, heading toward the camp. "They would not shake loose, no matter what I did."

"Sounds like you put on quite a show." Luc sent him an amused look, then turned back to look at the camp behind them. "They'll follow."

"Oh, yes. What will we do?"

"Ava's back there," he said. "Listening in. I need to loop back and get her."

"I'll come along. I've wanted to punch that smug bastard Harvey in the face all night."

Luc nodded, gave a low whistle.

Everyone went quiet and slowed their horses.

"Dak and I are going to make sure we aren't followed," he said, voice low. "The rest of you, go as fast as you can back to the others, and set an advance lookout around the camp, all directions. Take down anyone you don't know, blindfold and bind them."

With a whoop, Lucilla took off, the rest of the group right behind her.

Luc nudged his horse back behind the treeline on the side of the road, Dak by his side.

They were only five minutes from the camp, so they didn't talk, and when the horses began making too much noise walking through the dried leaves on the forest floor, they dismounted and tied them to a bush to continue on foot.

Luc's hand closed around the hilt of his sword as he moved forward.

"How many are there?" he asked Dak.

"Four. The three you saw, and one other, Fengal, who hid in the trees."

"Do you think that was a precaution, or was Fengal afraid of being recognized?"

"I don't know." Dak's soft reply was thoughtful. "Harvey's in charge, though. No doubt about that."

"You think they're Grimwaldian spies?"

Dak gave a nod. "I suspect they're well trained. Not quite a team, but they know each other well enough to work together. Something about us set at least one of them off, made them suspicious."

That was unfortunate, but not completely unsurprising. Just one or two slips, even though they had some genuine Venyatux in the group, and someone watching carefully might have decided to take a closer look.

"You think they're dangerous?" Luc asked.

"Oh, yes." Dak was holding his knife as he spoke. "We don't want them to find Ava."

They wouldn't, Luc assured himself.

But he moved up his pace, all the same.

CHAPTER 17

"That big one, the leader. He's dangerous." One of the three men left standing by the fire shook his head.

They were all moving toward the horses, and Ava guessed they were planning to follow Dak and Luc immediately, leaving their things behind for now.

That would mean she could go through their bags easily enough, but she had a feeling there would be more useful information from listening to them than whatever they had packed away in the saddle bags they were stepping over.

She pulled out one of the narrow, rectangular cotton strips she kept in her pocket, needle and thread already woven into it.

She worked quickly. She had to get them to stay first, then she could get them talking.

She moved in front of the man closest to her and tossed her working at his face.

The light fabric fluttered, caught by the breeze, and he caught it automatically.

"What's that?" The man Dak had addressed as Harvey asked.

The man held up his fist, looked at it. "A rag."

He didn't throw it away, though, he held it out to Harvey, who took it.

"If that leader's so dangerous, remind me why we're going after him?"

Harvey gave a sneer at that, but Ava noticed he didn't disagree. He looked at the scrap in his hand, then frowned. He set his saddle back down.

The third man, seeming to sense they weren't in the same hurry they'd been in a moment ago, set his own saddle down. "We should have guessed someone would come looking for them."

Ava took out another scrap, glad to see her first working seemed to be doing the job of keeping them from leaving. She worked the need to discuss their plans and orders into the rough cotton.

Harvey had moved back to the fire, crouching beside a pallet, and she moved around to him and threw the cotton strip onto the thin sleeping mat.

He stared at it, frowning as he picked it up.

As soon as he tightened his grip on it, she began to move back to the horses, heading for the pile of saddle bags.

She could rifle through their bags and listen to them at the same time.

"You thought someone would come find them, did you, Rabin?" Harvey asked. His tone was sarcastic but he settled down on the pallet, as if all urgency was gone.

Rabin shrugged. "They're Venyatux soldiers——or so they say. They were buying supplies in Illoa and I'm assuming someone was waiting for those supplies. When they didn't return to their camp, someone would have wanted to know why. We're on the road to Illoa here, they didn't even have to look hard."

A shadow stepped out from the trees and Ava froze.

She hadn't forgotten the shadow she and Luc had seen darting into the trees, but she had thought he must have run away, given how long it had taken him to reemerge.

She watched as he moved toward the fire.

She wondered if he would be drawn into the spell she had

created——a working that inspired a need to think and discuss before they acted——or whether he would agitate for immediate action.

It would be interesting to see.

Even if he wasn't drawn in, he would lose the argument, she believed, because it was three against one, and Harvey was the clear leader. Still, she had never had a chance to observe the way her magic worked in a group setting like this, and whether it could pull someone in who hadn't been a direct recipient of her working.

"Rabin's right." The man who walked out of the shadows tossed his own bag on the ground beside the fire. "We should have anticipated it."

He settled down, and she wished she could tell if it was of his own free will, or because he had already been drawn in.

"Where did you go, Fengal?" Harvey turned to him. "A little warning next time, if you're going to run off and leave us."

"I didn't leave you." Fengal's tone was calm. "I didn't want the newcomers to get a good look at my face. All it would take to cause serious trouble was for one of them to recognize me."

"Dak and his group already saw plenty of you," the man she'd given the first working to said.

"They were drunk," Fengal shrugged. He pulled his bag closer and pulled out something that he began to chew on. Dried meat, maybe. "The soldiers that came to get them clearly weren't. If any of them had seen me around in Fernwell, that might have led to uncomfortable questions."

"All right." Harvey made himself comfortable on his bedroll. "That wasn't a terrible idea. Did you recognize the big one? The leader?"

"I didn't get a good look at him." Fengal stretched out his legs. "Did you see how quickly they packed up, though? Like they might not have been as drunk as they pretended."

"You think the whole *I can't ride any further* story was a ploy?" Rabin asked.

"Now that Fengal mentions it, it was a little too convenient."

Harvey turned his head, looking in the direction of the road. "If we leave now, we won't be too far behind them."

It was as if he was discussing the weather. There was no urgency in his voice.

"They'll be watching for us." Fengal reached out and grabbed a pillow, using it to prop himself up as he got comfortable. "Your response to that leader would have made him suspicious."

"You criticizing me?" Harvey turned to look at him.

"Just saying. You might have tried to be a little more friendly."

Harvey half-lifted a shoulder. "If they want to watch for us, let them. We already spun a story that we're going to Venyatu. What can they do about it if we follow them?"

"They could kill us," Fengal said. "The Venyatux aren't known for their friendliness to outsiders."

Ava had been going through the saddlebags as she listened in, and her hand suddenly closed around a slim leather cylinder. She carefully drew it out, sliding it into an inner pocket of her coat. She crab-walked to the next pile of bags, began quietly rifling through them.

She still couldn't tell if Fengal had been drawn into her web, or simply didn't want to go chasing after danger anyway.

"We can't follow after them." The man who Ava had ensnared first shook his head. He had settled on his bed roll, leaning forward with his elbows on his knees. She wondered if he was going to give a reason for his statement——whether he had been able to convince himself of the logic, or whether her working was nudging him with no basis in fact. "This was supposed to be a quick diversion, because Harvey thought they might be Rising Wave soldiers nosing around Illoa, and thought it was worth a few hours to see if they were telling the truth. Aren't we supposed to be up at the Skäddar border in three days? That's a problem for us, because it's at least a five day trip."

So he had found a way to convince himself.

She felt a jolt of guilt.

Her magic was not something that she could ever be reckless with.

What she was doing now needed to be done, but it was good to remember that she was playing with peoples' minds.

"Whose fault is that, asshole?" Fengal asked. "We were starting to draw attention to ourselves, waiting for you in Illoa."

"Even I can't control the weather." The man sent Fengal an evil stare. "The pass through the mountains from the eastern seaboard was impassible for three days."

"Was it worth something at least, Kilmer?" Harvey asked. "Did you get any good information?" He paused as soon as he asked the question, and Ava guessed it was not something he would have usually done. He was wondering what made him ask.

Her working was steering him against his natural tendencies.

Kilmer lifted his shoulders. "Maybe. Maybe not. Who knows what the boss will find useful."

There was a moment of silence at that, and Ava decided they were all in agreement. Her hand closed over another cylinder and she slid it out to join the first one.

"The boss changed the plan. We were supposed to go to Taunen, and he diverted us. He'll know our timing can't be precise." Harvey reached back, almost touching Ava where she crouched behind him, and grabbed the bags she was about to rifle through. He placed them between his legs, out of her reach. "As long as we've got what he's looking for, he won't mind us being late by a few days."

"I saw the new queen when I was in Fernwell," Fengal said suddenly. "She was just walking around the market."

The others turned to watch him, and Ava thought with a frisson of shock that perhaps he *had* been drawn into her spell.

Offering up conversation about something off-topic. About her.

She wondered if the fact that it was her he was talking about made it easier for the spell to work.

"What did she look like?" Kilmer asked.

Fengal shook his head, then lifted his hands. "Delicate. Fragile."

"You should have grabbed her," Rabin said.

Fengal gave a snort. "My orders were to gather information on Kassia's alliances and stability, not steal their queen." He shook his head. "I wasn't set up for something like that. I wouldn't have made it out of the city."

"She have guards?" Kilmer asked.

"It didn't look like it," Fengal said. "But yes," he blew out a breath. "I think she did. They kept themselves out of sight."

"If you could have gotten away with it, the boss would have made you his right-hand," Harvey said. "Word is, he tried to grab her a couple of months ago himself."

"I heard. And if *he* tried and failed . . ." Fengal let his voice trail off and Harvey gave a nod.

Ava shivered. She knew now who they were talking about. The man with no name. The one who'd given Sirna the rope to bind her, the net to capture her, the tea to muddle the minds of the diplomats he'd used to get into the city.

She had only interacted with him once, but it had been enough. And Sirna had been frightened of him.

If he was these men's boss, she knew exactly what they were.

Spies.

"We should at least try to see how big this group of soldiers is, and if they're really going into Venyatu. The boss will definitely want to know that, even if it makes us a day or two late. Less Venyatux presence in Kassia means the Rising Wave is weaker."

"What does it matter to us? We're not going to war with them," Fengal said.

Harvey said nothing.

"You think we might be going to war with Kassia?" Fengal sounded aghast.

"We've just discussed how the boss tried to kidnap the queen a few months ago. Do you think the Rising Wave's commander will take that lightly?" Harvey finally stood, lifting his bags over his shoulder.

She had made her workings with a specific goal. To stop and consider their next move. To discuss their plans.

That had happened.

The working was coming to an end.

That was a relief in a way, too. She hadn't set them up to loop the same actions over and over.

"Luc Franck and the new queen live together in the same quarters. They're considered heart-bound," Fengal said. He got to his feet, the other two following him. "So no, he won't take it lightly."

"Does he know it was the boss who took her?" Kilmer asked.

"Not the boss, specifically, but the Rising Wave knows Grimwalt was behind it." Harvey began to saddle up.

"Everyone in Fernwell thinks Grimwalt was behind it," Fengal confirmed, following suit.

Ava moved back from the bags as the others did the same.

"I'm curious. Did the boss do it because he thought the Rising Wave was weakened from fighting for control of Kassia? Because that isn't what it looked like to me in the capital. They hardly had any casualties." Fengal tightened his saddle straps.

"I don't know why he did it. There must have been some logic to it, but I don't know what it was." Harvey swung onto his horse. "That's why the boss sent us out, I think. To see if there were any hints the Rising Wave was considering retaliating."

"I didn't hear any talk of war."

"Me, either." Kilmer also mounted up.

"In a way, that's worse." Fengal went back to the fire, doused it with sand. "It means they're talking behind closed doors."

"Nothing we can do about that." Harvey began to nudge his horse forward.

"Why do we have to go to the Skäddar border?" Fengal asked. "Why not Taunen?"

"Because that's where the boss is. He's got something going on there." Harvey stopped. "Look, he'll ask how many Venyatux soldiers are going home. Let's get close enough to their camp to see the general size of it. Then we follow the directives."

"But what's happening on the Skäddar border?" Rabin asked as they moved through the trees back to the road. Her working was still holding him, she guessed, forcing him to ask things, slow things down.

"I've been in Kassia as long as you have," Harvey said, his tone short as they rode away. "I know as much as you do."

The Skäddar border.

All roads seemed to lead there, it seemed.

Something big was going on.

Ava stood beside the smoking fire pit until she couldn't hear their voices or the sound of their horses' hooves anymore.

She slipped the scarf she'd used to make herself invisible from around her neck and put it back in her pocket.

Luc would have found it hard to justify coming back alone, she guessed, which meant there would be at least one other soldier with him, and she wanted to hold her secrets close.

"You there?" she called softly.

Luc appeared on foot through the trees, absolutely soundless.

Dak walked a step behind him.

"All right?" Luc reached her and she gave a nod. He widened his stance and tugged her to stand between his legs, holding her close for a beat.

"You hear any of that?" she asked, and then smiled as he took her hand.

"Some, near the end." He led her back the way they'd come, through the trees, rather than on the road.

Dak fell into step on her other side.

"Fengal, the one who darted into the trees, he was spying in Fernwell, and was afraid someone would recognize him."

"He was in Fernwell?" Dak sounded affronted. "I hadn't seen him before."

"He saw me," she said. "He told the others he watched me in the market."

Luc went very still. "And?"

"And he thought there were guards watching me, although he

couldn't see them." She sent Luc a smile. Because that guard had been him.

"And the others? Where were they coming from?" Dak's job was intelligence, so Ava understood the intensity of his tone.

"One was on the eastern seaboard. He kept the rest waiting for him in Illoa because there was apparently a storm that delayed passage over the mountains."

"I had reports of that," Dak nodded.

"The others didn't say where they'd been." She dug out the two leather cylinders. "But these might tell us something."

Dak took them carefully. "How did you get these?"

"Stole them out of their saddle bags while they were busy arguing over whether to follow us or not. I only had time to look through two."

"They might not even realize these are missing for a few days," Dak said. "Which means they won't necessarily tie the disappearance to this incident."

Ava shrugged. "What can they do about it, either way?"

They arrived where the two horses had been left to graze, and Luc swung up into the saddle, reached down for her, and lifted her up behind him.

She was always amazed at how effortless it seemed to be for him.

"We'll have to go around, if they're going to stick to the road and do as they say," she told them. "Did you hear the part about just wanting to know the size of the camp?"

"Yes." Luc headed away from the road. "We'll let them. Wanting them to think we're Venyatux heading home is exactly what we hoped to do."

"Speaking of which . . ." Dak leaned to the side and took something out of his saddle bag. "I have something for you."

He held out a parcel wrapped in brown paper to Ava.

"For me?" She was sincerely touched as she reached out to take it. "Cake?"

"No." He laughed softly. "I did get cake, but this is something just for you."

Ava squished the parcel in her hands, and she leaned against Luc's back as she looked over at his best friend. "Yarn?" She opened the top of the parcel and felt what was inside. "It's so soft. Thank you."

He gave an embarrassed duck of his head, and then fumbled for the cylinders, trying to read them in the weak moonlight as they took the long way back to camp.

It seemed the news was good for Kassia. Most people had relaxed after initial fears that the Rising Wave would seek reprisals for what had been done under the old queen.

The spies seemed to think the alliance between the Cervantes, the Funabi and the Venyatu was strong, and the tentative peace with Jatan was a major achievement.

All bad news for the Speaker, she assumed.

The spies had also outlined issues and people who could be manipulated. Could be turned to cause trouble and unhappiness.

She'd felt the weight of her power earlier, but hearing Dak muttering under his breath as he lifted the scrolls up to read them better, she didn't regret using it.

That was the line, she decided. She would protect those she cared for, those who she saw as her responsibility, like the people of Kassia and Venyatu.

But she would never play with people's thoughts and minds lightly.

She tightened her grip on Luc's waist.

"All right?" he asked softly.

She nodded against his back.

"From what I heard, there really is something going on at the Skäddar border," she said.

"What did they say about it?"

Dak edged his mount closer, as interested in her answer as Luc.

"That their boss was waiting for them there. They don't know what he's up to, though. It's a mystery to them."

"Who is their boss?" Luc asked.

"The man who organized my abduction," Ava said. "The man without a name."

Luc was silent for a while.

"He doesn't need a name to die," he said eventually.

CHAPTER 18

"You know what the Boss Man was looking for, don't you?" Massi knew it wasn't really a question, it was a fact. Duncan's reaction said it all.

Her gaze focused on where the three men had disappeared through the trees, leaving them alone outside the fortress. "You knew he wouldn't find it."

Duncan couldn't help the chuckle that escaped. "I did."

She gave an acerbic snort, which delighted him.

"Surely the rope was in the one bag he was holding so carefully," she said. "What was in the other?"

"The gloves he uses to hold the rope," Duncan told her, and his fingers brushed over the rough edges of the pine cones in his pocket again.

"But there was something else, or he wouldn't have looked so angry."

Duncan entertained the insane thought that he should tell her what the Boss Man had tried and failed to find.

He forced himself to keep quiet.

He suspected the pine cones were a way to track him, but he didn't know how they worked.

That kind of magic was foreign to him, and he knew his lack of knowledge there was dangerous.

Elemental magic like his own was thought to be gone from the world.

He'd been told he was the only one left, so when he'd met Lithwick, he'd been less cautious than he should have been, so happy to find someone to talk to who understood.

He'd been easy prey.

"He thinks you're going to the Skäddar border," she said. "Is that where you're from?"

He nodded. "The forest in the Dallir Valley."

"I need to know what someone like him is doing up there," she murmured.

"Why?" he asked.

"Because he's the Speaker's right hand. If he's going there, it's because there's something important happening. Do you know what that is?"

He didn't. And the urgency to protect what was his was a clanging bell in his head. "Come with me and find out." The thought of having her travel with him was . . . good.

"Tomas and Velda," she said, in response.

He owed the couple his loyalty, and so he inclined his head.

"I have to catch up to them. See them safe." She hitched her bow over her shoulder. "Want to join me?"

There it was again, that wildness, that dangerous edge. It was all but irresistible to him. The pull of this forest, the pull of her, was hard to fight against.

"I have to look after the safety of my own," he told her, and he could hear the rasp of regret in his voice as he spoke. "And I've been away for nearly two months, while the one who engineered my removal has been free to do whatever he likes."

She gave a nod. "Understood. When I'm done in Taunen, I might come up your way, see what the Boss Man is up to. Where is a good place to find you?"

He didn't know the situation, didn't want to give her a place that Lithwick may well have taken for his own.

He snapped off a scale from one of the pine cones before he could think about it too much, and presented it to her.

She narrowed her eyes as she stared at it. "A piece of bark?"

"A way to find me," he said. "I think. This is not my type of magic, but I think it will lead you to me once you're in my forest."

She took it carefully, wrapped it in a handkerchief and put it in the inner pocket of her jacket. "Thank you."

"Take the horse," he said. "It will slow me down where I'm going, whereas you can use it to catch up to the others."

She tapped her chest with a fist and bowed her head in thanks. "Good luck, Forest Man."

She moved to take a step away, checked herself, and turned. Her arm curled around his neck and she went up on her toes, brushed her lips across his cheek as her other hand rested on his chest. "Look after yourself."

And then she was gone, striding toward the clearing where they'd put the horse. When she reached it, she turned, gave him a jaunty wave, and disappeared.

He stood without moving for a minute, until even the sound of her and the horse had gone.

He wanted to follow.

He had never put anyone over his forest in his life. And he hadn't this time, either, he acknowledged. But he was tempted.

Very tempted.

He spun on his heel, looking toward the north.

He could make better time if he used the forest paths, not the road, especially without a mount.

There was a stretch of land with no trees far up ahead; he could feel it. But until then, the forest would help him, bolster him, and he would make good time.

What was Lithwick doing in his forest that would draw the attention of the Speaker's man?

Nothing good, he was sure.

Nothing good at all.

Massi eventually found a track wide enough to let the horse have her head, and bent low over her neck to duck the branches above.

It was hours since they'd parted, but she couldn't shake the memory of Duncan, standing absolutely still and focused on her as she gave a final wave goodbye.

He was everything she liked in a man.

Quiet. Intense. With a wild edge that would never be easily tamed or controlled.

And the sharp beauty of his face, the lean muscles of him, didn't hurt, either.

The way he'd stood absolutely still as she'd kissed him, as if afraid any movement would cause her to withdraw.

It was a pity their paths lay literally in opposite directions, but she never reneged on a promise, and she had told Ava she would make sure Tomas and Velda were safe.

She also wanted to get a message to Luc that there may be something happening on Grimwalt's border with Skäddar.

The path widened a little more and seemed to join up with a much wider track up ahead. She straightened in the saddle, trying to orientate herself.

The main road to Taunen, maybe?

She paused when she reached it, looking both ways.

Since she'd left the fortress she'd ridden south east through the forest, in the direction of Taunen, looking for the two carts, but Duncan's trick of obscuring their tracks had worked too well. She'd lost the starting point and never stumbled over any sign of them again.

She could be ahead of them, she realized, or just behind.

She had not made good time through the choked vegetation, but then the carts would have had an even more difficult time of it, and they had a lot more people as well.

The sun had nearly set, and if the carts were close by, they would be settling in for the night.

Which she should do, as well.

Her mount was tired, and so was she.

She was considering making camp where the narrow track met the road, but as the sun was swallowed by the horizon, she saw a flicker of firelight in the distance.

She rode toward it, murmuring promises of rest, water and feed to her horse, and then got off the road before anyone in the camp ahead could see or hear her. She led her mount to the stream she had heard burbling for the last ten minutes, and left it to drink and rest while she moved forward on foot.

As she got close enough to the fire to hear the low murmur of voices, a snap of twigs to her right made her go still. She moved back a little, ghosting toward the sound.

She found a horse tied to a bush.

It gave a quiet snort, and she moved past it, stepping carefully.

Someone shifted up ahead, and she crouched down, moving further right until she was at an angle to the person clearly watching those around the fire.

She couldn't tell who was hunkered down in the darkness, but it didn't matter, because he chose that moment to step into the flickering light of the fire, a crossbow in his hands, and reveal himself.

"Renard." Ventnor's voice was startled. "What are you doing here?"

Massi crept closer, saw Ventnor and the three soldiers in his unit were sitting around the fire, with Renard looming over them.

Massi supposed that transporting the bodies of Chart and their other two friends would have slowed Ventnor down, given Renard a chance to catch up to them.

It was still possible that Tomas, Velda and the others were ahead, but Massi thought probably not.

The soldiers had all taken the road from Waldrand, whereas the carts would have had to navigate the forest, at least for some of the way. They would have been much slower than soldiers with fast horses on an open road.

"What are you going to do? Kill us?" Ventnor asked.

Massi notched her bow, and moved a little closer.

"That's exactly what I'm going to do." Renard lifted the cross-bow. "But first, where are the prisoners?"

"Prisoners?" Ventnor sounded mystified. "The people in the carts? I have no idea."

"Edith." Renard angled his crossbow toward the soldier sitting next to Ventnor. "Where are they?"

"We last saw them about ten minutes after you did, Renard. There was a small earth tremor after you and Chart left, and our horses bolted. Why do you think we followed you to the fortress? We lost them."

"So they're still back in the forest?" Renard asked.

"Who knows? Who cares." Ventnor waved to where the three bodies were laid out, wrapped in their sleeping blankets. "You and that other man killed Chart. Killed the others. What's going on?"

"More than you'll ever understand." Renard lifted his bow, and Massi sensed he was about to shoot.

She shot him through the throat, and the bolt he was about to put in Ventnor shot up into the sky.

All four soldiers leaped to their feet as he fell, and Massi waited a moment, wondering whether to step forward or not.

Better to have more allies than less, she eventually decided. And Ventnor would owe her a big favor after this.

She stepped into the circle of light, another arrow notched but pointing down.

"Who are you?" Ventnor was holding a sword, but he kept it close to his side.

"Massi Joure. I helped the prisoners that you met earlier to escape."

Ventnor studied her. "I didn't see you among them."

"I was hiding, in case they needed protection from you." She lifted her bow a little and then pointed it downward again.

"You're responsible for the arrow in that man's shoulder at the fortress," Ventnor said. "The one who attacked the lieutenant?"

"Yes."

"You were following us?" Ventnor asked.

She shook her head. "I lost the rest of the group when I followed Chart back to the fortress. I've been playing catch-up all day, and stumbled on your camp."

"Thank you." He looked down at Renard. "I never liked him, but I can't understand why he would have turned on us like this."

"There'll be more of them," Massi told him. "Men and women loyal to the Speaker who are seeded in the army. The Speaker's aide ——the man who killed your lieutenant——activated him by using a code word. As soon as Renard heard it, he switched sides."

"What word?"

"I couldn't hear it properly. He called it out again when you and your team approached the gates. But none of you reacted."

"I heard him say something," Edith said, her voice thoughtful. "I couldn't make out what it was."

"So what now?" Ventnor slid his sword back in its scabbard.

"Renard's horse is back there, and so is mine," Massi said. "If you're happy to share your fire, I'll spend the night here." She might have to go back down the road to look for her lost lambs. Maybe in the light of day, she could see if there were tracks that would tell her if they'd been this way.

"You're not Grimwaldian, are you?" Ventnor asked. "Your accent is different."

"No." She left it at that, walking back into the forest to get the horses.

When she returned, Renard's body had been laid a little way from the other three and two of the soldiers were busy making food over the fire.

She settled down, and while there was no doubt plenty to talk about, she had neither the inclination nor the energy for it.

She caught Ventnor studying her a few times, but it seemed he was not inclined to talk much, either.

His colleagues were dead and they must have ridden hard from Waldrand.

No one was in the mood to share.

She ate what she was given gratefully, and was asleep almost immediately afterward.

She woke in the early hours of the morning, feeling rested, and revived the fire.

When it was light enough to see, she went down to the stream and washed, stripping naked and forcing herself completely under the cold water. When she got back to the camp, all four of her new companions were busy digging a grave to bury Renard.

"Good idea," she said, walking over to observe. "It's better if he simply disappears."

Ventnor pushed Renard's body into the shallow grave, and the others threw soil over him.

"We can't wait with you," he said, stepping back, hands on hips, as they patted the earth down. "Chart and the others need to be buried as quickly as possible, but I need to give them to their families first."

"Understood. My friends are heading for Taunen, so if you need witnesses to what happened at the fortress, Ranulf Harkonan will be willing, I think."

Ventnor gave a nod. "Tell him to find me. He knows where to go." He paused. "I'm sure there's a lot to this story, but there's no time to hear it. When you get to Taunen, you're welcome to find me, too."

She waited for them to tie the bodies back onto their mounts, swing up onto their own, and then watched them canter away.

They would let Tomas know where she was if the carts were up ahead, but given the speed Ventnor had been traveling, she was sure they were behind.

She doused the fire, tied Renard's horse to her own, and turned back toward Waldrand.

She had been riding for only an hour when she heard a yip from up ahead.

The first dog appeared, running toward her, tongue hanging out, and she gave a high-pitch whistle of greeting.

A howl of welcome was the response, and she dismounted as the pack raced toward her.

She crouched down to stroke heads and rub flanks.

When the carts appeared, Tomas shouted a hello and waved, and she saw with relief that all seemed to be well.

Suddenly she was surrounded by as many people as dogs, everyone eager for news.

"Where's Duncan?" Velda asked.

"He went his separate way," Massi said.

"And Lieutenant Chart?" Ranulf asked. He still looked like a homeless beggar in old robes, but his bearing had changed since yesterday. He stood taller, looked more authoritative.

"Chart is dead." As she told them the circumstances, silence settled over the group.

"So the Speaker has managed to turn some of the army, and it will be difficult to know who." Ranulf sounded shocked.

"This also tells us that there are plenty who don't follow him." Camille, the spell caster who'd put the guards in the fortress to sleep, reminded him. "I've never met General Ventnor, but I've only ever heard good things about her. Her son's eye witness testimony will go a long way to shocking Taunen into opening their eyes at last. At seeing what's really going on."

"We need to get to Taunen as fast as we can," Ranulf said. "Our presence, our own testimony, will add weight to it." He lifted the bag Massi had given him the day before. "As well as the records Massi managed to get from the warden's office."

Massi agreed. It would be a huge shift in the status quo.

And it would be in the Rising Wave's interests.

Not only would there be less chance of another attack on Ava, but no matter the circumstances, it was always dangerous to have a neighbor ruled by a corrupt leader.

But still, her promise was to Tomas and Velda, and she would honor it.

The couple stood together, worn and thin and with dust smudged on their faces, but with a calm dignity she admired.

She rose up from her crouch, walked over to stand close to them. "What do you want to do? Go home?"

Velda shook her head. "They abducted us from the estate. As Ranulf says, we need to be in the public eye, not tucked away where they can try to take us again in secret."

"They won't stop unless we make enough noise to expose them," Tomas agreed, and bent to scratch one of the dogs between the ears. "Ranulf will put us up in his house in the city. This is the only way to end the danger to everyone. Ava included."

Massi gave a nod, ran her eye over the bedraggled group, and felt a spike of humor at the beauty of such a ragtag bunch bringing down the Speaker of Grimwalt. "Then let's end it."

CHAPTER 19

They rode into Taunen two days later.

Massi worried they were pushing too hard, but it was as if everyone was determined to go as fast as they could, the months of confinement lighting a spark of rage in them that fueled their determination.

The leadership structure had settled into Ranulf, Tomas, Camille and Velda at the helm, with Massi acting as their guard, ranging ahead, the dogs around her horse, to check there were no threats waiting for them.

The guards at the west gate of the city let them through so easily, Massi pulled up beside one as the carts creaked under the portcullis. "Ventnor let you know we'd be coming?" she asked. The skin under her collar began to prickle and she touched a fingertip to Ava's embroidery.

The guard nodded, his gaze flicking over the group curiously as they moved passed him. "Mentioned there'd be a group coming behind him. Asked us to let him know when you arrived."

Massi didn't like it, and wasn't sure the reaction of Ava's protective workings were stirred to life by her own wariness of going into the heart of the Speaker's territory, or whether there truly was a threat.

Any of the people they passed as they traveled over the west bridge of the River Fei could be embedded allies of the Speaker.

Nothing she could do about it now, though, except be extra alert.

They reached the end of the bridge and the carts began moving through the streets of central Taunen to Ranulf Harkonan's home.

When the streets began to get narrower, Massi notched an arrow in her bow, her gaze going up, looking for threats from the windows above.

Fernwell was the biggest city she had ever been in, and while it had tall buildings, most were no higher than four floors, and the streets were much wider.

Taunen's architecture and layout had everything to do with the fact that the city was built on an island in the middle of the River Fei, a long sliver of land that ran north to south, like the river itself. While the town had spilled out on either side of the river, lining the banks and connected to the island via stone bridges to the east and west, buildings in the center of Taunen had gone upward out of necessity.

Massi felt a constant buzz of nerves, as well as the uncomfortable irritation of the protective spells against her skin. She kept her horse between the two carts, keenly aware that they made nice, easy targets, corralled by the narrow streets, with nowhere to run.

They were too exposed. She moved to the front of the group and got Ranulf's attention. "Take a different, less obvious route to your house," she said, gripped by a growing sense of threat.

Ranulf looked as if he wanted to argue, so she turned her horse, blocking the way. "Now."

With a slightly sulky nod he called directions, and Tomas turned to the right, moving them down a short street to emerge onto the island's east riverside promenade.

At least there was no threat coming from the river, leaving only the buildings on the left.

Massi felt a slight lifting of her sense of danger, and her hand lifted unconsciously to touch the collar of her shirt again.

It meant someone *had* been back there, and they had intended harm.

"How far from here?" she called to Ranulf.

"Not far," he admitted. "You saw something?"

She gave a shrug. "I'll stay back here, watch our rear."

They had done the unexpected, and whoever was planning to attack them would be coming up from behind now.

Ranulf searched her face and gave a nod. "It's ten minutes from here, maybe less." He gave her directions, and she turned her horse to face the way they'd come, moving close to the buildings.

She sat still in her saddle, waiting, watching.

It took less than a minute for the archer to come around the corner.

He was on foot, panting slightly as if he'd had to run, and she guessed he'd been lining up a shot from a few floors up and had to race down stairs to follow them.

He was not in any kind of uniform, but that didn't mean he wasn't in the military, just that he was not acting under the military's orders.

His gaze jumped ahead, looking for his targets, and she admired the smoothness of his lift of an arrow from his quiver and his draw on the bow.

"I wouldn't," she said, and he turned and shot her in one movement.

She bent to the right, following the tug of Ava's magic, and the arrow flew past and smacked into the stone wall behind her, then fell to the ground.

She shot back at him as she straightened out of her bend, aiming for his right shoulder.

Unlike the Boss Man——and herself——this one had no magical protection, although he only grunted when her arrow buried itself deep.

She admired his control.

He held a hand to his shoulder, his gaze on her as if he understood she'd hit where she meant to, that she did not plan to kill him, only disable him.

He would not be able to draw a bow for months.

She lifted a hand in salute, and with a baring of his teeth, he ran back the way he'd come.

"That was exciting," a woman said.

Massi turned, startled, and saw an old woman she hadn't noticed before sitting on the steps of a townhouse two doors down from her.

"Two warriors, battling it out. And almost not a sound out of either of you. And whose side are either of you on?" the woman wondered. "What battle is there, in Taunen?"

"That's a complicated question," Massi said.

"Most things are." The woman tilted her head. "Whatever is going on, I think I'd back you." The woman nodded at the carts, disappearing in the distance. "The one you hit, I saw him trying to find a specific person in that group you were protecting, trying to line up a shot. He was planning on getting one of your friends in the back."

Massi lifted a shoulder, impressed by the woman's reading of the situation. "He's a tool. And now he's out of the game."

Something scrambled near the woman's knees, and Massi saw a black hen poke her head up, then bob back down.

"Well, good luck to you." The woman, old in her wrinkles and in her dress, but sprightly enough in her movements, scooped up the hen and stood.

"Thank you." Massi gave her a polite nod and then urged her horse into a trot to catch up to the others. The woman gave a wave as she stepped into her house.

As Massi gained on her friends, she realized this was just the opening salvo.

She would protect them for as long as she could, but she had a feeling someone needed to go up to Skäddar and see what was happening there. It had a different flavor to the other plots the Speaker had launched.

Self-interest and naked power had been the simple drivers so far, but what could he hope to achieve up on the border?

Patience, Massi. She could almost hear Dak's teasing voice in her ear.

Hopefully there would be some word from Luc or Dak waiting for her. And she needed to send a letter so Ava knew her friends were finally free and safe.

A bell rang out from the river and Massi glanced over to see a sailing boat gliding toward her. She watched it for a moment before she turned back into the narrow streets, off the promenade.

She wondered if the river would be a faster route north to Skäddar than by horse.

She rubbed the top corner of her jacket, felt the bump of the piece of pine cone scale Duncan had given her, and wondered how he was doing——whether he was shadowing the Boss Man, or whether he'd gone home the fastest way he knew how.

Would the tiny piece of wood actually work in finding him once she got to his forest? He hadn't seemed sure of it himself.

It's not my magic, he'd told her.

So what *was* his magic?

She turned down the street, following after the carts, and realized she was counting down the hours before she could leave here.

There was going to be nothing but arguing and underhanded attacks in Taunen and it was not the type of conflict she enjoyed.

She had fought in some way or another since she was eight years old; since she'd been abducted from her village and forced into the service of the Kassian army.

Would she know what to do, if there was nothing more to fight against, she wondered?

A trip north, a mission to find out what was going on, appealed to her greatly.

And having Duncan Erdo as a host when she was up there . . . that was appealing, too.

CHAPTER 20

Duncan crouched beside the sick and dying tree, and felt his anger build.

This was the third one he'd come across as he'd moved through the narrow gorge that would lead him to the Dallir Valley.

To home.

The mountains loomed high above him, the snow-covered tops invisible so deep in the narrow gorge, the shadows they threw cloaking him in gloom.

Lithwick was responsible for this decline.

After what he'd done to get Duncan captured, it was the only explanation.

He ran his hands over the bark, trying to find out what was wrong, and found blight.

He touched a hand to the ground between the roots and poured healing energy into the soil, heard the trees around him sigh in relief.

He rose to his feet and began to move faster than he had, hands reaching out to touch leaves, bark, and branches as he ran, trying to get a sense of the overall health of the outskirts of his domain.

The forest was sluggish to respond, its voice quiet, and he couldn't work out if it was because he had been away for so long, or because Lithwick had done something to it.

If Lithwick had assumed his role of protector, using the power and the energy of his forest to keep it strong and healthy, Duncan would have understood it. Not accepted it, but understood. Power was seductive, and his domain had almost limitless amounts of it..

But instead, it seemed as if Lithwick had weakened what he had stolen from Duncan.

It made no sense.

He felt a growing urgency to reach the valley.

If this is what Lithwick had done to the outer-reaches of his forest, what had he done to the heart of it?

The gorge angled down suddenly, the last slope before it dipped into the gentle valley through which the Dallir River flowed.

Duncan used the trees to slow his descent, and when he reached the bottom, he looked through the trees on the flat valley floor to see the Mirror Mountains on the other side.

They were not an exact replica of the mountains that stretched behind him to the left and right, but they were similar enough.

Long ago, some force of nature had come through the center of this range and flattened it, leaving the wide, deep Dallir River in its wake.

For the Skäddar and the Grimwaldians, the river that ran through this valley made the perfect border between their two countries, but a map-drawn border was not something Duncan acknowledged.

Was he more Grimwaldian than he was Skäddar, he wondered?

His physical home was on the Grimwaldian side, but he moved without thought between the two.

His trees did not care which government claimed their soil. They answered only to him.

Or they used to.

He turned east, toward the center of his domain.

And almost immediately saw a stand of trees that looked dead.

He ran forward, and when he reached it, he leaned his chest against the closest trunk and closed his eyes, searching for a cause.

He could feel an actual tug on his strength, a weakening in his limbs, and he rested a little more heavily against the trunk.

This wasn't just a little blight. This was a serious depletion of the tree's life force.

Could Lithwick not understand how it worked? That the forest always gave more than it received.

All it took was a tiny piece of your soul.

He had left small pieces of himself all the way from Waldrand to here, his body not strong enough to make the trip quickly without the give and take of his magic.

But if Lithwick wanted no connection to the land, perhaps he had taken by force.

Either that, or the land would not share with him.

After all, it already had a partner, and that was Duncan.

What is wrong here? he wondered, and found the deep, hidden voice of the forest sluggish and quiet.

A whistle sounded a mere second before pain pierced him, and he gasped. An arrow had gone through his thigh and embedded itself in the trunk against which he was leaning.

He was pinned.

He twisted his body at the waist, trying to keep his leg still, and looked over his shoulder. Two men appeared from between the trees, both on horseback.

He took a deep breath and reached back, gripped the arrow, then pulled it out of the tree trunk and his leg.

He turned and leaned back against the trunk, breathing hard, the bloody arrow shaft in his fist.

His wound throbbed, and he could taste the sharp green tang of tree sap on his tongue as it seeped into the gash in his thigh by way of the arrowhead that had pierced the tree.

He watched the Boss Man and someone he knew very well approach, getting closer than he'd like.

"Norba." He snapped the arrow shaft in half to stop himself crying out as the sap suddenly began to burn him from the inside.

He kept hold of the broken pieces in case he needed to snap them again.

"Duncan." Norba looked frightened. His eyes were wide, and he couldn't stop looking between Duncan and the Boss Man. "I didn't shoot you. That was him." He moved his horse away from the Boss Man, almost going off the track.

The strength that had left Duncan when he tried to bolster and analyze the trees began to trickle back into him. Not in a gush, like when the forest was healthy, but a thin drip, drip, drip.

His chest heaved as he fought down the urge to take more than was offered, then throttled back on his need and tried to relax, the tree behind him propping him up while its sap seemed to scour and abrade his leg and then move upward.

"Was it my plan to let you out of your cell into the open air that allowed you to escape?" the Boss Man asked.

Duncan didn't know if he was going to get away yet, or whether he would be taken a prisoner again. If he was, it would be very handy for the Boss Man to believe the rope weakened him, rather than strengthened him, so he shook his head.

"It was coincidence. The woman who rescued us all arrived the day before you came, and was watching the fortress."

"Do you know who she is?"

Duncan shook his head again. "As soon as I was free, I left. I didn't wait around for introductions."

He would not give his enemy even the smallest piece of information about Massi.

"You look better," the Boss Man said. "Not as thin."

He wanted to have a chat about Duncan's health? Duncan tried to keep his face neutral.

He really was nothing more than a tool to this man and the Speaker, both.

"I've had a few days in the forest to recover." Duncan kept his voice even, resisting the urge to rub his wound, which itched now, as if the skin was healing.

It felt like it might have completely closed up.

Under his palm, he felt the bark behind him crumble, and he rubbed it, found it gave way into powder.

The tree had already been almost gone, and it had given the last of what it had to Duncan, so he could heal. It was close to fully dead, now, desiccated and stripped of all life.

Duncan held the broken arrow so tightly, his knuckles went white.

This was unacceptable.

Every tree was precious.

He eyed the Boss Man, saw he hadn't drawn another arrow.

The Boss Man's shoulder was bandaged. Duncan could see the white of it peeping out from the neck of his shirt. He held himself stiffly, so maybe it had hurt him to shoot the arrow in the first place.

That was something, at least.

He held the bow loosely in his hand, sure of himself now that he had injured Duncan.

He knew nothing of this place. Nothing of Duncan and his role here.

Unlike Norba.

The old trader, who Duncan had thought of as a friendly acquaintance, knew enough to be afraid.

"Your welcome is rescinded," Duncan told him.

"I thought you were gone for good," Norba whispered. "I was told you were dead."

Duncan eyed him. "By whom?"

"Lithwick."

"And you're taking this one to Lithwick now?" Duncan asked.

Norba shook his head, then turned to spit on the ground. "Going nowhere *near* that one. Nowhere near."

His vehemence took Duncan aback. Norba wasn't just avoiding Lithwick, he was terrified of him. "And why is that?"

"He isn't right." Norba tapped his head. He opened his mouth as if to say something else, but then closed it again.

"You'll see where he's taking me soon enough. You're coming with us." The Boss Man kept his focus on Duncan, but jerked his head to Norba. "Get off your horse. He won't be able to walk on that leg."

Norba hesitated, looking at Duncan as if for permission.

"You answer to me." The Boss Man had seen the look, and his voice was sharp.

"Why would you think he answers to you?" Duncan began to limp toward them, dragging his leg with each step. "You've just arrived, and have no authority here."

"What authority do you have?" the Boss Man asked.

"More than you." As he spoke, Duncan crushed the wooden shafts in his hands to splinters, and used the energy that had built up in him to blow them into the Boss Man's face.

They exploded outward with magical force.

The Boss Man's head snapped back, unbelievably fast, and Duncan suddenly remembered Massi commenting that he had some kind of magical protection.

I never miss, she'd said. But her arrow had only hit him in the arm, not in the eye, where she'd aimed.

Nevertheless, the Boss Man gave a shout of pain and lifted his arms up, and Duncan ran, dodging between the trees, where he drew on the forest to hide him as soon as he was out of sight.

He'd caught a quick glimpse of Norba just as he'd made it to cover, saw the old man had caught a splinter on his cheek.

He'd lifted a finger to wipe away the blood, and given Duncan an apologetic nod as he'd run past.

The sound of the Boss Man swearing behind him was sweet music to Duncan's ears.

As Massi guessed, he may be protected, but there were chinks in the armor.

Duncan got off the path and kept off it, curving around to the north and keeping his eyes peeled for any sign of Lithwick.

Home.

His body knew it was close, and the forest knew he was finally back.

He could feel the joy, the surge of interest all around him.

It wasn't all dead. Wasn't all corrupted.

Lithwick hadn't done as much damage as Duncan feared.

And he would make sure he did nothing more.

Nothing.

CHAPTER 21

"Y ou need to come up with a name for the fortress." Massi leaned back in the hard wooden chair set at Ranulf Harkonan's dining table, and found herself the focus of all attention.

It was dark, long after dinner, and the ten former prisoners who were staying with Ranulf huddled together in the dining room like they were planning a coup.

Which maybe they were.

The petition they had decided to submit to the Council, outlining the various crimes against them by the Speaker, lay spread out in front of Ranulf.

"A name?" Tomas asked her.

"Firstly, did it have a name?" she asked. "Originally, I mean?"

There was a general shaking of heads.

"Not that I ever heard," Velda said.

"Then you need to make one up. Something that will remind everyone who speaks of it that it is associated with the Speaker. Call it the Speaker's Secret Prison, even."

"Because?" Ranulf frowned at her.

"Because words matter. And concepts matter. A fortress with

no name is a place whose existence can be called into question. I was forcibly taken to what the Kassians called a Chosen Camp when I was eight. Chosen being a word they used to make it sound as if I had been honored, and was special, when what had actually happened was I had been kidnapped and forced into a child army." She saw the winces around the table and guessed most of those present had heard of the camps and what they were really about.

"Own the conversation from the start, it's a luxury not everyone has." Her people, the Cervantes, certainly hadn't been able to contradict the Kassian spin on the camps. They were too busy hiding their children.

Camille, the spell caster who'd helped Duncan bind the guards, slid her elbows forward on the table. "The Speaker's Secret Prison sounds like a very good name for it."

"And when you submit your complaint to the Council, give actual directions to it," Massi said. "Be specific."

Ranulf was studying her. "You are a good strategist. What is your rank in the Rising Wave?"

Massi hesitated, unsure if it was in the Rising Wave's interests for the Grimwaldians to know one of Luc Franck's three lieutenants was interfering in their business.

"That high?" Harkonan's eyebrows rose.

Massi grinned at him. "I don't know what you're talking about."

"What does it matter?" Tomas asked. "She rescued us. Protected us all the way to Taunen. What are your plans, Massi, now we're safe?"

"You aren't safe." She shook her head.

"What do you suggest we do about the archer who was trying to shoot at us earlier?" Ranulf asked.

"He was aiming for you, Ranulf." Massi thought the woman with the black hen had been right about that. "So be very careful. Hire some guards, maybe. Or wear protection."

Massi glanced down and touched the letter on the table in front of her. She'd managed to collect it earlier that evening from the old man Ava had advised her to use as her contact in Taunen——an old friend of her grandparents.

The missive was from Luc, had been written just outside Illoa.

Just over the Grimwalt border into Kassia.

He told her he and Ava were going to Skäddar, skirting Grimwalt and going up through Venyatu, then into the Dallir Valley and the Mirror Mountains.

The news left her feeling even more edgy than before.

No letter she sent now would reach him, not at the pace he was planning to set.

She wanted to go up there herself, from the Grimwalt side. Check out the situation and then make her way over the border into Skäddar to meet up with him.

"You won't accept an offer to be one of those guards?" Ranulf asked.

"No." She touched the letter again. "I'm needed elsewhere." It would be better if they didn't know exactly where she was going, although they could probably guess.

She was not exactly in Grimwalt legally.

"Give us one more day," Ranulf bargained. "Just long enough for us to submit this petition."

One day would give her time to send a letter to Fernwell, so at least General Ru knew what she was planning, and she could also restock her supplies for a trip up north.

She inclined her head. Turned to look at Tomas and Velda. "You'll have to promise me you won't go out alone once I'm gone."

"The Speaker wouldn't know us if we spat in his eye," Velda told her. "He sent someone to drag us out of the estate, but here in Taunen, we're just strangers on the street."

"Until tomorrow, when you submit a petition right in front of him," Massi countered.

"We'll not waste your rescue," Tomas said. "Trust us. We'll be careful."

As he said it, there was a pounding on the front door, and Ranulf stumbled to his feet, face tense.

Massi guessed this was how he was taken the first time, even though that had been at his country estate.

She moved before he did, slipping out of the room, the knife from her belt already in her hand.

A servant stood at the door, nervous and uncertain, reaching for the handle, and Massi held up a hand to tell him to wait.

Ranulf arrived moments later, and shooed the servant away.

"Who is it?" His voice was steady, even though he gripped his hands together.

"General Ventnor."

Ranulf visibly relaxed, pulled the door open, and then stepped back. "General, I'm pleased to see you."

The woman who stepped inside was accompanied by two familiar faces. Her son, who'd told Massi his name was Peter during the night they'd camped together, and Edith, one of the members of his unit.

The general didn't even notice Massi, her attention on Ranulf as he led his guests toward the dining room.

Massi contemplated whether to fade into the shadows and escape.

Then Peter Ventnor turned and looked her in the eye. "I hoped you would be here."

The general stopped walking and spun on her heel. She took Massi's measure, eyes narrowed. "You saved my son's life."

Massi inclined her head. "It was a case of being in the right place at the right time."

"And you're not Grimwaldian." His mother shot Peter a look, and Massi guessed he hadn't told her that part.

"She would prefer to keep her presence here low key," Ranulf said. "And given all she has done for us, we are happy to respect that."

The general paused, then gave a slow nod. "What are your plans from here?"

"I will be leaving Taunen the day after tomorrow."

"She has agreed to watch our backs when we submit a formal complaint to the Council tomorrow," Ranulf said.

They had reached the dining room, and Ranulf waved a hand expansively to invite their guests inside.

"That's why I'm here." General Ventnor's gaze swept the room as everyone at the table stood. She inclined her head in greeting.

"You know what we're planning already?" Tomas sounded shocked.

"I sent a servant around to ask when the Council was sitting tomorrow," Ranulf said. "And to borrow some of the books on protocol and law for the petition. Someone must have put it together."

"Someone did," General Ventnor agreed. "There is already noise about it. Fortunately I have eyes and ears in the chambers, myself, and heard the whispers. The guards at the gate informed Peter you'd arrived this afternoon. I decided it would be best for us to talk before you presented yourselves tomorrow."

"Talk about what?" Camille was obviously suspicious.

"About how to protect yourselves, because there will be more people like Renard, standing by to do the Speaker's bidding. Not just in the military, but in the court itself."

"You knew this was happening?" Ranulf asked. "That the Speaker had embedded his people in the military?"

"I knew something was happening." General Ventnor blew out a frustrated breath. "I knew my second in command was behaving strangely. That he would disappear and then shortly afterward, I'd hear someone had gone missing. I started to worry there was something serious going on."

"There was," Camille said.

Ventnor gave a nod. "I've been cultivating a group of my own, watching, collecting information. I haven't had anything concrete, until Peter came back from Waldrand. Every time I seem to get close, the leads fade away and I'm back to the beginning again."

"And your second in command?" Ranulf asked.

"He's dead." She shook her head. "He went missing, and then I received a notification from his family home in the north that he had been found dead on the road."

"Do you think there are others as high up as him that have been turned?" Tomas asked.

She lifted her shoulders. "I won't take the chance there aren't. Which is why we're meeting now, like this. And why I'm warning you about tomorrow, about what you might be facing."

"We understand the danger, but we can't let it stop us coming forward," Ranulf said. "Otherwise we might as well be back at the Speaker's Secret Prison."

The general frowned at the name, but gave a nod. "I'm not here to dissuade you. I agree you need to present yourselves, especially you, High Commissioner, but I'd like to suggest that all of you go." She looked around the room. "If you're only planning to take a few of those who were imprisoned with you, it will have less of an impact, and it will make any attempt to kill you much easier."

"You want me to surround myself with others so that they get killed instead of myself?"

To his credit, Ranulf sounded genuinely outraged.

General Ventnor shook her head. "Your death is one I'm sure the Speaker is after. If his assassins can't get to you, then I don't think they'll bother with anyone else. That would just put your guard up and make you more wary."

"They already tried this afternoon," Massi offered. "An archer in street clothes, but my guess is he's military."

General Ventnor spun to face her. "Description?"

"Right now?" Massi asked. "He has an arrow wound in the joint between shoulder and arm on the right hand side."

"Sentra." Edith said the name softly. "Claimed it was a training accident."

"You only wounded him?" Peter Ventnor asked, surprised.

Massi shrugged. "Might have been a bit difficult explaining a body in the streets. Besides, he won't be lifting a bow for at least two months."

"You're Rising Wave," General Ventnor said, voice even softer than Edith's. "Cervantes."

Massi didn't react. "It doesn't matter what I am. I'll be out of your way soon enough. What do you suggest should be my part in what happens tomorrow?"

"I can get you up in the gallery," Peter said.

His mother turned to him, a sharp movement of her head. "Peter."

"She has the skill to wound, not kill. There won't be dead bodies on the floor."

"I hope I don't have to lift a bow at all." Massi didn't like the idea of being trapped up in a gallery, with no good way down. "How will I even get a bow up there?"

"We won't go through the main door." Peter stared his mother down and with a sigh, she turned back to Ranulf, conceding.

"I'll fetch you a few hours before the others leave," Peter said. "Bring your bow and arrows, and wear a cloak."

After their guests had gone, everyone remained on their feet around the table.

"This is the start of something," Camille said. "The beginning of the end."

"Maybe," Velda said. "Let's make sure we're the ones who finish it."

CHAPTER 22

Peter Ventnor came for her after breakfast, meeting her at the stables as they'd arranged the night before.

Massi felt good.

She'd eaten, had a decent night's sleep, and a change of clothes.

She wore her cloak, now clean and smelling much less like damp forest and horse, and she pulled it tightly around her. The air was bracing, with a sharp, icy snap to it that hit the back of her throat and hurt her lungs.

It had been cold up in Waldrand, too, but since they'd reached the city the weather had turned, thrusting them into true winter.

"Did anyone ask after Renard?" She glanced at Peter as he led her through narrow streets made gloomy by the shade of the tall buildings around them.

"A few." He flicked her a look, and she wondered if she was imagining the spark of heat in his gaze.

Probably not.

She seemed to attract a certain type of military man.

There had been a few Jatan senior military officers who'd actually flirted with her while she was in an armed standoff with them not so long ago.

"Will his disappearance cause trouble, down the line?" She didn't feel guilty about Renard's death, but she'd like to know if there was a reason to avoid Grimwalt in the future.

Peter shook his head. "The official version we gave is we found Chart and the other two already dead and Renard gone. We looked for him, couldn't find him, and came home."

"Edith and the others can be trusted on that?" she asked. It was a good story, but stories could fall apart when there was more than one person telling them.

"I think they can." Peter steered her through a narrow gate, his hand brushing hers as he walked beside her.

"So, what's the plan?" She was holding her bow, her quiver of arrows hooked over her shoulder. "You're sneaking me into the gallery?"

"There's a secret entrance and a place to watch what's happening below, unobserved." He took her through a back alley that smelled of rotting food, and then opened a wooden door that led into a tiny courtyard.

It was dull, a little dingy, and looked disused.

The building it was attached to was the back of the parliament.

Massi recognized it immediately. She'd put up the missive accusing the Speaker of trying to assassinate Ava on its front gates.

The missive was a lie.

The Speaker had not planned to assassinate Ava. He'd planned to kidnap her and force her to use her magic in his service.

But Ava wanted to stay away from any hint of what he'd planned for her. She wanted her secrets to be kept safe.

And the Speaker *had* harmed Ava. She was no longer the strong, healthy person she had been.

So, even if it wasn't the whole story, it allowed Kassia to vent its outrage, and the Speaker was hardly going to quibble over the details.

"This is the only way in?" she asked as Peter opened a door set into the stone wall.

He nodded, lifted a finger to his lips, and then motioned her to follow him.

Massi closed the door quietly behind her and then walked up the narrow, twisting staircase of rough planks. It wound its way up and up, with no exits onto the floors they passed, until it ended in a tiny room with angled walls.

It was a secret tower, she realized. An enclosed cylinder that had been built into the back of the parliament.

Peter made room for her when she stepped into the small space and pointed to a slit in the wooden wall opposite.

Massi peered through it, saw a narrow view of the chambers below, now mostly empty. A few clerks walked briskly down the middle aisle, what little of it she could see, and placed jugs on the big table at the front of the chamber. This place must have been built especially to watch the councilors, as the only part of the room she had an unimpeded view of was the councilors' table.

There were ten chairs, all on the same side, facing down the hall.

"Who knows about this secret room?" she asked, glancing at Peter.

He was handsome, she thought, although she immediately turned back to the narrow window, keeping her gaze below.

Handsome, and yet, he did not draw her the way Duncan did.

No one had ever drawn her like Duncan did.

He hadn't answered her question, she realized, and she turned her head to look at him.

He was watching her, light hazel eyes intense under his straight brows. "I like the way you move," he said. "Like the ground has less of a hold on you."

She grinned at him. "Now, that is a pretty compliment."

He grinned back, but ruefully. "You aren't interested in me at all, are you?"

She lifted a shoulder. "It's nothing to do with you, everything to do with someone else."

"I'm too late, you mean?" He pondered it.

She didn't respond, leaving it at that. She was too unsure.

It was more than possible that she might never see Duncan Erdo again.

Her hand strayed to the chip of pine cone in her top pocket, and she brushed it with her fingers.

She decided she would make sure she did see him.

She hadn't done anything for herself in a long time, but after she went up to the border, if she hadn't come across him already, she would find him.

Find him and see . . . whatever it was she thought she might see.

"You didn't answer me. Who knows about this place?"

"The military." He spoke reluctantly. "A few of the top generals, like my mother."

"To keep an eye on what's happening with the council?" She didn't think badly of them for it. It was good to keep a finger on the pulse, especially if the military were going to be asked to enforce what was decided by the councilors.

"Yes." He shifted uncomfortably. "One of the generals' brothers was responsible for building this hall about thirty years ago. He slipped in the plans for it, and we've used it ever since."

"And it's definitely been kept quiet?" Massi asked. "Because word usually gets out."

"I don't know." He shifted against the wall as she watched two council members walk into view and take their seats. "I don't think so."

"You do realize that if I have to protect Ranulf this afternoon by shooting from up here, this place won't be a secret any more." She looked over at him, because it was a very real possibility.

He shook his head. "I'll be one floor down, in the gallery. It's just below this room. I'll say I saw someone come into the gallery if you do have to shoot. Just stay here until the panic is over if it comes to that. I don't want anyone to see you leave via the courtyard."

She didn't like it.

If someone did know of this place, she'd be trapped when they came for her. There was only one way in and out.

She liked how little range of view she had even less.

Still, it was better than nothing when it came to the problem of keeping Ranulf and the others safe. And the military had taken a massive risk letting her see this place, which they'd kept to themselves for thirty years.

"All right." She took her cloak off so she could shoot more easily, and stacked her bow and quiver against the wall. "But my view is so limited, even if someone does try to kill Ranulf, I might not see them."

Peter edged her aside, frowned, and pressed his face against the narrow opening. "You're right."

"If nothing happens, do I leave when Ranulf and the others leave?"

He gave a nod. "Give it ten minutes. My mother and I will most likely come back to Ranulf's house this evening to discuss the session."

He moved toward the door, hesitated, and she turned to look at him.

"Thank you, again, for saving my life," he said. "I don't think I'll ever forget seeing that arrow pointed at me, that look on Renard's face, and then he just dropped. You came out of the darkness, bow and arrow pointed down, your face so calm." His lips gave a twist. "It made an impression."

"He chose to put himself in your camp. He could have run," she said. "He was free of the Boss Man, and he had a horse and money. He could have gone anywhere, but he chose to follow orders, hunt you down and try to kill you to keep you quiet. He was planning to meet someone here in Taunen afterward to get a new assignment." She had forgotten that, she realized. Forgotten about that whole conversation.

"Who?" Peter asked the question too loudly, narrowed his eyes, and asked in a whisper, "Can you remember?"

She thought back to the conversation Renard had with the Boss Man. "Car- someone. Carvellis?"

Peter almost reeled back. "I know . . ." His eyes went thoughtful. "When did you hear this?"

"Just after you left the fortress. Renard complained that he had been outed, that he couldn't go back to the military. The Boss Man told him to kill you and your colleagues and then report to Carvellis to get his next job."

"He would have been put into a new unit," Peter said slowly. "Because Carvellis is the roster clerk. They would have slipped Renard in as if he had never been up to Waldrand, if all the rest of us were dead." He snapped to attention. "I need to give this information to my mother."

"I'll see you later then." Massi watched him slip quietly through the door, heard his soft footsteps on the rough wooden boards as he descended.

At least she would hear someone if they came up.

She'd have some warning.

A booming voice down in the hall below had her turning back to the narrow window. Something about the tone caught her interest.

The man who was talking was large, his shoulders wide, his chest a barrel. He was in black, with gold braid edging his cloak. He had a beard, and his eyes gleamed below bushy brows.

The Speaker, she wondered?

He had a big personality, talking in a jocular fashion that struck her as false. His slap on the back to the man he was speaking to was just a little too hearty, the laugh a little too loud.

He was trying too hard.

The two councilors already seated watched the exchange with faces that showed little emotion, Massi noted.

They clearly disliked him.

Interesting.

Ranulf was sure the Speaker had the capacity to influence people, that he had used that influence to gain power. Everything he had done, though, from his secret letters to the old Kassian queen, trying to bargain political and trade concessions for personal wealth, to his attempt to kidnap Ava, told Massi that his influence only stretched so far. He was far from all powerful. He wouldn't have needed Ava, if he was.

Or maybe, he had no power at all.

Maybe he was using the magic of others, just like Massi was herself.

She touched her collar, felt the soft bumps of Ava's silk thread embroidery under her fingertips.

Maybe the items he was using were losing their potency.

If he needed Ava's magic to keep his hold on power, if all he'd ever had to prop himself up were things he'd stolen from the vault, then now was the time to stand up to him, before he found someone else to help him keep his position.

Ava could not be the only one with the power he needed, and sooner or later, he would get lucky and find them.

More councilors walked in, some skirting around the Speaker as he stood in the aisle, passing him with a polite nod, one or two had a warmer exchange with him, but none lingered beside him.

Eventually he followed them up onto the dais, taking his seat in the middle of the table.

People began coming in, some going straight to a seat on the benches, some conferring with a clerk standing off to one side.

The petitions got off to a slow, meandering start, with many of the councilors looking bored or disinterested.

If someone had warned them that Ranulf was coming in with an explosive complaint, it didn't seem to worry any of them.

Maybe no one in the clerk's office had had the courage to mention it to the councilors.

Or the Speaker.

He was leaning back in his chair, his gaze down as if he was looking at something on the table in front of him.

A sudden murmur of voices from the entrance, which Massi couldn't see from her spot high above the hall, was the first indication something out of the ordinary was happening.

She cursed her narrow view again. It was almost useless to her for protection purposes and she couldn't see what was happening at the back of the room.

Unless the assassin jumped onto the councilors' table to shoot Ranulf, she wouldn't have a clear shot.

She was surprised to see Ranulf, closely surrounded by his fellow ex-prisoners, when he appeared below her, walking determinedly up the aisle.

She wasn't expecting him to arrive until a little later.

Massi wondered what had happened to move things up, and decided whatever it was, she was glad they had come now.

She wanted this to be over.

The Speaker froze at the sight of the group.

Massi watched him carefully as he turned his head, then he flicked a finger at someone to his right.

A clerk, perhaps. One of his embedded allies.

She couldn't see who was there.

"High Commissioner." One of the councilors scraped back their chair with a screech of wood and stood, leaning forward with both hands planted on the table. "We thought something bad had happened——"

"Something bad did happen, Jonquil. I was abducted from my estate by agents of the Speaker, and held in his secret prison with the other people who have come with me today."

"I object——" The Speaker rose himself, glanced right again, gave another finger flick.

Was he commanding someone to kill Ranulf, was that the signal?

Massi wondered who would dare in this crowded space, where getting away would be difficult.

Especially if the winds of power were starting to turn.

If the clerks in the parliamentary office who'd worked out Ranulf was coming today, and had informed General Ventnor about it, had not seen fit to let the councilors or even the Speaker himself know, that said a lot.

"You can object all you like," Camille stepped forward, and a few of the councilors reacted to her appearance as well, clearly recognizing her. "We were taken from our homes, held against our will in terrible conditions. We demand justice."

"This is a serious allegation." A woman rose to her feet, and Massi recognized her as one of the two who had watched the Speaker come in, and had barely repressed her dislike. "How many of you are there?"

"There are forty of us." Ranulf waved his hand. "We were held just outside Waldrand at the fortress the guards called the Speaker's Secret Prison, and we only managed to escape a few days ago."

The Speaker looked to his right again, and in frustration, Massi reached for her cloak and picked up her bow and arrows.

This was a secret listening post, not an archer's nest. If someone attacked Ranulf or any of the others directly in front of her, she could do something about it, but she had a feeling no one was going to be that obliging.

She hesitated a moment, then, making up her mind, she quietly left the room, closing the door silently behind her.

She ran lightly down the stairs, exited the building, and stopped short at the sight of a man waiting in the shadows thrown by the high wall of the tiny courtyard.

"Who are you?" she asked, taking his measure.

"Did you use that bow and arrow?" the man responded, gesturing toward her weapon.

Massi frowned at him, thinking through the implications.

"No," she said.

He frowned.

"You're supposed to grab me after I've shot someone, is that right?" she asked.

Well, well, well.

It seemed there was either a traitor close to General Ventnor, or the general herself was untrustworthy.

Whoever it was, they knew about this secret entrance, and wanted to protect it.

They'd set someone to wait for her to come out, so they could say they caught her escaping down the back alley, which would keep the listening post secret.

The problem for the man in front of her was that it would do the Speaker very little good to bring her in if she hadn't killed or wounded anyone.

He clearly knew it, too.

"Are you lying to me?" He looked a little nervous, now.

"No." Massi lifted a shoulder. "Why don't we both go into the parliament and you can see for yourself?"

She wanted to get inside anyway. This man could probably get her exactly where she needed to go.

"All right." He said it slowly. But really, what choice did he have? He needed her close at hand to 'capture' her. And he needed to find out if she was telling the truth.

"Lead the way." Massi smiled at him.

"You lead the way."

"I don't know where I'm going. You do." She lifted her shoulders again.

"Stick close." He stepped to the door, opened it, and when Massi walked toward him, he grabbed her arm in a tight, bruising grip.

She let him lead her along the back alley and then up to a side door, biding her time.

It came as he fumbled one-handed for a key.

Eventually he had to let her go, but relaxed a little when she leaned against the wall, arms crossed, waiting for him.

As soon as the stiff lock turned, she struck, slamming his head into the door, then throwing him down the three steps they taken to reach the side entrance.

He landed hard, winded, nose bloody where it had smashed against the door. She leaped down after him, flipping him over and taking the restraints she had seen hanging from his belt and tying him up.

He would be able to shout in a few minutes, when he had his

breath back, as she had nothing to silence him with, but no one had come past while he had been working on the door, so perhaps no one would hear him.

She took the key out of the lock anyway, and locked the door behind her when she stepped inside.

She was at the rear of the building, and she made her way to the hall.

Whoever the Speaker was looking at to help him, they were this way.

She thought about the implications of the man she'd just dealt with.

The Speaker *must* have known about Ranulf's arrival.

Why else would he have someone waiting for her? Who else would be interested in grabbing her?

Her arrest would embarrass Kassia, the army, and Ranulf. It was an excellent ploy, she had to admit, but only if she had killed someone.

Otherwise, she was just a tourist, watching proceedings in an unusual place.

If someone had shot at Ranulf and succeeded, and then she had killed the assassin, her arrest would be an excellent move for the Speaker.

Ranulf would be gone.

Kassia would be on the back foot.

The Speaker would have some confusion and distraction from what he'd done to Ranulf and the others in his fortress prison.

And yet, he had seemed genuinely surprised to see Ranulf and the others.

She hadn't thought he was acting.

So he must have expected Ranulf later. Perhaps he'd been taken by surprise, and he didn't have what he needed in place.

Maybe the flick of the finger had been to send the man she'd just incapacitated to wait for her.

She slowed her step as she pondered that. It was possible, although he'd gotten there pretty fast, if that was so.

That would mean whatever assassination plan the Speaker may have had in play was also not ready to go.

She might be able to take advantage of that.

She turned a corner and found a wall of richly carved panels, with a door cleverly fitted into one of them.

She slid it open, found to her relief she had gotten it right, and this was the Chamber.

Every one of the councilors was standing, and there was shouting from all sides.

The Speaker looked . . . diminished, Massi thought.

He was not being ignored, precisely, but he wasn't in control, either.

"Silence!" One of the councilors managed to shout over everyone else, and to Massi's surprise, silence did fall.

"Ranulf, this is a crazy story," the councilor said.

"Is it, Jean-Guy?" Ranulf tossed back. "I disappeared, just after I started looking into the mysterious disappearances in the Artifacts Vault." Ranulf paused, nodded toward the woman on the far end of the councilors' table. "Florence can attest to it. We were together, discussing it, before I went to talk to the Speaker about my concerns. He asked me to travel home to my estate to look through some inventories I had in my personal library, and I was taken shortly after that."

Everyone turned to Florence, and she gave a slow nod of her head.

"What are you saying, that there are artifacts missing and the Speaker abducted you to prevent you from investigating what had happened?" A third councilor lifted his hands in an exaggerated, dramatic fashion, as if he were mocking Ranulf. Massi recognized him as the one the Speaker had been talking to in low tones earlier.

"Yes." Ranulf's voice was a drawl. "And given your attempts now to minimize what is a serious matter, I have to ask, did you help the Speaker steal them, Francis?"

The woman who Massi had noticed held the most enmity for the Speaker turned slowly to face Francis. "If the Speaker is involved, so is Francis." She glanced at each of her colleagues. "I saw him steal something for the Speaker and then lie about it."

"What did you see me steal?" Francis spluttered it out, too late realizing his question seemed to confirm he had stolen something.

"Enough." The Speaker hauled himself up on his chair, and then walked to the very edge of the stage.

If she'd still been above, Massi realized, she would have lost sight of him. The move from his seat at the table must have been beyond protocol, because the eyes that followed his path were shocked and surprised.

Massi had been edging her way between two rows of benches since she'd stepped through the door into the hall, trying to get to Ranulf, Tomas, Velda and the others. While she was moving, she swept the room for anyone that seemed more focused on her own group than the antics of the councilors up ahead, but so far, everyone seemed to be watching the front of the room.

"Enough?" Ranulf took a step away from the others. "Speaker, your misdeeds have been exposed. You've imprisoned——"

The Speaker's face was interesting. As Ranulf started talking, Massi could see true indecision in his expression, and his hand hovered near a pocket.

He had an ace-in-the-hole, clearly, but he didn't want to use it unnecessarily, which told Massi he only had one.

It was obviously something he was saving for desperate circumstances, and she could tell he couldn't decide if he was in those circumstances now or not.

Another thing she understood was that she couldn't shoot him preemptively.

That would destroy all the progress Ranulf had just made.

So if she couldn't shoot him, she would make sure no one could say she had even the slightest intention of doing so.

She adjusted her bow on its strap, tightening it so it lay flat against her shoulder blades, her quiver of arrows firmly over her shoulder, her hands completely free.

Then she stepped out, moving swiftly through the group

standing in the aisle, and she reached Ranulf just as the Speaker seemed to come to the conclusion he was in dire enough straights, and had to use whatever was in his pocket to get him out of it.

With a roar, he pulled an item out and threw it at Ranulf.

Massi leaped to intercept, turning her back so that the——was that a milk jug?——bounced off the quiver on her back and landed with a crash on the floor.

She spun back around, her gaze on the Speaker, who was staring wild-eyed at the smashed pottery on the floor.

It hadn't just broken into a few shards, it had disintegrated into a brown and cream powder.

"That's . . . from the vault." Florence's gasp was clear in the surprised silence of the room.

The Speaker held a handkerchief in his hand, and he let it go to flutter to the floor.

He couldn't touch the milk jug with his bare hands, Massi guessed. She was very pleased she had remembered the spoon that had killed one of the Grimwaldian envoys who'd presented themselves to the Kassian court. That it had killed on contact with bare skin.

"Is there a whole deadly set of tableware?" she asked, looking over at Ranulf.

"Yes," Ranulf answered, interest at her question lighting his eyes. "It's called the Last Rites Tea Set." He focused his gaze up to the Speaker. "You would have murdered me in front of a sitting council session? How did you think you would get away with it?"

The Speaker looked out over the crowds, opened his mouth, and Massi suddenly knew he was about to say the strange word the Boss Man had used to activate the soldiers at the fortress.

Before she could move, he shouted it, a strange, almost sibilant word, and again, silence fell as surprise froze people in place.

She watched the councilors first, worried about the power they wielded, but only one jerked in reaction. Francis.

"He has called on those who have pledged allegiance to him to step forward and help him." Massi shouted the information while everything was still quiet.

It seemed to wake everyone up.

There was a flurry of movement.

The councilors on either side of Francis grabbed him, and there were a few struggles from among the crowd. In the end, only three people made it to the Speaker's side.

He began to back away, stumbling as he dropped down off the dais, while his three protectors formed an arc around him.

He moved to the side door that Massi had come through, and just as he reached it, it was yanked open, and Massi caught a glimpse of Peter Ventnor just before he hauled the Speaker by the collar into the passage, and someone else slapped restraints on his wrists.

"I think this is over," she said, careful to step around the spell-infused pottery on the floor. "Quicker than you were expecting."

"Have you seen a piece of the Last Rites Tea Set before?" Ranulf asked, dismissing the victory with a wave of his hand.

"There was a recent Grimwaldian envoy that came to see the queen in Kassia. Two of them had pieces of it with them. A spoon, which killed one of the diplomats in the envoy, and a fork, which was used to try and kill the queen."

"A Grimwaldian tried to kill the Queen of Kassia with a fork from the Last Rites?" Florence's voice was quiet as she stood above Massi on the dais, eyes sharp under severe brows.

"That wasn't the first attempt at the queen's life by your Speaker, and it wasn't the last," Massi said.

"You were the one who put the demand about the attempt on the Queen's life up on the Parliamentary Gates?" one of the other councilors asked. "You are Kassian?"

Massi considered that. She thought of herself as Cervantes. Then Rising Wave. Kassian last, and only because Kassia had annexed Cervantes to begin with. "I represent the queen of Kassia," she said eventually.

"And what are you doing, mixed up in the affairs of today?" someone called.

"She helped to rescue us from the Speaker's prison. She protected us when his assassins tried to kill us here in Taunen. And now, she saved my life when the Speaker himself tried to kill me in front of all of you." Ranulf's words caused a stir in the room.

"And why would you do that?" Florence asked. "How did you even know about the fortress to rescue the Commissioner?"

"She was sent by the queen of Kassia to rescue us," Velda took a step to stand beside Ranulf, with Tomas at her shoulder.

"And who are *you*?" one of the councilors called, indignation clear.

"I am the housekeeper for the Yngstra estate," Velda said, with quiet dignity.

"Forgive me," Florence looked down at Velda, her face not haughty, only confused. "Why would the queen of Kassia have an interest in the housekeeper of the Yngstra estate?"

Ranulf held up a hand, and every eye turned to him. "Because the new queen of Kassia is Ava Yngstra."

There was a beat of silence, and then the room erupted into chaos.

CHAPTER 23

In the three days since the Rising Wave unit had broken camp and crossed into Venyatu, they had headed north, keeping close to the border with Grimwalt.

The landscape of Grimwalt, a continuous line of forest to her left, had tugged at a part of Ava she hadn't realized she had within her——a homesickness for the dark green of the woods, the sweet scent of pine on the air, and the rattling whisper of the wind through the branches.

She'd enjoyed the journey, the creak of leather saddles, the company of the soldiers all around her.

The Venyatux who were bound for home had turned east and waved goodbye two days before, and now they were a smaller group, faster and more focused.

They skirted the foothills of the Mirror Mountains that rose up on the Grimwalt side, and finally the mouth of the Dallir Valley came into sight to the west.

Venyatu stretched many miles further to the north, but the Dallir River was an obstacle to cross first, especially if they wanted to enter Skäddar, which lay north and west of the churning meltwaters.

There was a bridge.

Ava studied it as she crested a gentle rise and it came into view below.

Luc, Britta and Dragir had already reached it, all three of them off their horses, inspecting it.

Ava didn't think she had ever crossed a wooden suspension bridge before.

She didn't like the way it was swaying in the wind, but given how high the rocky banks of the river were, it was clearly the best way across.

Helmi had told her earlier that given their pace, they would easily be in Skäddar by nightfall, and it seemed she was right.

The path into Skäddar was clearly visible beyond the bridge, on the left.

Tomorrow, they would reach the place where Britta and Dragir said the Gathering was going to take place.

And they would come before the Skäddar Collective.

Ava hadn't been a queen for long, but she had already represented Kassia to the Jatan. She knew she hadn't convinced them she had a good hold on her throne, and had been lucky Luc, as well as Kikir, her friend from the Skäddar, had stood solidly at her back as she'd negotiated.

She needed to look more the part this time.

The Jatan had needed the settlement they had negotiated, but the Skäddar were not in the same position. They could walk away from the alliance with the Rising Wave, especially if they didn't think she had the power or authority to uphold her part of the bargain.

She had to project strength, so it was a good thing she was stronger every day, and no longer as exhausted every night.

She could feel her magic was stronger, too.

It no longer took as much concentration when she worked something, and she had begun asking the soldiers for items of clothing to embroider, weaving protection and healing into as many as she could during the stretches where the paths were rough and they had to go slowly to keep the horses safe.

The men and women in the unit seemed to delight in the tiny, colorful birds, flowers and insects she worked into their collars or cuffs, although she wondered how pleased they would be if they knew she was using spell craft.

Some would be honored, she guessed——work such as she created came with a hefty price tag to those who sold their skills.

Others would be more wary.

It didn't matter, because they would never know.

She worked on her woolen tunic at night, using the soft wool Dak had bought her in Illoa, and it was nearly done.

Sirna, the man who'd abducted her from Fernwell months ago, had destroyed all her clothing when he'd taken her, including her cloak.

She had spent so much time working so much into it, it had been a massive blow to lose it, especially as she had not been able to work at the same strength when she'd gotten back to the palace. The cloak she had now was nothing like the one she had lost.

With every day that passed, though, she sensed her power growing, and it made her work long into the night, until the fire light got too low to knit by.

The tunic was less likely to be taken from her than a cloak, and would lie closer to her skin.

In time, she would start working on her cloak again, but for now, she sensed the magic was deeper-seated in the wool, in the weave of the garment itself, as she knitted it into existence.

She made sure to weave magic protections into her hair each morning, as well.

She wished the Cervantes favored the long, braided hair of the Venyatu, so she could do the same for Luc, but he liked his hair short so no one could get a grip on it, and most of the Cervantes soldiers with him followed suit.

Luc looked up as she began the downward descent, and he lifted his arm to wave at her.

She waved back, aware of the grins from the soldiers riding around her.

It wasn't as if she and Luc hadn't ridden together most of the day, with Luc only going ahead with Britta and Dragir an hour before.

Still . . . her heart was as happy to see him again as if they had spent the day apart.

When she reached the bridge, everyone was dismounting, taking the time to stretch and get a bite to eat.

"Is it dangerous?" Ava asked, stepping onto the first plank and giving it a test bounce.

"We crossed it, no problem, coming to you," Britta said.

"The wind is worse now, though," Dragir said, watching it sway with narrowed eyes.

"Do we wait until it dies down?" Dak came to stand beside her, arm reaching up to give the hessian rope above their heads a tug.

"I don't want to," Luc said. "We can't know it isn't going to get worse, and I'd prefer us to be on the right side of the river when we camp tonight."

"Then let's go." Dak stepped back.

Ava turned, found Luc's hand out to her.

She took it, stepped delicately off the plank. Gave him a smile.

He smiled back, and for a moment the others, the river roaring at her feet, the sharp bite of cold in the air, all disappeared.

Luc drew her closer, his big hands warming her own, and she went up on her toes to kiss him.

Someone gave a piercing whistle, and with reluctance they drew back from each other.

Ava curled an arm around Luc's waist, and he tucked her up against him, his hand stroking her arm as he held her close.

There was a moment of silence, and she realized everyone was looking at them.

Britta cleared her throat delicately. "Dragir and I walked our horses across one by one last time. It's probably the best way to do it again."

There was some jockeying amongst the more competitive soldiers as to who would go first, so Luc asked Britta and Dragir to decide between them. "They know how to do it, so watch them carefully," he ordered.

Britta went across, her horse shying twice as the wind jerked the bridge beneath their feet.

She nearly lost the reins near the end, but managed to hang on and get across.

No one was as keen to go, all of a sudden.

"I'll go." Ava patted the trusty, dependable mount the stable master in Fernwell had given her.

Luc nodded, and she guessed he wanted her across as soon as possible, in case the wind got stronger, or the bridge got weaker.

She knew the others thought of her with varying degrees of pity since she'd returned from her abduction. She was so clearly not herself.

If she went across, the others would have no excuse.

She caught hold of her horse's reins and urged her up onto the first wooden plank.

The wind seemed to die down for the first part, and though her mare didn't like the way the planks moved beneath her, or the creak of the ropes on either side, she walked forward, tossing her head now and then to show how unhappy she was.

"You are so clever and good," Ava murmured, stroking her flank as she focused on Britta, standing up ahead, rather than looking down, or taking any notice of the fine spray coming up like smoke from below.

When they reached the halfway point, the wind grew stronger suddenly, swinging the bridge from side to side as it gusted.

The mare panicked, and Ava admitted she wasn't far behind as she felt the ropes cut into her back as she lost her footing and was thrown against them.

The horse reared, ripping the reins from Ava's hands and headed toward Britta, screaming in rage and distress.

The bridge swayed even more as it was thrown from side to side as the mare ran, and Ava stayed where she was, hands gripping the nearest rope to steady herself.

It was a good thing she did.

As the mare took a final kicking leap onto the far side of the river, the rope on Luc's side gave way on the bottom right.

The whole structure tilted, flinging Ava off the planks.

She swung for a horrible moment, suspended over the water, and then she got her arm through the rope and waited for the worst of the swinging to stop.

The rope twisted her toward the far side, where she could see Britta's face in stark relief, eyes wide, and then it twisted her back, so she was looking at Luc.

He was hanging over the edge, checking the ropes. As she faced him, he lifted his head, his face drawn.

"I'm all right." She swung her body, trying to get momentum so she could land back on the tilted planks, but although she managed it, it was only for a second, and then she slid off again, swinging madly above the river.

For the first time, she looked down and considered her options.

The water below looked treacherous. Strong, wild, and dangerous.

But she did not have the arm strength to pull herself across to Britta.

"It was almost cut through." Dragir's voice was suddenly clear as the wind dropped again.

He was bent down, looking at where the rope had given way.

So, someone had weakened it.

She was glad Britta had gotten across safely, and so had her mare.

The rope had turned her back to face the lone Skäddar warrior on the other side. Britta was now crouched down, checking the ropes on her side. She looked . . . worried.

"Ava." Luc's voice was intense.

She tried to get the rope to twist back toward him.

He was kneeling at the edge, hand out as if he was planning to crawl across and get her, when the rope on the right, attached to Britta's side, suddenly gave way, too.

Luc threw his weight back in time and Ava plunged downward, an involuntary scream wrenched from her throat. She lost her arm hold and scrabbled as she fell, just grabbing the rope before she tumbled into the water.

For a moment, she swung with her eyes closed, simply happy to be holding on.

Then she opened her eyes again, twisting back to Luc.

He was studying the bridge.

Her arms just weren't going to last, Ava realized.

They were shaking under the strain of holding up her full weight, and her fingers were burning against the thick rope.

She could feel the prickle of magic against her scalp where her braids touched her skin, and at her neck and wrists, from her shirt.

Her protections were trying to work out what they could do. She tried to flex her hands, get a better grip on the rope . . .

Rope.

She could work with rope.

Almost at the same time, Luc seemed to work it out, as well.

He knelt on the left side, took out a knife, and began to cut the bottom rope. "Get ready, Ava. It's going to swing across."

She couldn't respond.

Her hands burned as if they were on fire, and her arms shook so badly, she had seconds, she realized. Less time than Luc could give her.

She felt her magic surge up, and with an audible snap, the left side of the bridge that Luc was trying to cut gave way.

The bridge was now attached only to the left side on the opposite bank.

The whole thing swung across the river and Ava curled up, bracing for impact with the cliff on the other side.

Her bones rattled as she hit, and then she was flush against the rock face, scrabbling for a foothold.

The wooden planks that made up the bridge were thick, hacked from sturdy trees, and she was easily able to fit the toes of her boots between them.

The relief in her arms was instant.

She closed her eyes again, leaning her cheek against the cold stone.

Had that been her magic, or Luc, who'd cut the rope? Or both?

Her magic had changed minds, tricked eyes, and diverted weapons. But this was a proactive magic, a severing of thread.

If that's what had happened.

She would have to talk to Luc.

"Ava!" Luc's shout was clear across the roar of the water. "Speak to me!"

She turned, making sure she had a good hold on the rope, and blew him a kiss.

The single rope was thick enough to hold her weight, and she began to pull herself up.

Britta grabbed her when she reached the top, hauling her up onto the lip of the cliff.

She sat, arms behind her for support, and then let them give way, so she was lying on her back, looking up at the sky.

"I can't believe I got across alive," Britta said. "And I really can't believe you did."

Ava struggled back up, studied the ruins of the bridge structure on the other side. "We were lucky."

She got to her feet, dusting her hands on her trousers, and saw Luc was still watching her.

"He was going after you. If the other rope hadn't snapped, he would have." Britta's voice was soft.

"I know." He told her he would always come for her.

He always had.

"What do we do now?" Britta asked.

"The others will have to find another way to cross, and I'm guessing there isn't a good place close by on the Venyatu side?" They wouldn't have built the bridge here if there was.

"Our border patrol has mentioned there's a good place to cross further down the valley, but that would mean . . ." Britta trailed off.

"That would mean they'll have to enter Grimwalt to reach it." Ava looked down the valley.

Was that why someone had sabotaged the bridge, to force them to go onto the Grimwaldian side?

Was there a trap waiting for them there?

She wished she could warn Luc, but from his grim expression, from the way he was looking from her and then down the valley, she guessed he understood all too well.

He pointed to her, to himself, and then down the valley.

She nodded back.

She agreed.

They needed to travel together, on opposite sides of the river, never losing sight of one another.

It wasn't safe, but it was the best way forward they had.

CHAPTER 24

Luc stopped at the border——according to the map it was where the forest began——and looked across the river to where Ava and Britta sat on their horses, watching him and the group.

His arms and neck still prickled with the adrenalin, the terror, of seeing Ava dangling from rope over the roaring waters.

His hands still felt the sting of the rope snapping beneath his hands as he'd tried to saw through it.

He didn't understand how it had done that. He hadn't been close to getting all the way through.

He had been too slow to work it out, too late.

Even while he'd hacked at the thick hessian, he'd known that she would fall, and he would lose her.

And then he'd felt something, a shiver of . . . he couldn't describe it. And he didn't care if it was the forces of darkness itself.

Ava was alive, in sight. Safe, for now.

"Someone knew we were coming," Dak said, drawing level with him. "Do you think they were trying to force us to go this way by damaging the bridge."

"Yes." There was no question in Luc's mind.

And they had nearly taken Ava from him with their trap.

They would not like the consequences of that.

"Risky." Dragir said. "They surely couldn't have predicted when the bridge would go." He shielded his gaze and looked through the narrow gap in trees ahead, the pathway into Grimwalt.

"If they expected a Rising Wave unit, they would have known it would have come down some time during the crossing." Luc glanced at Dragir, and wondered if the Skäddar warriors traveling with them realized someone on their side had betrayed them.

Because as far as he knew, only the Skäddar and the Rising Wave knew about this meeting. Knew to expect a unit traveling this way.

"You say there's an easy place to cross on the Grimwalt side," Luc said, keeping his thoughts to himself for now. "But how far in?"

"About an hour's ride," Dragir said. "I've never seen it myself, but we were given information from the Skäddar border guards before we made the journey to you, and the crossing was mentioned, in case something happened to the bridge."

"Helmi and I got that same information," Pilar confirmed. "You think we can expect something bad there?"

"There," Luc agreed, "or between here and there." He studied the tree line. "Maybe they're watching us right now."

His words caused a ripple through the group.

"No sense waiting. We're just giving them more time to prepare." He turned in his saddle. "Combat ready," he called, and the soldiers of his unit drew themselves up.

He could see the battle light gleam in their eyes.

The Cervantes were trained for this. Were very good at it.

And they had been lounging around in Fernwell for months.

They would be looking forward to a melee.

He looked over at Ava, and she gave a nod. Her and Britta's path was an easier one, as the trees had been cleared back from the river bank on the Skäddar side.

They would lose sight of each other when he reached the trees, but he had to assume the path curved back to the river soon after that.

"Go." He urged his horse forward, and Dak kept pace beside him, with the three Skäddar warriors right behind him, and then the rest of the unit.

He had his sword out by the time he reached the forest, his gaze sweeping the dense brush for any sign of an ambush.

If it was him, he would wait until the whole unit was inside the forest before attacking.

He rose up in his saddle and looked back, but nothing seemed wrong, and there was no buzz, no warning of danger.

He looked toward the river, but it was shielded from view by the trees.

He urged his mount faster, unwilling to have Ava out of his sight for even a moment longer than necessary. As he turned a corner, a wall of green blocked his path, and the horse managed to dance and rear to a halt just before they hit it.

He slid off the saddle, throwing the reins at Dak and ducking under the low branches of the trees that formed the barrier in front of them.

The path was still visible around the trunks and roots, and it looked to him as if someone had magically grown trees that would usually take years to reach this height overnight, sprinkling them across the path to bar the way.

The trees only grew three or four rows deep, and then the path continued on, as open as it was on the other side of the strange green wall.

Luc moved back, straightening up just as Dak dismounted.

His friend blew out a breath in relief at the sight of him. "Well?"

"Someone's blocked our way." He glanced over at Dragir. "You said someone was growing thick stands of trees on the Grimwalt side of the border, way more than could be accounted for by nature itself?"

Dragir gave a nod, then lifted his gaze to the trees in front of them. "You're saying . . .?"

"We're nicely hemmed in." Luc wondered if the way back had been blocked since they'd entered, either with more trees, or with the soldiers of whoever wanted to attack them.

Whatever the answer, the horses wouldn't be able to move forward, and going back wasn't an option.

He looked left and then right.

His inclination was to go right, toward the river and Ava, although the path to the left looked the easier, more open one.

"This way?" Dak pointed left and Luc shook his head.

"Too obvious."

There were grumbles, but he organized for some of the soldiers to bring up the rear with the horses, and began on foot to the right, clearing the way as he went.

A few members of the unit had machetes for just such a problem, and they were passed forward so that Dak and Luc could hack an easier path.

Luc lost himself in the swing, chop, swing motion as they opened the way, and the tingle of warning came too late, just one beat before he broke through onto the river bank, too late for him to pull back as his arm swung down to clear the last branch.

A monster rose up, as if a wind blew the debris on the ground in front of him into a loose shape made of sticks and dead leaves and the loamy soil of the forest floor.

It rose up and up, towering over him, as if the very act of stepping out of the tree line had caused it to spring to life.

As if he had triggered a trip wire, or crossed a magical line.

The wards that Ava had sewn into his shirt, into his tunic, into his very skin, flared to life.

He had sheathed his sword to wield the machete, so he parried the first blow of a strangely bulky fist with it, felt the vibration through his arm as his machete blade struck hard wood and stone.

The monster——faceless, almost formless——reared back, but Luc stepped closer, taking another swing until he felt the blade bite into wood again.

He leaned in, pressing harder, until the wood cracked and gave way.

He had broken what could loosely be called its arm, he saw, and as it reformed in front of his eyes, suddenly everyone was around him.

He sensed their shock, their fear, and from the corner of his eye, saw more than one take a step back.

He gave a battle cry and leaped at the monster again, and then Dak leaped forward with him.

After a beat of hesitation, everyone else joined in, hacking with swords and knives, chopping away at the strange creature.

It struck back, sweeping more than a few soldiers off their feet, but it never seemed to get a solid blow in.

He would have said it was the formless, lumbering shape of it that was hindering it, but when it hit out again and only just clipped one of his soldiers when it looked like it should have been a solid blow, he suddenly knew.

Ava.

Luc started to laugh as he swung the machete again.

She had woven her magic over all of them, with her flowers and her bees and her birds sewn into collars and cuffs.

He caught Dragir looking over at him, frowning, as he lunged and spun as he laughed, chopping away at the creature someone had made from the detritus of the forest.

"Force it into the river," he ordered, and his soldiers moved into an arc, advancing as they dodged and struck out, until the monster was at the very edge of the cliff.

Luc didn't dare look over to see if Ava was on the opposite bank, needing every ounce of concentration to deal with what was in front of him.

The monster stood in the sunlight, out of the gloom of the forest, shocking in its strangeness——a nightmare of someone's darkest dreams.

Small rocks and stones, dead branches and leaves, coalesced together to make a bipedal creature with no face, no definition.

Luc wondered at the mind that had conceived it.

Was he or she close by, powering the entity they had created somehow? Or had the energy already been embedded in it, so that once the trap was sprung, it would go on until it had used up all its power?

He looked up at where the head should be, but it was just a misshapen blob, a wobbly approximation of a person.

No eyes looked back at him. No intelligence.

He bent and sliced across its ankle, and before it could reform, it overbalanced, falling backward into the river.

He stood on the edge, looking down, and saw the water churn it into pieces that tried to stitch themselves back together again and again as the water ripped it apart.

It was swept away, and the others came to stand beside him, breathing hard.

Luc lifted his gaze, found Britta and Ava standing on the other side, faces shocked.

Ava looked so worried, he looked down at his hands and saw they were covered in small cuts and nicks.

His face began to sting, and he lifted a finger to his cheek, and it came away bloody.

"Small cuts," he called across the water. "I promise."

She didn't look convinced, and Luc noticed the others were in a similar condition to himself.

Everywhere their skin was bare was abraded, but everyone was standing.

Some had leaves and bark in their hair——he did himself, he realized as he lifted a hand to rub his head——and there were a few rips and tears in his clothing, but nothing serious.

"Where did it come from?" Dak asked, bending at the waist, hands on his knees.

"I think it was waiting for us to cross some invisible line," Luc said. "I think this was the trap." He hoped it was the only one.

"You always laugh when you battle monsters?" Dragir asked, coming to stand beside him.

Luc smiled. "Always."

THE MONSTER LUC HAD TOPPLED INTO THE RIVER WAS ABLE TO re-form less and less of itself as it was swept away.

Ava watched it until it was out of sight, and guessed that whatever spell craft had powered it had run out of spark.

Despite that, it was impressive.

She had never seen anything like it.

"A skovva." Britta was also watching the monster as it tried to reconstruct itself over and over on the water's surface, only to be ripped apart again. "I thought they were myths."

"What are they?" Ava asked.

"A bad forest spirit. But in the stories, they don't attack groups of people. They sneak up behind a lone woodcutter, or a traveler, and drag them away." Britta finally turned to look back over at the rest of their group.

"What does it do to the people it catches?" Ava asked.

Britta frowned. "I don't know, specifically. Nothing good. It kills them, I think."

"Is the myth of the skovva well known?" Ava asked.

"In Skäddar, yes. Maybe in Jatan and the north of Grimwalt, also."

Ava had worried that whoever had murdered the villagers in the mountains and threatened the treaty between Kassia and Skäddar had used magic to do it, but before she'd seen the skovva, she'd assumed she would be dealing with someone like herself.

A spell caster.

The stories of a gilla being spotted by the border guards——a man turning into a fox or a stoat——had made her wonder if it was the same person, switching from murder to mind games.

But she could not create something like the skovva. Had no idea how it had been done, when usually she could see how a spell was worked, and could find a way to relate it to her own magic.

This was alien to her.

And formidable.

If whoever had killed the men, women and children in Skäddar was the same as the person who'd created the monster that had attacked Luc, she felt a real sense of fear.

She was used to feeling in over her head, but this time, she might actually sink.

CHAPTER 25

They pitched camp an hour's ride from where Luc and the others had finally crossed the river.

No matter how tired they were, no one felt safe enough to rest where an ambush party from Grimwalt could easily reach them.

And at the back of everyone's minds was the fear that another skovva could rise up, and maybe this time get across the water.

Ava hadn't shared her idea that the skovva had been created with magic. They had all ridden away, fast as they could, as soon as they'd made it into Skäddar.

No one had said much until they'd found a camping spot.

"Not knitting tonight?" Helmi asked.

She shook her head. "Too tired."

That was a lie.

Her hands were injured from the rope, the skin still abraded and tender, but her magic had already done a lot of healing work, and by tomorrow, her palms would most likely be unblemished.

She would rather not draw attention to it, when it would soon be gone.

"You had an exciting day." Britta hunched a little, and Ava reached out and patted her shoulder.

"We all did. On both sides of the river."

"Just a bit." One of the soldiers leaned forward, elbows on knees.

They all wanted reassurance, Ava realized. Someone to tell them it wasn't as bad as they thought.

"Was there enough balm for everyone's cuts?" she asked. "You all look like you walked through a whirlwind."

"Dust devils, they call them in the east," someone commented.

"Did anyone catch a glimpse of the spell caster working the debris?" Ava asked.

A few of the soldiers seemed to sit a little straighter at the question.

"Not me," Lucilla said.

"Britta and I only had eyes for the fight, and I could kick myself now that I didn't look beyond that." Ava glanced at Britta. "Unless . . .?"

Britta shook her head. "It was like a skovva come to life. I couldn't take my eyes off it."

"If there's a next time, we should try to see the puppeteer, instead of the puppet," Ava said.

No one contradicted her, but some looked skeptical that there was a puppeteer at all. At least she had sown a kernel of doubt that they were up against an actual monster.

It would have to be enough for now. She had nothing left in her.

She stood, stretched. "I'm going to bed."

There was a general murmur of agreement, and as she headed for her tent she saw a number of others drift away from the fire and follow suit.

She crawled in, wrestling her clothes off, and curled up naked on one side to make room for Luc when he joined her.

He had found it difficult to settle after the day they had had.

She knew it wasn't the skovva. She had a feeling he could fight monsters all day.

It was seeing her dangling by her fingertips over a raging river that had him jumpy.

He had sat beside her at dinner, and then gone off to do a circuit of the clearing they had settled in for the night.

He needed to move, to protect.

She waited, and when he finally crawled in, she pulled him close, enjoying his hum of pleasure at finding her naked.

He ran a hand down her back, then up her arm, and gently cupped her hand to look at her palm.

"Still sore?"

"A little." She used the back of her hand to brush his cheek, which was criss-crossed with healing scratches. "It will be gone by morning."

He kissed the fine skin on her inner wrist, and then moved to her neck, then up to the side of her temple.

"Was it you who broke the rope?" he whispered in her ear. "I wasn't close to cutting through it when it snapped."

"I . . . think my magic did it. I thought about it, and then it happened. I wasn't sure if it was you or not."

"It wasn't me." He sounded regretful.

"I'm not sure it would have worked if you hadn't already been cutting it." She tilted her head, trying to see him in the dark. "My workings have never done anything like that before."

"Do you think you're getting stronger?" He moved so she could push his shirt off his shoulders.

"I'm stronger than I was after the abduction. I didn't think I was stronger than I was before that. But maybe . . ." She had been so focused on getting stronger, maybe she had surpassed what she had been before. Stretched herself without knowing it.

"Whatever the reason, I'm glad. You would have been washed away if you'd fallen in."

"Maybe." Her hand went to the buckle of his belt. "But I was still protected. I think I would have survived if I'd gone in the river."

"Maybe isn't good enough for me when it comes to your safety."
He lifted himself over her.

"I had to watch that skovva attack you, while I stood, useless,
on the other side of the river, so I understand."

"You weren't useless. Your workings protected me and every
single person in the unit. The monster couldn't get a direct hit on
any of us."

"Really?" She raised her brows in surprise.

"Really. That is why I was laughing. I realized that when it came
down to your magic against whoever created that thing, yours was
winning."

She blew out a breath and felt a surge of hope. "That's good to
know." She thought about what he had just said. "You think
someone created that thing? That it wasn't a real skovva."

He shook his head. "I felt the trap as I sprung it. Your magic
buzzed. And there was no intelligence in that monster. It was like a
mechanical toy, released from a box to go until it ran out of energy."

"That's what it seemed to me, too. But some think it's real. That
it's a myth come to life."

"Someone's hoping that's what we all think."

"We will have to try and change their minds. It's hard to fight an
enemy if some don't believe they exist."

"That's a problem for tomorrow." Luc bent his head to the tip of
her breast and she surged under him.

There were no more words left to say.

And tomorrow would come soon enough.

THEY ENCOUNTERED THE FIRST SKÄDDAR GUARD HALF A DAY'S
ride from where they'd set up camp.

Luc saw movement through the trees moments before Britta let
out a yip of greeting and rode forward.

Dragir, Helmi and Pilar followed close behind her.

The guard emerged from the small wood, the blue and green design on his face marking him as a warrior.

He met their Skäddar friends in an open meadow where they formed a huddle, talking in low voices.

Pilar turned and waved to Luc to signal that all was well.

Luc raised a hand in acknowledgement.

There was a lot of trust resting in this encounter, and Luc hoped it was not lost on their hosts.

They had both the queen of Kassia and the commander of the Rising Wave at their mercy.

Hopefully it would prove the extent of his and Ava's goodwill and commitment to the alliance.

He had ridden slightly ahead of Ava when he'd noticed the guard, but now he waited until she was level with him before continuing on, and was pleased when Dak fell in on her other side.

He could sense other Skäddar around them as they entered the woods, a quick movement here and there, on both the left and the right of the narrow path.

The whole Rising Wave unit was boxed in, and again, Luc hoped the Skäddar appreciated the trust being placed in them.

The woods were not deep, merely a ribbon of trees that curved along the top of a gently-sloping hill, and they emerged back into the open in less than ten minutes, into another meadow, the grass winter dry and crispy under the horses' hooves.

Below was a shallow valley, covered in large tents in hues of dark rust orange, dark grays, and murky blues.

The Dallir River curved into the valley and then out again in a neat loop at one end of it, and the foothills of the Mirror Mountains rose up behind the camp and on the other side of the river, thick with dark pines broken by granite cliffs.

"The Gathering," Ava murmured. "It looks like they've just arrived."

Some of the tents were still being set up, and at others, saddle bags were being unpacked, and things carried inside.

"Good timing," Helmi said, riding back up to them. "Most of the Collective have only just arrived."

"Would they like time to settle in before we talk?" Luc asked.

Helmi lifted her shoulders. "I don't know. Why don't you pick a spot for the unit to set up camp, and I'll find out what's going on."

She rode back down the hill, and Luc scanned the terrain.

"Will they object to us being above them?" Dak wondered. He pointed to a nice wedge of flattish ground just below the top of the hill they were on, to the right.

"I'm sure they'll tell us soon enough if they do," Luc said.

They began pitching their small traveling tents and creating fire pits, and more than one of the soldiers voiced their approval at their distance from the river.

Some were still thinking about the monster that had gone into the water the day before.

"It was a construct, not a living thing," Ava said to Lucilla, who was one of the soldiers talking about it. "Britta and I saw it trying to reform but it had less and less energy as the water kept swirling the parts of it away from each other. It's in pieces now, floating far down the river from us."

"Let's just say, even if that's true, I'm happy to be here, rather than there." Lucilla pointed to one of the tents that was being set up close to the river bank. "Because if someone could make one, they could make another."

"True enough." Luc was not going to minimize things. "But it has to take a lot of power and time to work a spell like that. I can't imagine it would be easy to do."

Yarlun, his senior officer, gave a slow nod. "It was nothing like I've ever seen, ever even heard about."

"Britta says it looked like a mythical creature described in folk-tales from around these parts called a skovva. And they've been seeing another magical creature across the river——they call it a gilla. It appears to be a person who changes into an animal." Ava crouched in front of the fire pit and added a few sticks. "I think someone is trying to use the Skäddar myths and folktales to frighten the Skäddar away from our alliance."

"You think the same person is responsible for both?" Yarlun asked.

Ava nodded. "It would be a huge coincidence if two mythical creatures are seen in the same area for the first time ever, just when the Skäddar have been warned off of their friendship with us."

"And to be clear, neither Ava nor I believe in coincidences. Not like this," Luc said.

"We've been played, too, then, haven't we?" Lucilla said. "Setting that thing on us. Trying to frighten us with monsters."

"And not even very dangerous monsters," Luc kept his voice even. "While we all got a few cuts and bruises, we hardly came out of it with any major injuries."

Maybe it would have been different if Ava hadn't spent so much time making sure everyone was protected, but she had.

He would use that to keep his people calm and clear-eyed, not in a fog of fear.

"Shock and awe," Dak said suddenly. "First lesson of war."

A few of the soldiers began to nod.

"Trying to make us so on edge, we're jumpy and unfocused." Lucilla spoke slowly. "Damn. That makes me mad." She paused. "I'm still glad we're not camped by the river, though."

There was a ripple of laughter at that, and then everyone got back to setting up camp.

Luc was hammering in the last peg of his and Ava's tent when he saw Dragir and Britta walking up the slope toward them.

He straightened, dusting his hands, waiting for them to approach and pass on whatever instructions they'd been given.

Up until the Skäddar met their own people earlier, they had been part of the Rising Wave unit, but now they were setting themselves slightly apart.

Luc couldn't blame them for it. They were Skäddar warriors, part of a different chain of command, and now that they were on home territory, things were different.

Helmi and Pilar were nowhere in sight, and he guessed they were being debriefed, as they had spent over a month in Fernwell.

He was fine with that. He'd known they were visiting as representatives of the Skäddar, and both he and Ava believed transparency and friendliness were the best ways to secure the alliance.

"The Collective has asked if you would meet them now, before the evening meal," Britta said. "Then after the discussions, we can share food together."

Luc nodded. He glanced across at Ava, and she came to stand beside him.

Britta glanced at them both, and at the tent. "Do you want to change?"

Luc looked down at himself. He was wearing his rough trousers, his embroidered shirt under the woolen tunic Ava had knitted him, and his cloak. His sword was on his belt. He was a little dusty, but not too bad. They had had a chance to wash off two days ago, and most of his things had been cleaned.

Ava was dressed in a similar style. She had on trousers, embroidered shirt and a jacket under her cloak.

She hadn't finished knitting her own tunic, and when he tried to give her his, she told him the magic was specific to him, that his would do her no good.

He wasn't sure that was completely right, but he was pleased to see her complex braids were still in place, crisscrossing her head and falling in thin plaits to below her shoulders.

"There is nothing to change into that isn't just more of the same," Ava said, with an apologetic shrug.

The Collective were getting the queen in her riding gear.

They followed Britta and Dragir down the slope, and Dak and Yarlun trailed behind them, not close enough to indicate distrust, but close enough to remind the Skäddar they were there.

Britta glanced at them, and frowned. "No one will harm either of you here."

"We know. But Dak worries." Ava softened his and Yarlun's actions with a gentle, indulgent smile, and Britta gave a slow nod.

"I can understand that."

"We're all a little shook up after what happened yesterday." Luc tipped his head at the river.

"Yesterday." A warrior who'd been watching them approach the big rust red tent Britta was leading them to, and who Luc had been watching in turn, stepped forward a little, holding up a tent flap in a huge hand. "What was it that happened yesterday?"

Britta looked startled at the question, then glanced through the opening into the tent itself. "I think our guests can tell the Collective that, Johan. Not explain to you in the entrance."

Johan gave a smile that was all teeth and stepped aside, and Britta led them through the entrance.

"He's heard rumors after Pilar and Helmi were debriefed, most likely," Luc heard Britta whisper to Ava as they ducked under the low canvas door. "He's as curious as a cat." She glanced back at the big, burly warrior, and then forward again.

Luc gave the man a nod, but there was no friendliness in his expression as he let Luc pass.

Luc came to a stop, eyeing the cool, gloomy interior. The Collective seemed so similar in structure and style to the Cervantes own system of government, Luc felt a tug of nostalgia for the days before he'd been taken by the Kassians, when his mother had been head of the village, and he had sat through many a long, boring meeting as she had consulted with the other elders.

He bowed to them in respect, and Ava put her hands together, and dipped her head.

"This is Ava Yngstra, Queen of Kassia," Britta said, introducing them. "And Luc Franck, Commander of the Rising Wave."

"You are sure?" One of the older men on the left end of the semi-circle the Collective had formed asked, voice a touch querulous.

"I am sure, uncle." Britta stepped back, giving the floor to Ava and himself.

Luc wondered if the man was actually her uncle, or if it was just a term of respect.

"They don't look very important."

It was always good to know exactly what your friends, as well as your enemies, thought of you. Luc kept quiet, and so did the Collective.

"They have traveled for many days, over difficult terrain, and even fought a skovva and won," Britta said, her voice slightly agitated. "They wear the clothing of warriors."

More than one of the members of the Collective seemed to straighten at her words.

"Pilar and Helmi have told us of this skovva." The woman at the center of the semi-circle said. "I am Tuva, and I am most interested to hear what you have to say about it."

"But first, you wanted us to meet you here to discuss our alliance?" Ava spoke for the first time.

"We did." Tuva's focus moved to Ava, and they stared at each other for a moment. "I thought you might be simply a figurehead, Ava Yngstra. I had never heard of you before you became queen of Kassia. But you don't look like a puppet."

Britta gave a snort, and Luc tried to keep a straight face, himself.

"I see that you very much are not a puppet." Tuva sent a sharp look at Britta, and she swallowed and stood a little straighter.

"I have the power to negotiate, if that's what you're asking."

"Then why is the Commander of the Rising Wave with you?" Another member of the Collective asked.

"Aside from the fact that you specifically asked him to be?" She held the man's eyes until he looked away. "I have the power, but so does he," she said, voice serene. "I will never do anything to weaken the Rising Wave. We work together, and every decision we make bolsters what we have achieved."

There was silence as the Collective absorbed what she said.

"And what have you achieved?" Tuva asked.

"We have brought down a corrupt queen and her even more corrupt Herald. We have freed the region from ambition without responsibility, and ended a war with Jatan, which we could not have done without the help of the Skäddar. We have united the east, drawing in the Funabi and the Venyatu, to create the strongest region in the history of both our countries."

There was silence at Ava's list of accomplishments.

"And you, Commander?" Tuva turned to Luc. "What do you say to this?"

"I could have taken Kassia without Ava Yngstra. Like you, I had not heard her name before as a possible heir to the throne, but our alliance meant that we were able not just to take Kassia, but to hold it with minimal bloodshed. We managed to transition from one government to another with very little resistance. I did not bring down the walls of Fernwell, although I could have done. Instead, they opened the gates to me and mine."

Helmi and Pilar had probably told her this already, because she did not look surprised at what he said.

"And this alliance between you? How long will it last?" one of the Collective asked.

"It will last forever." Luc turned to Ava, and she slid her hand into his.

"Many people in love think that is so," Tuva said. "It doesn't always work out like that. And you are not heart bound, although you have had time to do so."

Luc lifted their joined hands. "Not because we do not want to."

"Then why?" Tuva asked.

"Politics. Kassia exists in a state of nervous repose. They accept Ava as their queen. They accept that I and my army have won the war. To them, we are in balance."

"And your heart's choice ceremony may make some even more nervous?" a woman amongst the Collective asked. Her eyes were sharp, her expression thoughtful. "Too nervous?"

"They may think a queen in love could be manipulated. Or a warlord could be swayed by pillow whispers." Ava inclined her head. "We have chosen to wait until things are a little more . . . settled to declare our bond."

"Yet you want us to back you, although you are not 'settled'."

The querulous old man asked.

"Even walking a careful path, we are far from powerless," Luc said. "We are being honest with you, laying out the full reality. But we have still managed to achieve many things, and the foundations of a new Kassia get stronger all the while."

"So the question is, why would someone try to hold you to ransom?" Ava asked them. "If we are weak, unsuitable allies, why threaten the lives of your people if you continue to uphold our agreement? Who benefits?"

They did not like that. They did not like that at all.

Luc could see the frowns, the quick downward turn of mouths.

They didn't like this situation being described as them being held to ransom. He could tell they thought it made them appear weak.

Ava had chosen just the right words to prick their pride.

"Grimwalt benefits," Britta said.

Luc was surprised she'd spoken up. It was interesting, because although she was a warrior, charged with fetching them to the Gathering, she was surely too young to participate in the Collective.

Maybe the old man really was her uncle.

"Grimwalt, and the Furla," a voice called out.

A man standing near Tuva flinched back as if struck. "The Furla would never harm a Skäddar village," he hissed, outrage in every line of him. He turned to whoever among the group had spoken out. "We may have had doubts about this alliance, but we've brought our questions and our reservations to the Gathering, into the open, as is proper. We would never stoop to murder, and certainly not commit the blasphemy of trying to make it look like a garanda was responsible. We are part of the Patchwork, just as the rest of you are. More isolated, perhaps, with less bountiful resources, but part of Skäddar all the same."

There was an uncomfortable silence.

He was protesting too much. Luc didn't believe him, and from the looks on the faces of others in the Collective, they didn't either.

"No one believes you're responsible, Jens." Tuva eyed the accuser with a gimlet eye, but even her words lacked conviction. She turned back to Luc and Ava. "How would Grimwalt even know about our alliance?"

"Because they have spies everywhere. There was at least one in Fernwell, we know for sure, and perhaps a few amongst your own people, too. The fact that Kikir fought with us, and Helmi and Pilar spent time with us in Fernwell, might have been all they needed to work it out. Perhaps one or more of the Jatan passed on the information to Grimwalt, after Kikir and his unit helped us during our confrontation with them? It is not a mystery how the word could have spread."

Tuva gave a slow nod. "That is true. But what possible reason would the Grimwaldians have to stop our alliance such that they would kill a whole village?"

"They are cut off now," Ava said. "A lone territory in a sea of allies. The Speaker tried to do a quiet deal with the old queen of Kassia before we took Fernwell, offering trade concessions in exchange for personal advantage and wealth. It would be hard for him to fill his coffers if he is surrounded by countries in a strong alliance, where he has nothing to offer that is worth more than our own partnership."

"You are saying the Speaker of the Grimwalt Court could be personally behind this massacre? That the reason for it could be his own advantage and lining his own coffers, not the Grimwalt council acting in what they think is the best interest of their country?" The woman who'd asked about their heart choice ceremony sounded shocked, and skeptical.

"It's possible," Luc said. "But to be honest, it seems too indirect to me. The Speaker has tried to kill Ava, has tried to bribe the old queen. He has kidnapped his enemies and locked them up. But arranging to kill a village in the hopes that you will walk away from our agreement? It seems out of character for him."

"What is the alternative?" Tuva asked.

Luc lifted his shoulders. "Perhaps between us, we can find out?"

CHAPTER 26

Duncan lay still, tucked up close against a tree, while Lithwick hunted him.

He had finished healing one of the biggest trees in the forest, and it had drained him completely.

He had only just managed to stagger away and fall into the undergrowth, rolling under a bush out of sight.

If Lithwick found him now, he was dead.

There was something almost unhinged at Lithwick's reaction to his reappearance.

It was as if he had lost control of himself and hadn't been able to get it back.

Norba had said he wasn't right in the head, but even knowing what a back-stabbing, power-hungry bastard he was, Duncan was shocked at Lithwick's reaction to their first encounter.

He hadn't seen Lithwick's face——he was going about in a hooded cloak——but he'd known it was him, the forest had told him who it was before he'd even seen him. And Lithwick's scream of rage as they'd stared at each other between the trees had struck Duncan with something he didn't feel often.

Fear.

Lithwick had run then, shouting curses as he went.

And he kept away while Duncan was strong, only hunting him when he was weakened by healing what Lithwick had tried to destroy.

Somewhere in his head, Duncan berated himself for giving more to the tree than was safe, but he had not been able to pull away.

This was an ancient one.

A being deserving of everything Duncan could give.

Now he was shattered, and the forest was only able to respond sluggishly, giving him energy and power back in a meagre drip, drip, drip.

Not enough. Not nearly enough to help if Lithwick caught up to him.

This was the third time Lithwick had come looking for him after such a big use of power, and Duncan guessed he must be able to feel when the balance of the forest changed. He was hoping to catch Duncan weak and unable to defend himself.

And maybe he had.

And still, he couldn't regret it.

He could not let an ancient tree die.

He lay still, trying not to gasp for breath as Lithwick stalked around the big tree he'd saved. He made no attempt to soften his footsteps.

He wanted Duncan to know he was there.

"Come out, Duncan. You have to be near death after this one." Lithwick waited, and Duncan wondered if he really thought Duncan would just obey. Would just give himself up.

"You can fix this one like you fixed the ones you did yesterday and the day before, but you can't fix them all, Dunc. You will kill yourself trying."

Was that nerves he could hear? Duncan wasn't sure if he heard correctly or not.

What could make Lithwick nervous about his saving the big trees?

He had looked at the extensive damage and had had to work out a triage of sorts. He had chosen to save the ancient giants of the forest first.

The worry eating at him since he'd gotten back was that after expending everything he had on saving them, Lithwick might just come back and suck the big trees dry again.

So far, he hadn't done that, and now Duncan wondered why not.

Lithwick sounded tired. So far, he hadn't managed to catch a good look of the tall, thin man who'd once been his friend, but he didn't think it was his imagination that he moved less energetically, and Duncan thought yesterday he had stumbled a few times.

Still, he was walking upright, and that wasn't something Duncan was currently capable of.

He was so exhausted, he could barely concentrate on Lithwick's threats.

The ground below him was cold and hard, and he shivered against the tree.

"Lithwick? You found Duncan?"

Duncan turned his head a little as the distinct voice of the Boss Man called out.

"Taggar. I wondered when you'd show up. And to answer your question, no. He has to be close, though."

"You know my name." The Boss Man sounded absolutely shocked.

"The Speaker told me, when we met in Taunen."

Taggar said nothing for a long moment. "Can't you feel Duncan? Through the ground, or something?"

Taggar's question was a good one.

Duncan had been wondering for days how Lithwick hadn't been able to find him, depleted and weak.

Duncan could certainly feel Lithwick. That's how he'd gotten away each time.

"This forest gives me nothing for free, Taggar. Everything I've gotten, I've taken."

"I'm sorry to say, but it shows. You are not looking yourself, Lithwick." Taggar sounded slightly disgusted.

"The fungus and the moss?" Lithwick asked, his tone sarcastic. "You need a stronger stomach, Taggar."

"It's reversible?" Taggar asked.

"I got this in service of your master. It was the price I paid for him to take Duncan and keep him away. And look how that turned out."

"And what was that price? The massacre of that Skäddar village?"

There was a long silence.

"What do you know about it?"

"That's why I'm here, Lithwick. I had to go out of Grimwalt on some business, and while I was away, my boss made his little deal with you. A deal I would have been very much against if I had been around to advise him. I recently got news from my spies in Skäddar of a mysterious incident in the mountains, and given the details, and your particular brand of magic, I thought it best I come up here and make sure you haven't started a war with our neighbors."

"A war with your neighbors?" There was a considering tone in Lithwick's voice. "Why not? That would serve him right."

"What are you talking about?" The impatience in Taggar's words was clear.

"It means I took an irreversible step, you fucker. I was told to do something that would really get the Skäddar's attention, make them rethink their alliance with the Rising Wave, or at the very least give the Speaker's spy in the Collective the excuse to call for the queen of Kassia to travel up to Skäddar to reassure them and save their little alliance. And it all worked out exactly as requested.

"Although the Speaker said the Skäddar spy wasn't happy with the method I'd chosen. I'd gone too far, apparently. But it was already done. All for a promise that your precious lord and master didn't keep. And while I want to bring down Duncan, by any means I can, I want to hurt your boss just as much. He and I had a *deal*."

"You killed those villagers to make the Skäddar rethink their alliance?" Taggar's tone was exasperated. "You were both playing with fire. And the Speaker did *not* let Duncan out. He escaped. I'm looking for him. My guards at the camp are, too. When we find him, we'll get him out of the forest."

"About that camp of yours. I withdraw my welcome. The camp has to go. You all do." Lithwick ground the words out through what sounded like clenched teeth.

"That's not going to happen." Taggar gave an almost surprised laugh. "You don't own these forests, much though you'd like to think it. This is Grimwalt, and the Speaker rules Grimwalt."

"The terms of our deal have been broken. You got the camp in my woods as a concession. That is over now."

"You want to talk about broken deals?" Taggar sounded quiet now, silky-voiced and dangerous. "Much though I thought it was a stupid idea, part of the deal was that you were supposed to be our defense against the Skäddar up here——a green line the Speaker called it——making sure there could be no incursion by the Skäddar across the Dallir River. But they've noticeably increased their patrols since you've been here, my guards report, the opposite of what should be happening, and now they're having their annual Gathering right on the border line."

"Have they set foot in my forest?" Lithwick's voice shook. "No. And neither will you any longer."

"What about the queen of Kassia and her entourage that our spies in the Skäddar Collective say are coming to this Gathering?" Taggar asked. "You have a way to deal with them?"

"I forced them into my forest, and they met one of my constructs."

"They're dead?" Taggar asked.

"They got away."

Taggar made a sound of frustration. "Who is reneging on deals now, Lithwick?"

"The deal is over." Lithwick sounded strangely high-pitched, and suddenly Duncan felt a pull on the forest, a tight, dark tug that spiraled up leaves and soil and rotting bark.

Taggar gave a shout of . . . rage? Fear?

And then the pull vanished, and Duncan could hear both men breathing heavily.

"That should have hurt you," Lithwick said.

"I've got protection, you idiot. Do you think after all the enemies I've made I can walk around without it?" Taggar's voice was low and furious. "What was that thing?"

"A taste of my power," Lithwick said. "I'm rather proud of it. I've perfected the shape into something the Skäddar myths call a skovva."

"These are the games you're playing with them?" Taggar scoffed. "No wonder they're curious about what's happening here. And what's the logic of it? It's not going to stop them aligning themselves with the Rising Wave. They're hardly going to blame the Rising Wave for a creature they already consider their own."

"No. But what I did in the village *did* make them rethink the alliance. Why else did they demand the queen of Kassia come up to speak to them? And my games, as you call them, keep them out of my forest." Lithwick sounded winded. "It'll keep my domain clear of them. And you."

"I think it would be best if you didn't issue threats." Taggar's voice was slow and thoughtful. "Don't come near me again, Lithwick. We are done. Our business is over. And the camp stays as long as I say it stays." He walked away.

"You don't come near *me*, Taggar!" Lithwick shouted after him. "Stay out of my way. I've sacrificed too much to give this forest up." He went silent but Duncan could still feel him close by. Standing quietly, listening.

Eventually, he started to move.

"Hear that, Duncan? I'm not giving this up!" He raised his voice and spun as he shouted the words.

Duncan closed his eyes, feeling Lithwick get further and further away, but he had no energy to move, to find a safer place, and so he tucked up closer to the tree and let it give him what it could.

Leaves brushed Duncan's cheek and he opened an eye to see a vine had stretched from the bush shielding him from view to twine around him. The ground seemed to soften, and he felt the velvet of moss under his hand.

The forest was taking care of him as best it could.

As he fell into sleep, he rested in the knowledge that its best was very good, indeed.

Using the river had cut over a day's ride from her journey up north. As Massi haggled for a horse with the stable master in the tiny town where the river hit the mountains and swung west, she decided no matter how unpleasant being cheated by a horse trader was, it was infinitely better than dealing with the politics of Taunen.

She had left the capital city not exactly in turmoil, but certainly not stable.

Ranulf Harkonan had used the incident in the hall to gather allies on the Council, and the Speaker had been jailed pending an enquiry.

Whether that would come to anything, Massi didn't know.

She'd prefer the Speaker to be held to account by his own people, but if he wasn't, Luc would make sure he paid, one way or another.

Massi would help him.

She had left quickly, that same afternoon——before either Peter Ventnor or his mother had a chance to speak to her after everything that had happened.

She had no patience left with them.

Someone in the military had leaked her position, had set her up for death or imprisonment, and she didn't have the time or the energy to work out who.

"I care for my horses," the stable master was saying. "The forest as it is now is no good for them."

Massi had already given the stables a critical once-over, and it looked as if it was going through hard times.

She could see the stable master did look after his horses, though. She wouldn't have dealt with him, otherwise.

The whole town of Bergtor had a slightly seedy air about it. As if it had fallen from grace.

It sat, tucked up against the foothills of the Mirror Mountains, the forest a green canvas behind it, looking small and lost.

"If you won't rent me a horse, just say so." Massi had had enough of this time wasting. Either she'd find a private seller, or she'd walk.

She was sorry now she hadn't brought the dogs, but Tomas had insisted on keeping them, and had told her he'd take them back to Ava's Grimwaldian estate as soon as he and Velda were able to leave the capital.

She turned away, and was walking out when the stable master's hand came to rest on her shoulder.

She turned, and he snatched his hand back quickly.

"You'll have to buy, not rent." He took a step back. "There are things in the woods these days. Bad things. If you don't come back, or the horse dies . . . "

"What's going on in the woods?"

His mouth formed a straight line, his lips pinched. He didn't answer.

"Fine, I'll buy." As long as it was healthy, it didn't matter too much what mount she had. Even the swiftest steed would struggle to run in the dense forest that started just beyond the town, an unending line of green that crept up the side of the mountain.

She knew stable masters. There was no way this one was going to sell her his best horse.

They haggled over the price and eventually came to an agreement.

"You should take a guide, if you're going in there," the stable master told her, saddling up the sedate mare he'd eventually decided he could bear to part with. The saddle was his smallest and had no side bags, although that didn't matter to Massi.

She traveled with everything she needed on her back.

"Can you recommend a guide?" Massi asked. She didn't know if she trusted anyone enough to lead her into the forest, and she wasn't sure she wanted an audience when she got there, but it might be worth her while to talk to someone who knew the way.

"Norba." The stable master jerked his head toward the local inn. "If he isn't there, he'll be in that old cottage at the end of the street."

Norba wasn't at the inn, so she moved down the street to his house.

He came to the door of his cottage while she was tying the mare to the railing of his porch.

"I'm not taking people into the forest anymore," he said. There were cuts and scratches on his cheeks, she noticed——a few days old by the looks of the scabs.

He seemed . . . beaten down, Massi thought. Or sad.

"The stable master says you're the guide."

He shrugged his shoulders. "Not anymore."

Massi tilted her head, studying him. "Have you seen Duncan Erdo recently?"

He reacted, jolting as if he'd been hit by lightning. "You know Duncan?"

"I do."

Norba took a step back into his house, so the gloom of the interior almost swallowed him whole. "There's more than just Duncan in the forest now. It's not pretty." He shuffled back a little more, became nothing but a silhouette.

"Can you at least tell me where I'll be likely to find Duncan if I go in there?" She resisted the urge to touch the piece of pine cone in her pocket.

Norba shook his head. "Before, *he'd* find *you*. Now . . . something else might find you, and you won't like it."

His hand was shaking as he lifted it to grip the edge of his door.

"Don't go into the forest. You won't come out." Then the door was slammed in her face.

She stared at it in surprise.

It creaked back open, just an inch. "If you see Duncan," Norba whispered. "Tell him I'm sorry."

"Is he all right?" Massi asked. "Do you know where he is?"

The door snicked shut and there was silence.

A shoe scuffed the ground behind her, and Massi turned slowly.

Two of the patrons from the inn, a man and a woman, had followed her out. They stood a little way away, careful not to crowd her.

The woman shifted her weight. "I heard you say to Norba that you know Duncan?"

Massi nodded. "He's a friend."

The woman blew out a breath. "Where was he, do you know? These last months?"

"A prisoner," Massi said. "He was taken down south."

"Who?" The man was shaking his head in bewilderment. "How?"

"I don't know the how. The who was the Speaker of Grimwalt. Who is now imprisoned for his crimes."

Both their faces went almost blank with shock.

"Why?" the woman asked eventually.

"I think the Speaker wanted to use his power."

Massi wasn't sure she was making the right decision here, but she was not a game player. To her, the truth was the least complicated path, although it was often the hardest.

"But he's back now?" The man asked tentatively.

"He escaped the Speaker and was coming here last I saw him. I think he's back. Norba asked me to apologize to him, so I think he's seen him."

Both of them flicked their gazes up to the door. There was annoyance along with anger in both their expressions.

It seemed like Norba had not shared that with the town leadership.

"When you find him, please tell him the citizens of Bergtor are sorry, too. Lithwick said he was dead."

"Lithwick?" Finally, she was getting somewhere.

"Lithwick came to town, a few weeks after Duncan disappeared. Told us he'd replaced Duncan." The woman glanced over at her companion. "Duncan earned his keep here. We're a timber town. We make our living, almost all of us, either directly or indirectly from the forest. Duncan made sure we had good timber to work with. Kept the forest healthy. Marked the trees we could cut, gave us free passage in the woods."

"And since he's been gone, that's all stopped?" That would explain the town fraying around the edges.

The man gave a nod. "Lithwick won't give us access. Won't part with a single tree. But he still wants the supplies we gave to Duncan. He threatens us now, rather than cooperates."

"When last did you see Lithwick?"

The woman shook her head. "Not for over a month." She pointed to the wooden house closest to the forest, and Massi saw the walls were rotting away, the structure about to collapse.

"He did that?"

"We thought him not coming around was the end of it, but then he did that to Luther's house, and left a note. We must leave supplies just inside the tree line every two weeks, or he'll damage every house in Bergtor."

"Do you know where I'll find Duncan?" Massi untied her mare, readjusted the saddle.

Both of them shook their heads.

"He came to us, always. He hasn't lived in the village since his aunt and uncle passed away," the woman said. "He doesn't mix with us anymore."

Massi wondered why Duncan kept himself apart. He hadn't been unfriendly in the prison. He'd made a close connection to Tomas and Velda. To herself.

There was no reason for him not to be part of this community.

"Be careful in there." The man cleared his throat. "The man that

Norba took into the forest less than a week ago . . . " He glanced behind him at the forest, to a section where the trees were placed a little apart, like the start of a track. "He hasn't come back out, and Norba won't speak of it. Won't come out of his house, come to that."

"Did this man have a bandage on his arm?" Massi asked.

"Yes." The woman's gaze on her face sharpened. "You know him?"

"He works for the Speaker. He's hunting Duncan most likely. To take him back."

At least if they understood that, then the Boss Man would find no succor in this town.

A small thing, but Massi knew sometimes small things led to bigger ones.

"Are you the reason he has a bandage?" the man asked.

Massi swung into the saddle, and patted her bow. "Yes."

"He said to expect four men," the woman said, suddenly. "Gave the innkeeper instructions to tell them to wait for him to come back to town."

"I can't tell you how to deal with them," Massi said. "But the man Norba took into the forest works for the Speaker, and if the four you're expecting are his men, they are Duncan's enemies, just as much as he is."

"Understood." The man gave a decisive nod.

Whoever the four were who were planning to meet the Boss Man here, they were not going to enjoy their welcome.

"I have to say, in good conscience, that for your own personal safety, you shouldn't go into the valley." The woman didn't look at her friend as she spoke, as if she knew he would prefer her to keep silent. "Either Lithwick or something else in there has killed more than one woodcutter in this town. And there are three others like the one Norba took in a few days ago. Soldiers or mercenaries. Norba was their guide into the forest nearly two months ago, just after Duncan disappeared. They come into Bergtor now and then for supplies, but they don't say anything. They've set up a camp somewhere in there."

Massi appreciated the honesty. She gave a nod of acknowledgement, clicked her tongue to get her horse moving, and headed for that break in the treeline.

Danger. Mystery. Warnings of impending doom.

She smiled and broke into a trot.

CHAPTER 27

The mare didn't like being among the trees.

Massi couldn't blame her. There was something wrong here.

A smell of decay seemed to be in the air. Not always, but it came on puffs of icy wind that made her mount dance sideways and blow air from her nostrils.

They had passed through a narrow gorge, thick with trees and with high mountains on either side, and had finally made it out to a more gentle downward sloping hill.

She had reached the Dallir Valley.

She couldn't see the river below, the forest was too thick. She couldn't even see the Mirror Mountains on the other side.

She touched the pine cone scale every now and then, but got nothing from it, and began to think that Duncan had been wrong about its ability to locate him.

Or maybe someone with some spell casting ability needed to use it, and that person certainly wasn't her.

She wondered if she should abandon her search for him for the moment and simply head for the river. It was clear from what the people in Bergtor said that the Boss Man had arrived, so there was definitely something going on, and she couldn't imagine he'd been interested in the trees. It would be the river, the boundary with Skäddar, that he'd be interested in.

Her original plan after receiving the letter in Taunen had been to discover what the Speaker was up to here, then find Luc on the Skäddar side, let him know what she'd found, and then afterward take time to find Duncan.

He had invited her, and she was pleased to be invited.

That was rare enough to explore.

She sighed, touched the pine scale again, and when nothing happened, turned the mare north, toward Skäddar and the river.

It looked like she was going to have to sort out her Rising Wave business first.

While the Speaker may be out of the picture for now, she couldn't bet on him staying in prison, and it was unlikely the Boss Man had heard the news.

The horse turned eagerly under her hands and as they took the gentle decline, Massi sensed a lift of the dread she hadn't even realized had been sitting on her shoulders.

She turned in the saddle, her bow in her hand, looking for watching eyes or some form of danger from the gorge they had just come through, but all she saw were the trunks of trees.

She had to slow as the slope became steeper, and the sound of the wind in the trees tricked her a few times into thinking the river was close by, the swish of the leaves sounding just like fast-moving water.

Eventually she stopped at a small stream trickling downhill with a sense of relief. She kept having the feeling she was turned around.

All she would have to do is follow the narrow trickle of water and she should come to the river.

She slid off the horse and let it drink. She set her pack down, pulled out her water bottle and finished what was in it, then crouched to fill it, pleased to see the water was crystal clear and fast-moving.

It felt good to rest for a moment. Some sunlight filtered through the branches above her, and the touch of the rays was warm on her face.

She sat, leaning against a tree trunk, watching her horse, and absentmindedly brushed her fingers over the pine scale.

She felt a sudden, sharp pull to the east.

She stood as she turned in that direction, and then bent to scoop up her bow, fitting an arrow and aiming it in less time that it took the Boss Man to step out from behind the tree where he'd been hiding.

They stared at each other for a moment.

"You're the one who shot me," he said.

"Even with your protection," she agreed.

His sudden silence felt like shock to Massi.

"My protection?" He tried to sound as if he had no idea what she was talking about.

Massi laughed at him. "The spell you're wearing."

She wondered if he was alone, or whether the feared Lithwick was around, as well.

She tried to sweep the area without showing nerves.

"Who are you?"

She shook her head. "That's rich of you, given you won't even tell those who work with you what your name is, Boss Man."

He blinked at that. "You hold yourself like a warrior, but I know most of the archers in Grimwalt's military and you aren't one of them."

Massi lifted a shoulder.

"Skäddar?"

"I'm sorry, am I supposed to answer all your questions, while I'm the one with the clear shot?" Massi strained her ears to see if there was anyone else around, but the breeze was brisk and the rustle and clatter of leaves made hearing anything very difficult.

"I'm protected, remember," the Boss Man said with a shrug.

Massi gave another laugh. "Like the Speaker, that protection is fading. How did I get a shot in last time, otherwise?"

His slight smirk disappeared. "What do you mean, 'like the Speaker'?"

"The power of the things he stole has faded. He can't use mind tricks anymore. He's in prison in Taunen." She didn't know if the items he'd stolen gave the Speaker the power to trick and convince others, but Ranulf suspected it, and she guessed he knew what he was talking about.

She decided she'd guessed correctly when the Boss Man didn't answer right away.

Would he believe the Speaker was no longer in charge, she wondered.

"Imprisoned, how?" The Boss Man spoke cautiously, as if trying to work out the best questions to ask. "Who had the power to do that?"

"I took the prisoners back to Taunen after I rescued them. Ranulf Harkonen, the High Commissioner, was one of them. He has friends in the military, on the Council, in every walk of life, really. And he was very convincing." Massi lifted her shoulder again. "And as I said, the power of the Speaker's spell-cast items was either already used up or so faded that he couldn't turn any more minds in his favor."

The Boss Man swore. "I don't believe you."

"You believe me. You're just wondering what you're going to do now. And I don't blame you, Boss Man. You've left a trail of very unhappy people behind you and whatever protection the Speaker gave you is fading away." She gave a chuckle. "Too bad."

"Why would the Skäddar send a warrior into Grimwalt? How did you even know about the secret prison?"

She assumed he was still trying to work out where she was from.

"You have a spy on the Skäddar side, why shouldn't we have one in Grimwalt? Maybe a Grimwaldian spy told us."

"What are you doing here?" he asked. "Looking for Duncan?"

"Who's Duncan?" she asked.

He narrowed his eyes at her, then his gaze flicked over her shoulder.

At the same moment, she smelled the rot again, felt the sense of being studied by an unfriendly eye.

Her mare screamed in terror and reared up, blocking Massi's view of what was behind them for a moment before it turned and ran, scrambling up the hill and disappearing through the trees.

A monster stood a little way back.

It moved as if powered by a small whirlwind, pieces of fallen leaves, soil and bits of wood undulating in a rough person shape.

Bad things in the woods, the villagers had said.

That was an understatement.

Massi already had her bow ready, and she shot the thing straight through the heart.

The arrow flew through it as if there was no resistance, but instead of going out the other side, it was sucked back into the whirlwind, and she saw her arrow become part of the monster's chest.

The thing lumbered toward her, swinging wildly with fisted hands.

She easily ducked it, and given she had no other weapon, used her hand to grab a piece of wood from its side as she slid under its arm. Surprised she was able to pull it out, she threw it into the stream.

The thing reached for the missing piece of itself, stumbling toward the stream, and as it did, it seemed to notice the Boss Man.

She almost physically felt its focus switch from herself to him, and as it stepped over the narrow channel of the stream, the piece of wood she'd thrown flew up, spraying droplets of water, to become part of its torso again.

It lumbered toward the Boss Man.

"Lithwick!" The Boss Man backed away. "Lithwick, call it off."

A sound behind her, just the faintest hint of movement, had her spinning to look, afraid there might be a second monster.

She got a look——just a quick flash——of . . . something. Someone?

She saw gray-green skin, with what looked like shelf mushrooms growing down the briefly-glimpsed cheek.

Then it . . .they . . . were gone.

The Boss Man ran——the monster lumbering after him—— screaming Lithwick's name as he went.

Bits of the monster fell as it got further away, and it seemed to lose its center the more distance it put between them.

It took her a moment to realize she was alone.

She could hear her own breathing, harsh and uneven.

What had just happened?

She swung her pack onto her back, held her bow in one shaking hand, and gently brushed her finger over the pine cone scale again.

Again, she felt a strong tug to the east.

The Boss Man was running toward the river and she didn't know where whoever she'd caught sight of——maybe Lithwick?——had gone.

She turned east and began to jog through the trees toward what she hoped was Duncan.

CHAPTER 28

S he initially overshot.

After she had walked for half an hour, she touched the pine cone scale again and, frustratingly, felt a pull back the way she'd come.

Unless Duncan was moving around, or was messing with her.

She started walking in a circle, slowly and carefully, touching the scale often.

She was circling a massive tree, she realized after a few minutes, a giant that rose too high for her to see the top.

"Duncan?" She whispered his name. He didn't answer, but the magic said he was here.

She set her pack down, slid her bow over her shoulder and began to look more carefully through the undergrowth.

Eventually she got on her hands and knees, and there . . . just under the branches of the bushes beside the big tree, she saw a hand.

It lay still. Unmoving.

Feeling slightly sick, she lay on the ground, crawling forward on her elbows, ducking her head to squeeze through.

A vine caught her wrist, curling around it with a pale green, flexible stem, then paused, almost as if it were . . . considering what to do with her.

She jerked her arm back and it let go, slithering away in a way that made her heart beat just a little faster.

"Duncan." She hissed a little louder now, and heaved her way through the branches, felt a twig dig into her cheek, and then suddenly, there he was, tucked deep in the bush.

She was almost on top of him.

He looked . . . ill.

He was clearly unconscious.

Had the monster got him?

She noticed a green tinge to his cheek, and had a moment of pure terror that he had been the mysterious figure she'd seen earlier, but when she brushed his skin with her thumb, the green came away, and she saw he was lying on a bed of moss.

"What happened to you?" She wondered it aloud.

The sound of a whistle close by had her remembering her pack, sitting out in the open, and she tried to slide back out as silently as possible to grab it.

Before she'd got very far, the vine reappeared, dragging her pack.

It dropped it next to Duncan and she inched back under cover and lay still.

The whistle came again, and then someone further away returned it.

Signaling to each other?

Eventually she heard footsteps and then the whistler walked away.

When it had been silent long enough, she shook Duncan's shoulder.

He opened his eyes in a sudden jerk, saw her, and dropped his head back down again.

"Massi?"

She was suddenly aware she was pressed up tight against him, with nowhere to move to.

"Are you all right?"

He gave a nod. "Just used up all my energy." His voice was hoarse, as if he'd been shouting.

She narrowed her eyes. "Sounds dangerous."

"I like to live dangerously." He gave her a weak, disarming grin.

"I think it's safe to move. It's been nearly ten minutes since I heard footsteps."

He gave a nod, and the bush just parted, as if it were a curtain, and she was able to get easily to her feet. She put down a hand and he grabbed it, let her help him up.

"Who was it you heard? Lithwick?" he asked.

"I don't know. They were whistling to each other."

He gave a nod, as if he knew who they were.

"I saw the Boss Man. And I think I caught a quick glimpse of Lithwick. And some kind of forest monster attacked me. Then it saw the Boss Man and went for him, instead."

"Interesting." He was swaying slightly, and she tucked under his shoulder to support him.

"Which way?"

He pointed and they began to make their way slowly even further east.

She didn't ask him any more questions. There would be time for that when they were safe, but right now, she didn't know who was running through these woods, hunting them.

They moved in silence, and she realized she liked being so close to him, liked the feel of him against her side. The scent of crushed pine coming off him was addictive.

It felt longer, but it was probably under an hour when they came to their destination——a dense stand of trees. Duncan stepped away from her and reached out to one of the trunks.

Suddenly there was a dark slit in the tree.

Duncan stepped in, held out a hand, and she took it.

He pulled her in, and the way behind her closed.

It was utterly dark inside, although she'd managed to catch a glimpse of a spiral staircase carved out of the wood before the tree shut them in.

She stumbled a few times as she followed Duncan up, stepping out of the tiny antechamber where the staircase ended onto a tightly woven platform of branches.

She turned in place, gaze going upward, and saw they were in the center of seven or eight trees, and the ceiling above was a similarly woven cover of branches, like the floor they were standing on, but it arched up, as elegant as the Fernwell palace itself.

Light came from openings on the sides, filtered green by the leaves, and it was surprisingly warm in here, despite the bite in the winter air. Beautiful chairs and a table, a bed, and few low cupboards seemed to rise up from the floor as if they were a living part of the space.

She stared around in wonder, remembering the bed the forest had made for Duncan back at the fortress. This was a more complex version of that.

She turned to ask him about it, and realized he was no longer stumbling or weak.

It was as if the short climb up the stairs had restored him to an even stronger, more muscular version of himself than he'd been when they'd parted ways.

"You're healed," she murmured, inexplicably tongue-tied.

He touched one of the tree trunks. "They give me strength."

He meant that literally, she realized.

"What did you do that you were so weak before?"

"Saved the big tree I was lying near." Something dark passed across his face, something cold and furious.

The part of her that understood vengeance pricked up its ears in approval.

"Lithwick nearly killed it. It took a lot from me to restore it to health."

"Who *is* Lithwick?" She moved to one of the chairs and lowered herself down into it, gave a sigh of relief when it turned out to be comfortable.

"He's someone I met about four months ago. He came into the forest, and for the first time, I met someone with the same magic as me." He shook his head. "Thought I had, anyway. I was probably too pleased to meet him to notice the subtle differences. He said superstitious villagers had hounded him out of his own forest. That he needed a place to stay until he could move on to a new forest of his own."

"That was a lie?"

Duncan lifted wide, muscular shoulders. "I did wonder how he could have been hounded out of a forest. No one could have made me go without my cooperation." Then he ran a hand through his hair and shook his head. "Not in a fair fight, anyway. Because I was taken out, but in chains and by trickery."

"Since I've met you, I've been curious about how someone managed that." Massi hoped he'd tell her, but he didn't seem inclined to right now.

"Lithwick was clearly in league with the Speaker, helping him get rid of me, and waiting to take my place. Why he's chosen to destroy the trees, destroy the place he sold his soul to take, I have no idea."

"Shouldn't he and the Boss Man be friendly, then, if Lithwick is working with the Speaker?" Massi knew they definitely were not friendly, from what she'd seen earlier.

"That was back when I was first captured. Since I've escaped, Lithwick is no longer on friendly terms with the Speaker or his flunkies." Duncan rubbed a hand down his thigh, as if massaging an old injury. "You said you saw the Boss Man. When?"

"Shortly before I found you. We had a little back and forth, and then someone came up behind me."

"Lithwick?"

"That's what I guessed. Whoever it was aimed a monster made of forest debris at me, but then it caught sight of the Boss Man and went after him instead." She sent him a quick grin. "He was screaming Lithwick's name as he ran away."

"Did you see Lithwick?"

She started to shake her head, then moved it side to side. "I saw something. I thought I saw part of his face, but it looked all wrong."

"Wrong, how?"

She heard the intensity in his voice.

"Like his skin had gone a green-gray. And there might have been those mushrooms that you find on trees attached to his cheek . . ." She knew it sounded mad, but maybe no more mad than a monster made of bark and dead leaves.

"That's what he was talking about." Duncan moved to a low counter, turned a handle that was set in the wall and water poured out into a wooden bowl. "He said something about fungus and moss."

"Maybe he's rotting, like a log in the forest." Massi realized she could be way off. She lifted both shoulders. "Or maybe he was using camouflage?"

"No." Duncan pulled his shirt over his head, tossing it on the bench and then bent his head, scooping up water to wash his face. "He's afraid of what's happening to him. Bitter about it. I heard him tell Taggar he'd taken an irreversible step." He turned, droplets of water catching on his beard, his eyes intense. "Taggar accused him of killing some villagers a couple of months ago. It was somehow supposed to make the Skäddar withdraw from the alliance they'd gone into with the Rising Wave. He didn't go into specifics, but Taggar said that's why he came up here. News of the deaths in the village, how they died, made him suspect Lithwick was involved, and he wanted to make sure Lithwick didn't get Grimwalt into a war with Skäddar because of it."

"Who's Taggar?" Massi frowned.

Duncan's eyes gleamed with sudden amusement. "Taggar is the Boss Man. He actually does have a name." He went back to the sink.

"Ha!" She thought back. "Was it that report he got, outside the fortress? The one that sent him north?"

Duncan nodded. "I guessed the same."

"Why didn't he just go ask the Speaker?" Massi wondered. "Why come all the way up here to confront Lithwick?"

"Because I don't think he was confident of getting a straight answer out of the Speaker. He told Lithwick he thought the deal he and the Speaker had made was ill-advised. My guess is he also knew I'd be coming back here, and it wouldn't have done his reputation any harm to return with me in tow."

"Not anymore," Massi said. "That ended when the Speaker was arrested."

"The Speaker was arrested?" Duncan turned, towel in hand, and she forced her gaze away from the muscles in his chest, the washboard of his flat stomach, to the arched opening in the wall.

"Yes, but Taggar said he didn't believe me."

"He won't want to believe it. It'll mean life as he knows it is over."

"It *is* over. Ranulf Harkonen turned out to have a lot of influence. And the Speaker turned out to have used up all of his." She tapped her lips, still not looking his way. "He'd stolen items from some artifact vault in Taunen, that's how he established his power base, but that magic only lasts so long, especially as some of it was very old."

"Taggar really wouldn't want to believe that."

"No." She thought back to the closed-mouth hardness in Taggar's face.

With a snort of amusement, Duncan went back to the water bowl.

Massi finally turned her gaze on him again. She, who had lived so much of her life in a traveling army, where men and women stripped naked beside her all the time, felt a blush rise up to heat her cheeks.

She was glad he was facing away from her, thrusting his arms into the basin and scrubbing them. She cleared her throat. "The Boss Man——Taggar—— guessed it was me who shot him. I suppose from the description the man from Waldrand gave him. Do you think he understands that with the Speaker in prison, the game is over and whatever plans he has in motion, they're dead now?"

"He's intelligent enough to know it. Whether he can accept that he's done is another thing." Duncan tossed the towel aside, took a fresh shirt from a little open cubby built into the wall and pulled it over his head.

She went silent, watching him turn up the sleeves with deft, quick movements.

He lifted his gaze, fixing it on her face.

"I'm very glad to see you," he said, voice still a little hoarse. "I wanted to stay with you when you left for Taunen."

She realized she was staring at him silently, and felt the heat rush up to her cheeks again. She was usually more composed than this.

Suddenly, she remembered the pine cone scale, felt a flood of relief at the distraction. "Oh. This worked." She took it out of her pocket, held it out to him.

He studied it for a moment. "Keep it. If it works, it'll be useful if we get separated."

She nodded, slid it back. "I'm glad to see you, too."

He caught her gaze again, and she fought down the sense of being flustered.

She fidgeted in her chair. "I hoped the pine cone scale would work, but it didn't for hours, so I was going to see what the Boss Man was up to, and then come looking for you afterward. Do you know what he's doing here?"

He shook his head. "I've only had one face-to-face with him, the day he arrived. He tried to take me prisoner." He tapped his fist against his thigh. "Since then, I've been too busy repairing the damage Lithwick has done to my forest. All I know is he's staying in a spy camp close to the river, and I think they're watching activity on the Skäddar side. The whistlers you heard earlier were probably the guards from the camp. They're also helping Taggar look for me."

"Do you know if there's a lot of Skäddar activity to watch?"

He shrugged. "I haven't had time to go over to the Skäddar side yet."

"Do you think Lithwick's been hurting the forest on that side as well?"

"We know he's been over there, if he's responsible for those deaths. But there are actual guards on that side, unlike here, so he doesn't have the same free run."

"I came through Bergtor, and I think he's used his monsters to keep the villagers out of the forest." She leaned forward, propping her chin in her palms. "They say they're sorry, by the way."

His face hardened a little. "I'm sure they are."

"They said Lithwick said you were dead, and then he infected one of the houses with rot to get them to put out supplies for him."

He gave a tiny nod.

"Norba says sorry, too."

He gave an amused grin at that, the humor coming suddenly and lighting up his face. "I bet."

"He hasn't come out of his house since he got back from taking Taggar into the forest. Is that why he's sorry, because Taggar tried to take you prisoner while he was there?"

Duncan gave a nod. "I was a little angry at the time. I revoked his welcome."

And Norba's living was guiding people into the forest. No wonder he was sorry.

She didn't doubt for a moment that if Duncan banned someone from the wood, they were banned.

"Can you revoke Lithwick's welcome? And Taggar's?" Probably not, as he would surely have already done it, if he could.

"I don't even know if I can revoke Norba's." For the first time he seemed agitated, shoving a hand into his hair, the dark strands longer than when she'd last seen him. "Everything is in flux. Lithwick's moved the balance enough that I can't get a good grip on it." He finally sat, leaning back in a chair which expanded, growing higher armrests and a higher back, accommodating his long-legged slouch.

She tried not to stare, but it was not the kind of magic she was used to.

This was happening in front of her eyes, like the forest monster earlier.

This was something other than Ava's brand of spell work.

"Do you think you will get a grip on it, eventually?"

His lips twisted. "Yes. But I have to give so much of myself each time, I'm afraid Lithwick's going to catch on eventually, kill me right after I've restored what he's destroyed." He gave a bitter chuckle. "That's how he caught me the very first time. I didn't realize it was him who'd caused the tree to start dying, I thought he was helping me fix it. Next thing I knew, I was in a cage lined with stone, in a cart headed for the fortress."

"Why did he send you to the Speaker?" she wondered. Lithwick must have known Duncan would always be a threat to him, as long as he was alive.

"Why didn't he kill me, you mean?" Duncan gave a nod. "I'm sure he wishes he had now. But there was some deal between him and the Speaker. He captured me for the Speaker and did whatever he did to those Skäddar villagers, and in return, the Speaker gave him free reign."

"He doesn't seem to have free reign." She remembered the way he'd run away.

Duncan thought about it. "The forest feels . . .different now. But it still helps me. Gives me what it can. If he has taken control, it's only of part of it. And it isn't an equal exchange, like it is with me."

"An equal exchange?"

"I give, it gives back." He folded his arms over his chest. "Lithwick doesn't give. He just takes."

There it was again, that dark, cold flash of emotion on his face.

If Lithwick was wise, he'd cut his losses and run.

Because Duncan was coming for him, and he was as implacable, as unstoppable, as nature itself.

CHAPTER 29

She was here.

Just thinking the words lifted Duncan's spirits.

He had been sinking into darker and darker waters, he realized. Getting caught in the strange cycle of healing trees, falling down, dragging himself back home, and doing it all again as soon as he was healed enough.

And dodging both Lithwick and Taggar while he was doing it.

At least those two were actively working against each other now. If they'd remained united, helping each other locate him, then he may already have been caught.

But Lithwick wanted him dead, and Taggar wanted him alive.

He turned his mind to Taggar's business here for the first time. Massi wanted to know what it was, but to him, it had been of secondary importance to healing the giants before they were lost forever.

Today, he'd saved the last one in danger.

He should go across the river, check to see if there were any in need of help on the Skäddar side, but he didn't have the same power base there that he had here. If he was too weak to swim back, he would be very vulnerable on the Skäddar side. And if a

Skäddar guard found him, he gave himself a very small chance of not getting stabbed.

Massi would want to go down to the river, he guessed.

She needed to see what Taggar and his little camp of thugs were up to, what mischief they were making on the Skäddar side.

And then she would have to go report back.

He forced himself to shrug that fact off.

She was here now, and she would stay for at least a few days.

He could hear her behind the screen he'd asked the tree to pull up in one corner so she could change and wash in private, and when she stepped out, she was bare foot and her dark hair hung to her shoulders, wet and curling at her forehead, her face glowing and her eyes the kind of deep blue that spoke to him of the sky just before dusk.

He couldn't pull his eyes away, and she stilled under his gaze.

Then she made a sound, just a little gasp at the back of her throat, and he moved, pulling her close.

She went without resistance, her arms sliding around his back as he ran his hands up her sides, along her shoulder blades, and into her hair, flexing his fingers against the delicate shape of her skull.

"Yes," she whispered into his mouth, and it sounded as if the branches whipped into a frenzy outside as he bent his head just the smallest fraction, so their lips were touching.

Then, with a groan, he deepened it into the hungry, voracious beast it wanted to be.

She licked into his mouth and he suddenly found himself lifting her against a wall, mouth on her neck, on her collar bone, on her breast.

They fought each other's clothes, half removing one thing, half removing another, coming back around to finish the job.

It was an exquisite game of hide and seek, and when she hooked her legs around his waist and he had his hands on the sweet, firm curves of her naked bottom, he had to fight for control.

He could barely speak as she arched her back, her breasts

pressing against his chest, and when he slowly pushed into her, he didn't care if he never spoke again.

WELL.

Massi stretched, looking over to where Duncan had just disappeared down the stairs.

She felt pretty smug.

It had been a very, very long time since she had last taken a lover, and the wait had been worth it.

She felt the heat rise again in her cheeks, a habit she was getting into around Duncan, and with a groan at her own train of thought, got out of bed and went behind the screen Duncan had coaxed out of the floor for her yesterday.

The water that splashed out of the tap was crystal clear, and she felt cool and refreshed when she stepped back into the clean clothes she'd worn for less than five minutes last night.

She pulled on her boots and shrugged on her jacket, then took the stairs. Duncan had said to come down when she was ready, and she was more than a little curious what he was up to.

She'd just reached the bottom, and was staring at the wooden wall, wondering what the trick was to getting out, when it opened suddenly and Duncan stood in the doorway.

"Good morning." His voice rumbled in her ear as he pulled her close, out of the dark staircase and into the chilly morning air.

The light was magical, pale gold and dancing on the ground between the shadows of the leaves.

"Mmm. Good morning." Her voice was husky, and she felt his grip tighten for a moment as if he was suddenly thinking of better things they could be doing.

She grinned, opened her mouth to speak, then stopped suddenly when she saw the bower.

It had sprung up from the ground, delicate arches lined with leaves, and in the center, a table and two chairs that had sprouted like mushrooms from the forest floor.

As they walked closer, she saw wooden mugs filled with water sat beside a neat heap of berries and nuts.

He had found her breakfast and had used his magic to make a place for them to eat it.

"It's beautiful." She stopped, tightening her grip on his hand so he had to stop, too. "You didn't use up too much energy——?"

"For this?" He looked at the bower in surprise. "No."

She sat, enjoying the quiet as they ate and drank, enjoying simply being there with him in the dancing light.

"You want to scout around today, check out Taggar's camp?" He leaned forward, elbows on the table.

She nodded. "Are you still busy saving the trees?"

He shook his head. "I've got to all the giants now. There are still trees to save, but it's not as urgent anymore. I'll come with you."

He watched her, his gaze holding her in place.

She faced the fact that she was more than a little infatuated with him.

She looked at his hands as he held his cup, remembered them on her body last night.

He set the cup down, reached out and linked his fingers with hers.

"What are you thinking?" She tightened her grip as she asked the question, felt a flutter of nerves and excitement in her belly she hadn't had in a long time.

"That I like you here." He drew her hand to his lips, brushed a kiss on her inner wrist.

"That's good, I like me here, too."

He suddenly smiled at her, that transformational smile that made him achingly, utterly transfixing. "In how much of a hurry are you, this morning?"

"Depends what I'm in a hurry about."

He rose suddenly, stepping around the table and swinging her up into arms as strong and hard as branches.

She found she had nothing to say, unless it was 'faster', but he was already moving as fast as he could, reaching the tree and stepping them into the dark, small space.

She expected him to take the stairs but instead he put her down three steps up, so she was close to level with him, and found her lips unerringly. His hand snaked under her shirt to rub her breast, his other hand sliding down the front of her trousers to rub between her legs.

She gasped at the onslaught, breaking apart under the clever dance of his fingers.

When she could think again, she wriggled out of her pants in the darkness, reaching for the front of his and unbuttoning them.

She swallowed a cry as he thrust inside her, leaning back on the step with her elbows, eyes closed.

He moved faster, pulling her close as he shuddered inside her, his mouth on her throat, and she turned her head, brushed a kiss on the bulging bicep of his arm.

"You are addictive," she told him.

"You are like sunshine to me," he said.

He lifted her up as if she weighed nothing, holding her against him one-handed, and walked up the rest of the stairs.

He looked rumpled and satiated, and she had to guess she looked the same.

They eyed each other.

"No. Absolutely not. We need to find Taggar." She was firm, but she was so, so tempted.

He hesitated, looking like he was about to try quite hard to change her mind, when he turned sharply to the west, face suddenly still.

"Lithwick?" she asked.

He nodded.

"Does he know this is your home?" She tucked in her shirt, fastened her pants and collected her pack and bow.

"This isn't where I lived when I knew Lithwick before. This is a new place. He doesn't know we're here." He had straightened himself up while she was busy, and when she stood, ready to go at the top of the stairs, he hesitated, stopping in the middle of the room.

"If we end up on the Skäddar side today and if I find one of the ancients on that side needs my help, will you guard me?"

"I will." She didn't even have to think about it.

He gave a nod, touching her cheek gently as he passed her to lead the way out. When she stepped into the forest, she saw everything he'd created for breakfast had sunk back into the ground, leaving not a single trace.

She was sad to lose it, but nothing would help Lithwick more in his mission to hunt them down than a breakfast bower growing out of the forest floor.

"Who will I be guarding you against?" she asked. "Lithwick?"

"Maybe," he said, standing in a pose that made her think he was listening with more than just his ears. "But more likely the Skäddar guards."

As she fell into step beside him, she wondered if she would be met with friendship if she encountered any Skäddar on their side of the river, or whether they would shoot first and ask questions later.

Luckily, Ava had made sure she was impossible to shoot.

CHAPTER 30

The day after they'd met with the Council was a frustrating exercise in waiting.

The councilors did not move fast or with any sense of urgency, and Ava had to force herself not to pace.

She had studied the patterns on Tuva's hands last night, a sign of her seniority on the Collective, and so she channeled her impatience into embroidering a scarf to match it.

She knew by now that the nature of her magic meant whatever she did for Tuva would affect the councilor in some way, so she concentrated on wishing only that the head of the Collective be protected from harm and give the Rising Wave a fair chance.

She could manipulate her more than that, but she had chosen the lines she would not cross, and she kept to them.

Every now and then she would look up from her work to watch Luc and some of the other members of the unit spar and train.

The Skäddar were also very interested in the practice, and moved closer and closer to watch.

Ava had considered joining them herself——for the first time in a while she felt she had the energy and strength to do so——but even though it would have helped direct her impatience, she held back. Something told her it would be better if their new allies thought Luc was the brawn, while she was the negotiator.

Kikir, the Skäddar's best warrior, wasn't here to set them straight about her prowess with the fighting sticks the Skäddar favored.

She had beaten him, once. Or nearly——Luc had arrived just before she put him on his back, spiriting her away and nullifying the match.

When they were done with their training, they packed away their practice weapons and Luc caught her eye, pointing to the river.

He joined in the light-hearted banter between his soldiers as they all headed down to the river to wash off after their exercise.

Ava rose up and followed them down, her embroidery still in her hand.

She didn't know what she would do if the spell caster she was worried about created another skovva to attack Luc and the others, but she would rather be right there than watching from the hill, too far to do anything at all.

When they reached the river bank, Ava guessed some of them finally remembered their previous worry about the water, and hesitated.

Luc didn't, though. He pulled off his boots, pulled off his tunic and dived in still wearing his shirt and trousers.

He went under, then came up, flicking water from his short, dark hair.

The others jumped in more sedately, some cautiously lowering themselves in close to the bank, and keeping to the shallows.

"Some of your people are afraid of the water?" Johan, the curious guard from the day before, asked her, coming to stand beside her to watch.

Ava had noticed he had watched Luc and the others training, as well.

"After what happened on our way here, some of them are worried the thing they fought might still be in the river."

"The skovva?" he asked.

"I don't think it was a true skovva," Ava said. "But Britta says it seemed like the mythical creature from your folklore."

"What do you think it was, then?" Johan asked.

Ava wondered if he was simply curious, or asking for one of the councilors on the Collective. Either way, she was happy to answer.

"I think it was a magical construct, created by a spell caster."

She caught Luc's gaze as he stripped off his shirt and wrung it out, wading closer to the bank to toss it on the grass.

He was the most beautiful man she had ever seen.

The first time she had laid eyes on him, he had been thrown into her prison cell, bleeding from many wounds but the worst had been a cut on his forearm, down to the bone.

As he moved forward, waist deep in the water, she wouldn't even have been able to tell which arm the injury had been on if she hadn't sewn the wound herself.

There was no scar, nothing marred his smooth, golden skin, including the wound in his chest from an arrow strike he had taken to divert their enemies away from her. In fact, there were no longer any scars on his body, anywhere.

And he swore to her that even without the tunic she'd made for him and the embroidery on his shirt, he was still protected by her magic. That she had sewn strength and speed and health into his very body.

"You only have eyes for him, I notice."

She turned her head, saw Johan watching her curiously.

She lifted her shoulders. "He *is* my heart's choice."

"We wondered whether that was just a fiction to explain your strange alliance," Johan said.

"We?"

He shook his head, clearly not prepared to answer, his gaze going back to the river, to the Rising Wave soldiers who were wading back to the bank and hauling themselves out, water pouring off them as they wrung out their clothing.

The sun was at its highest, the light warm and golden, although there was a definite bite in the air, and the temperature had sunk to almost freezing in the night.

The river water had to be very cold and no one had stayed in too long.

Still, Luc waited until everyone was out before he climbed onto the bank.

He had thrown his sword down beside his boots, and Ava walked to stand beside them, waiting for him to shrug into his wet shirt and join her.

"Is that the famous sword?" Johan asked.

His question stirred interest from both the Skäddar and the Rising Wave soldiers.

"What do you know about the Commander's sword?" Lucilla asked, her tone friendly.

"Heard it was magical," Johan said.

"Heard from where?" Britta was watching her fellow warrior, her head tilted in surprise.

"Helmi and Pilar told the Collective about the rumor," he said, suddenly realizing he had everyone's attention. "They said they didn't believe it, though."

He looked a little embarrassed to be sharing a debriefing so publicly.

Ava hadn't realized the rumors were still circulating in Fernwell.

She knew what Lucilla had suspected with her too-sweet question.

Ava had suspected it, herself.

The rumor about Luc's sword was one of two they suspected had been started by a Kassian spy, Haslia, in the Rising Wave column. Haslia had since disappeared, but she had gotten her information from her handler, the general who'd been in charge at the fortress where Ava had been held prisoner for two years. The place where Luc had taken the sword from.

Anyone trying to revive those rumors was suspect.

But Helmi and Pilar had most likely been actively looking for information on Luc and herself while they spent time in Fernwell. Someone may well have dredged up the story about the sword.

"What kind of magic?" one of the other Skäddar asked.

"Yes, Johan. What kind of magic?" Britta crossed her arms over her chest. She was angry with him for running his mouth, that was clear.

Luc had pulled his shirt back on, and used his foot to flick the scabbard up, catching it and pulling the sword out.

He held it out to Johan. "Want to look?"

"I do." Johan gave Britta a quick look and then took the sword, giving it a practice swing. "It's well balanced."

Luc gave a nod. "I like it."

"Feel any magic?" Britta asked Johan.

He had the grace to look slightly shame-faced. "No."

"Can I?" Britta asked Luc, and at his nod, she took if from Johan, turning it in her hands. "I like the gold detailing on the hilt."

"Me, too," Luc said.

"Where did you get it?" someone asked.

"From the fortress I was taken to after the Kassian army ambushed me," Luc crouched to pull on his boots. "I found it on the way out of the fortress, when Ava and I escaped."

"You were in the fortress, too?" Britta obviously hadn't heard the story.

"My cousin, the Queen's Herald, was holding me there." Ava shrugged away two years of tiny cells and constant fear of death.

"So you rescued her?" Britta's gaze went to Luc, eyes wide.

Luc shook his head on a chuckle. "No. Ava rescued me."

Their eyes met, and Ava wasn't sure if she reached for Luc's hand, or he for hers, but they were suddenly standing close, hands clasped.

And then her magic ran down her skin in a prickling wave, and it must have done the same for Luc, because they both dived to the ground together as a volley of arrows flew just where they'd been standing.

Panicked shouting ensued, but they both rolled to their feet, and while Luc pulled on his tunic, Ava studied the trees on the Grimwaldian side of the river.

Dak had come to stand in front of them both, shielding them with his body, and she saw him and Luc exchange a look.

"At least three archers. Maybe more." Johan was crouched down nearby, his gaze also fixed across the river.

Ava glanced back, saw four arrows embedded in the ground.

The shouting had brought more Skäddar toward them.

"There they are," Britta said, eyes shielded against the glare of sunlight off the water, arm extended.

"They're moving west," Luc said.

Ava had caught a single glimpse of someone moving quickly through the trees, but she guessed Luc had noticed more.

"You want to go over there and track them down?" Tuva had appeared out of her tent, and Johan frowned in concern at the sight of her. "They're not after me," she said, forestalling him. "But I'd like to know how they knew the queen of Kassia was here, with her Commander."

"That," said Luc, "is something I'd like to know, too."

CHAPTER 31

There were too many people milling around.

Luc signaled his own unit and they spread out, focused on the forest opposite. Most were unarmed, but with a flick of his hand, his four best archers had run back to camp for their bows. No sword or knife would help at this distance, anyway.

He eyed the river. The current was strong but he was a good swimmer. He could be on the other side in ten minutes.

"You're planning to cross?" Tuva asked.

"Do you have an objection to that?" Ava had taken a step back, giving him space to get the unit in place, but now she stepped forward again.

"It'll be messy if you're caught," Tuva said. "And as we are still allies, if anything happens, we'd be obliged to go after you."

"Understood." Ava inclined her head. "Ready?" she asked Luc.

He loved this woman. She was indomitable.

He inclined his head.

"We will try not to be caught," Ava said to Tuva. "But I think we're capable of getting ourselves out of trouble, if it finds us." She held out a neatly folded cloth. "I made this for you."

Tuva was clearly confused as she took it, letting the fabric unfurl. It was a scarf, the fabric fine and delicate, and along the edges, Ava had copied the pattern of greens and blues on the backs of Tuva's hands.

Her artistry never failed to amaze him.

The head of the Collective gave an exclamation of surprise.

"This is . . . wonderful." She wound it around her neck. "When did you have a chance to make it?"

"I have been working on it since this morning." Ava bowed her head. "I am very pleased you like it." She crouched down and removed her boots, shoving her socks inside them, and then wound her cloak high around her shoulders.

"I think it's deeper than that," Luc told her regretfully. "You won't be able to touch the bottom in the middle."

"Oh." She grimaced. "Let's go now, then, while there is still some sunlight to dry out."

He nodded, walked over to where Dak and Yarlun stood, talking quietly.

"One of you has to stay and command the unit here. We can't take all fifty over." He wanted no more than fifteen, and even that was probably too much.

"I'll stay," Yarlun said. "I'll keep my ear to the ground here. Someone must have tipped off the Grimwaldians you were here."

"Agreed." Dak looked over the camp, his gaze cold. "And they were giving us the run-around. Making us wait all morning. Setting us up, maybe?"

"I truly hope not." Luc wanted this alliance to work. Was this morning's delay deliberate, or just the result of an argumentative Collective full of old councilors who loved to disagree?

"We'd like to come, too." Britta walked up to them, Dragir just behind her.

Luc hadn't seen Dragir since yesterday afternoon, and he wondered where the warrior had been. "Your commanders all right with that?"

Most likely they'd been ordered to keep an eye on the Rising

Wave group, but Luc had seen both of them fight in training, and Dragir had fought the skovva with them yesterday. He'd be happy to have them along.

Dragir gave a nod. "We asked to accompany you, and they agreed it was a good idea."

Luc nodded. Behind him, Dak and Yarlun were giving out orders, and when he turned back, he had his tight group, twelve, he saw with approval.

Ava walked over, Tuva close beside her.

"I've been trying to persuade Ava to stay with us, but she says she will go with you." Tuva looked a little nervous, and Luc guessed she did not want to have to explain to anyone from Kassia that their queen had died on her watch.

"She and I fight together," he said, with a smile, and then he picked Ava up, ran at the bank and leaped into the water.

She gave a shout of laughter as they went airborne, then a shriek as they hit the freezing water.

With a whoop, the other twelve ran after them.

Luc glanced back just in time to see Britta and Dragir exchange a look and then jump themselves.

Tuva stood, open-mouthed, watching as he kept Ava lifted as much out of the water as he could.

When he lifted her onto the opposite bank, she turned, kneeling, and leaned down, kissing him on the mouth. "Show-off."

It pleased him that he'd managed to keep most of her dry.

He grinned up at her, kissed her back, and then he was out of the water, gaze scanning the trees.

Dak hauled himself up beside them both, handing Ava the stick Luc had asked him to get for her.

It was in a sheath that strapped to her back, and she took off her cloak to buckle it on, then fastened her cloak again, so the end poked up over her right shoulder.

The rest of the team swarmed the bank, silent now, the fun over.

When everyone had a weapon out, they moved carefully forward, spreading out among the trees.

Luc looked for Britta and Dragir, and saw they were near the middle of the group, just as focused on finding the attackers' escape route as anyone else.

The few small disturbances indicated a westward direction, following parallel to the river.

It would be very interesting to find out how their attackers had known where to find them.

If someone among the Skäddar had betrayed them, he would rather know now than later, when the alliance was even closer than it was now.

"It has to be one of us, doesn't it? A Skäddar." Britta suddenly spoke out loud. "We invited you to the Gathering less than two weeks ago. Even if a spy in Fernwell found out about it, they couldn't have gotten here much faster that you."

"Yes." Dak's answer was implacable.

"We don't like it either," Dragir told him. "Tuva wants to know if we have someone spilling secrets to Grimwalt just as much as you."

"Fair enough," Ava said. "We have the same goal. I just hope the truth is palatable to both sides when it comes out."

"You think it might be someone powerful, someone that Tuva will be reluctant to accept is at fault?" Britta gave a nod. "I can see how you would worry about that, but there is no acceptable reason to share information about the Gathering to Grimwalt. And when we accept guests, they are under our protection. The whole of Skäddar will be embarrassed by what happened today."

"It also means that whoever killed those villagers set up the chain of events that led to us being brought here." Dak kept his voice low.

"That hasn't escaped us. If they were killed as part of a plan to lure you up here, that is unforgivable. No matter who they are." Britta's response was just as low, and she sounded like she was struggling to keep her tone even.

After that, no one spoke again. They moved through the forest silently, parallel to the river, looking for any sign the archers had come this way.

When they'd been walking for more than ten minutes, Luc felt the strange buzz he associated with the protections Ava had sewn into his skin, a prickling down his forearm and across his chest.

He raised a hand and everyone stopped, listening.

A man stepped out between two trees, a hooded cloak shielding his face, the dark color of it blending with the shadows so it seemed he materialized out of the gloom.

He gave a sudden yip of sound and the cloak seemed to collapse to the ground as if it had been held up by air.

Dragir made a sound as a fox appeared as if it coalesced out of that same air. It stared at them all, ears swiveling, and then it turned tail and ran, disappearing amongst the trees from one moment to the next.

"A gilla," Britta breathed. "Just like the guards saw."

Luc glanced over at Ava, saw her gaze was still fixed on where the fox had disappeared.

She walked forward, coming to a stop where the man had stepped out, and crouched down.

She studied something on the ground.

"What is it?" Luc moved over to her.

"A fox hole." She glanced up at him, then rose. "The magic might be that he can call animals to him, rather than turn into them. But it's still magic, nonetheless."

True. But being able to transform into another creature, another shape, was far more frightening, in Luc's mind, than being able to call animals to you.

"It might be a tame fox. One he's trained."

Ava gave a nod. "Also possible."

"What about the disappearing trick?" Dragir had been listening to them, coming over to look at the fox hole himself.

"Trick of the eye in the shadows." Luc shrugged. If the spell caster could make himself invisible, that was a problem.

But then, Ava could do the same. Or rather, her magic made people not see her.

He began to search the ground for any sign of the direction the man had gone, Dak walking to his right, Dragir to his left.

He glanced back at Ava, signaled her to wait a moment.

He wanted to make sure their strange visitor was gone before she went any further.

As he moved forward, the ground beneath his feet suddenly trembled.

He froze, spinning back to Ava. He caught a glimpse of her shock, and then she and the others disappeared, swallowed by the earth.

He didn't waste his time shouting, he raced toward her, came to a stop at the lip of a deep hole.

Ava stared up at him from the bottom of a steep-sided pit, and all around her, the others were picking themselves up off the ground.

"We're all——"

Before she could finish, a tree root seemed to reach out and try to grab her by the waist. With a shout of horror, Lucilla, who was standing beside her, began hacking at it with her sword.

Another root snaked out and smacked Lucilla's sword arm to the side.

Luc saw roots emerging from the ground, and from the sides of the hole.

He spun, looking for the closest tree to tie the rope in his pack around and when he couldn't see anything that was close enough to give him the length he needed, he threw the rope at Dak.

"You and Dragir hold me."

He tied the end around his torso and ran back to the edge of the hole.

It was chaos below, everyone was hacking roots or dodging them.

"Ready?"

Dak and Dragir were standing right behind him, braced to take his weight.

He crouched, then pushed off the edge, sliding down, grabbing roots as he dropped to slow his descent.

As his feet hit the soft, crumbling ground at the bottom, his sword arm was already swinging.

CHAPTER 32

Taggar's camp was empty.

Massi followed Duncan into it without any hesitation.

He could sense where people were in his forest, she was sure, and he had become less and less careful as they approached.

"Can you tell where they've gone?" she asked as she studied the tents. They were similar to the small travel tents the Rising Wave used when it was on the move, but pieces of canvas had also been strung between branches to create covered seating areas, and logs had been placed around the well-dug fire pit, to make a more permanent living space.

Four tents, so the three that had been here a while, plus the newcomer, Taggar. She could even tell which tent was his, it looked less worn than the others.

"They went that way," Duncan said, pointing east along the river, which ran just below the camp site, wide and deep, by the sound of it.

There was very little to learn here.

"I wouldn't mind seeing what they're up to." Massi caught Duncan's eye and he gave a nod.

Then he went still like he had earlier that morning.

"Lithwick?"

"He's pulling power again." He tilted his head. "Also to the east."

"You don't think he's cooperating with Taggar and his guards?"

"They didn't sound very cooperative the other day, but he is looking for me, and he knows Taggar is, too. Maybe he's just following them around, hoping to get lucky."

Massi gnawed on her lower lip. "Maybe you shouldn't come."

He shot her a look, gave a snort. "I don't hide from Lithwick."

She raised her brows, thinking of how she'd found him, and he gave a chuckle in response.

"All right, maybe I do. But only after healing a massive, ancient tree. Not when I'm at full strength."

He turned and loped off, and she had no choice but to follow. He knew the way, and she did not.

And he was not currently in the same condition as she'd found him yesterday, she had to concede.

When she caught up, which she did easily because he was waiting for her just beyond the camp, he pulled her into a quick, fierce kiss, and then began to move silently.

It was as if the forest moved every twig and leaf out of his way, so he disturbed nothing as he made a path through the trees.

She stepped on a dead leaf, which crunched beneath her boot, and he looked back as if surprised.

He crouched down, palm against the ground, then stood again.

Massi was sure he had asked the forest to do the same for her, because her feet did not make another sound.

Duncan stopped suddenly and pointed toward the river, then put his finger to his lips.

"They'll be on their guard now." The voice that drifted up the slope was Taggar's. "But it was worth it for the chance of getting her, especially."

"I've never seen anyone move that fast. How did they know?" The man who asked the question sounded aggrieved.

"They're wearing spell work. Have to be." Taggar sounded grim. "It's not going to be easy to get to them again."

"I thought protective spell work was really rare." A third voice sounded skeptical.

"Rare but not unheard of." Taggar's voice was firm.

He would know, Massi thought. He was wearing some himself.

She fingered her collar. It certainly came in handy.

And it clearly wasn't *that* rare. Everyone seemed to have it. Including whoever Taggar had just attacked.

"I wonder who they're talking about," Duncan whispered.

Massi was wondering that, herself.

"Do you think the Skäddar will come after us?" The final guard of the group asked. "They looked ready to."

"Doubtful." Taggar again. "They won't want a border incident."

"Except we did try to kill the queen of Kassia."

Massi reached out and grabbed Duncan's arm, squeezing hard.

Shit.

Ava and Luc were already here.

Massi wanted to laugh out loud.

Taggar was right. The people he'd just shot at, if they were Ava and Luc, and she didn't believe for a moment Luc wouldn't be with Ava, were probably covered with spell work from head to toe.

And Luc would be coming after them, Skäddar permission or not.

He would not let an attack on Ava go.

She held Duncan in place, letting the group pass by on their way back to their camp.

She knew where to find them when she wanted them. She had more important things to do. Like find her friends.

"What is it?"

"If they shot at who I think they did, then my friends might be here."

"Someone is." Duncan lost focus as he faced east. "A group. More than ten."

She couldn't help the wide grin at the thought of it.

"Come." She tugged him along. "*Now* we can find out what's really going on."

"Lithwick's that way, too, don't forget. Pulling power." Duncan was suddenly sharp and feral again.

That was probably not good.

"He has no reason to harm them, does he?" She frowned.

"He said he wants these woods to himself. I think he'll harm any stranger he sees." He glanced at her. "Don't forget he set one of his monsters on you the moment you came into the forest."

She *had* forgotten that.

They both picked up the pace.

She liked this silent running. She wondered how long it would last.

Duncan slowed suddenly, hand up to warn her, and she heard shouting in the distance.

If this was Luc, they hadn't been far behind Taggar and his guards.

But they had obviously encountered trouble.

"Lithwick," Duncan said. "He's close."

She took a step past him to look between the trees, and he bent suddenly at the waist, as if in pain.

"What is it?"

He put out a hand to the nearest tree, breathing out. "Something. Never felt it before." He turned his head to look at her, and his eyes were darker, less focused.

"What do you want to do?" She felt the tension of needing to be in two places at the same time.

"I need to see what he's doing."

She slid under his shoulder, just as she had done the day before, but after a few steps he could take his own weight again.

"He's forcing something to happen. I'm not sure——"

They both stopped.

Two men stood up ahead, holding a rope, and the shouting intensified.

Massi recognized one of them immediately as Dak.

"Where's Lithwick?" Better to know where he was lurking.

Duncan pointed south. "Not far, though. He's watching this."

Suddenly something that looked like a massive vine wound its way around Dak's waist and began to pull him into what she could now see was a hole in the ground.

The other man planted his feet, fighting to keep Dak from being dragged in.

Massi pulled her knife. "I've got to go."

As she ran forward, she shouted the battle cry she'd used ever since she and her friends had fought their way free of the Kassian army.

The answering cry came from a dozen throats, and she whooped as she reached Dak, sliding on her knees beside him, knife arm raised.

"Wait."

Duncan was suddenly on Dak's other side, eyes closed, face contorted as he thrust his hands into the soil. "Tell them to stop cutting the roots." He spoke through gritted teeth.

"Stop!" She peered over the side. "Luc, stop cutting."

"Massi?" Luc stared up at her, sword raised, his expression stunned.

"Tell them to stop cutting." She could see some of the unit hadn't heard her, they were too caught up in the fight.

"Swords up." Luc's shout had everyone going still.

The roots didn't stop, though, they snaked around ankles and arms.

She looked up at Dak, saw he was staring at her with as much shock as Luc.

Duncan drew in a deep breath, lowered himself flat against the earth, and the root around Dak slowly withdrew.

She peered over the edge, saw the same was happening below.

"Stay." Duncan put his hand out to grab the root that had come for Dak, and it stopped moving. "They can use it to climb back up." Finally he opened his eyes, looked over at Massi.

He looked . . . better, she thought.

"You took it back?" she asked. Then she remembered Lithwick, and she scrambled to her feet, bow ready. "Where is he?"

Duncan pushed himself up on his hands and knees, and then leaned back on his heels. He pointed. "But he's moving away."

"Mas." Dak hauled her into his arms. "How are you here?"

Luc pulled himself out of the hole, then leaned back in and pulled Ava out like she weighed nothing.

"She was always in Grimwalt. We're the ones who aren't where we're supposed to be." Ava smiled at her, then went on her knees to offer a hand to Lucilla.

"Would you like to introduce us to your friend?" Luc was watching Duncan in that quiet, waiting way he had.

She had been so pleased to see them, Massi had forgotten how suspicious he and Dak were, and how territorial Duncan was.

She pulled out of Dak's embrace, caught Duncan's eye and stepped over to him, sliding her hand in his.

She needed them to see that Duncan wasn't just an ally, he was far more.

"This is Duncan," she said. "I found him in prison with Tomas and Velda and helped him escape."

She knew there was no surer way to bring Ava over to his side than to put him with Tomas and Velda.

"The prison is near here?" Ava looked at her sharply.

"No. It's a long story. This is Duncan's forest. I came up here to meet you after I got that note, and also because the man who abducted you is here, too. I think he shot at you earlier?"

"That was Himself?" Ava's eyes narrowed.

"Are you the one Massi told me about who burned the old rope, made a new one?" Duncan's voice was low and hoarse.

Ava went still, turned to look at him. "Yes."

"I thank you." Duncan bent his head. "When Taggar put it on me, he thought it would make me weak."

"Was this in the prison?" Ava asked. She was looking at Duncan as if braced.

Everyone was out of the hole now, hanging on their every word.

Was Ava worried he would say something? Expose her, maybe? The new rope hadn't been inert. If Massi had understood her correctly, Ava had spelled it to help her heal. It had done more than just not made Duncan weak, it would have given him strength.

All Duncan did was nod.

Ava stepped up to him, and there was something on her face, almost too hard to look at.

"I did it for myself, to save myself, but if it has also saved someone else . . ." She gave a nod. "That is very good."

She reached out a hand and Duncan extended his own.

They touched only briefly, pulling back straight away. Neither said anything, but Massi guessed they were doing the equivalent of a magical taste test.

"Massi." Dak blew out a breath.

She turned to him, grinning in delight again to see him. "Yes?"

He looked from her to Duncan. "What the fuck is going on?"

CHAPTER 33

"This is the camp?"

Luc Franck, the commander of the Rising Wave, crouched beside Duncan, his eyes narrowed as he studied the cluster of tents up ahead.

Massi had called Luc and Dak her brothers.

The family she had forged in the hell of the Chosen camps.

Both men had thrown quick, suspicious looks at him the whole way back along the river as he led them to Taggar.

At least the Rising Wave unit was quiet and clearly well-trained.

Duncan was impressed with their silence, and the way they moved, but then, he'd always been impressed by Massi, and these were her people.

He led them south of the camp, so it lay between their small group and the river, with a good view from the slope above.

Ava Yngstra, Luc Franck, Dak, Massi, and two Skäddar warriors, Dragir and Britta, clustered around him. The leadership team.

The rest of the unit quietly found a place to watch along the ridge.

Duncan was the outsider in this little group, but he had Massi on his side, and Ava Yngstra was certainly friendly enough.

She had said nothing about what she had felt when they had touched hands.

He didn't know why he had reached out to her, and thought he saw the same surprise in her eyes.

It had been instinctive.

And enlightening.

Her magic felt like patterns. He wondered what his had felt like to her.

Whatever it was, she was content to keep it to herself, and was happy to crouch right beside him, relaxed and obviously pleased to see Massi.

Below, Taggar and his three guards moved around, talking softly enough they couldn't hear what was being said, and then ducked into their tents.

Luc had wanted to go down and question them, but Massi convinced him they might discover more if they eavesdropped first.

The Rising Wave Commander had exchanged a quick look with Ava at that, and Duncan saw her give a tiny shake of her head.

"So, do you think the Speaker will stay in prison?" Luc rubbed the back of his head, his focus fixed on Taggar below as he asked the question.

Massi had shared all her news quickly and concisely on their way to the camp, and Duncan could see they were all trying to come to terms with the massive change to Grimwalt's power structure.

Massi shrugged. "Harkonen has every reason to keep him there. And I think his time is finished. The magic he was using to manipulate those around him has faded away." She glanced across at Ava, and the queen of Kassia gave a slow nod in response.

"Taggar can't know, can he?" Ava asked. "Not if it just happened."

"I told him." Massi's lips quirked. "He didn't want to believe me. Either way, he obviously thinks the situation in Taunen can be reversed, or he's going to try and cause some chaos and make things uncomfortable for Harkonen and whoever else takes the reins in Grimwalt in revenge for the Speaker's imprisonment."

"That sounds just what the vindictive bastard would do." Ava spoke as if she had personal experience with Taggar, and Duncan realized she must have done.

"And this Lithwick is working with him?" Luc asked. He had a spray of mud on his cheek, and his eyes were the same blue as Massi's.

Even if they weren't actual siblings, they had the same look about them.

Duncan shook his head. "Lithwick's broken with the Speaker and with Taggar because they couldn't keep me locked away. He hasn't taken my return to the forest well. At all."

"So that attack wasn't to help Taggar?"

"No. We passed Taggar on the way to you. He was talking about how he wanted to try for you again——catch you off guard."

Luc's gaze swung sharply in his direction. "Is that so?"

"Then why did Lithwick attack us?" Britta asked, speaking up for the first time. She was crouched as far from him as it was possible for her to be and still be part of the group.

She was afraid of him, Duncan realized. So was Dragir.

They had seen him take back control of the forest, and it . . . worried them.

"He hates anyone being in the forest."

"Then he's in for a sad, frustrated life," Dak said, voice incredulous. "How's he going to stop people coming into the forest?"

"He sets monsters on them. They look like lumbering giants made of sticks and leaves," Massi said. "He steals energy from the trees to make them."

"The skovva." Britta gasped. "That's him doing it? This Lithwick?"

Duncan nodded at the same time as Massi.

"We saw a gilla, too, just before the ground collapsed," Dragir said. "He seemed to turn into a fox."

Duncan shook his head. "Lithwick again. He said he was playing tricks to keep people out."

"How does he do it?" Ava asked.

"Like Massi says. He steals from the trees. Didn't you notice the stand of trees near where the sink hole formed? He killed it." Duncan had touched the trunks before he'd led the group in the direction of the camp, anger fighting with sorrow when he realized there was no saving them. Lithwick had taken everything.

"And your power?" Luc asked. He didn't sound demanding though. He sounded concerned. "I saw you turn those roots from enemy to friend."

Duncan looked up at him, then his gaze swung to Ava as she made a face.

"You don't have to answer," she said. "Your magic is your private business."

And suddenly he understood the look of frozen fear she'd given him when he started discussing the rope, and her silence since they'd touched hands.

Ava Yngstra had not told many people what she was, whereas he had turned a forest attack around in the most public way.

But then, everyone had always known his power, since he had started disappearing into the forest as a child, and coming out, days later, wreathed in vines.

His parents might have shielded him if they had been alive, but his aunt and uncle had looked after him from when he was only six, and they hadn't known what he was. By the time he'd discovered his magic, everyone else had, as well.

Maybe it was an easier way to live, but it was more lonely.

He glanced over at Massi, and she looked back at him, steady and calm.

Letting him make up his own mind what he wanted to share.

He'd been afraid she had abandoned him, just for a moment, by the sink hole, and then she had stepped over to him and taken his hand in her own. Had aligned herself with him.

She trusted these people, and Ava had trusted him in return, sharing a glimpse of her power with him.

"I give to the forest, and the forest gives back." He reached out a finger, touched the tip of it to the ground and a flower curled up from where he'd touched, tender leaves spreading, tiny bud unfurling.

"And Lithwick doesn't do that?"

"Lithwick takes by force, and he pays the price for it."

Duncan would have to stop him. He'd danced around the issue since he'd returned home, but there was no other way. Lithwick could not be allowed to continue killing the forest.

"What price does he pay?" Ava asked.

"Not enough." Duncan hadn't seen what Lithwick was becoming, but however disfigured Massi had described him, that could not make up for what he'd already done.

"He looks less . . . human," Massi said, and he thought it was a warning. "If you see him, you'll know what I mean. He's becoming part of the forest itself."

"Like a garanda," Britta said. "The master of the forest who kills those who disrespect the woods."

Duncan had heard of the garanda——this close to the border, the myths and folklore of the Skäddar were well known.

"Just like that," he agreed. "Except in his case, he's the one disrespecting the forest. He is not its master, he's its abuser."

There was something niggling at the back of his mind about Lithwick when it came to the Skäddar, but Duncan couldn't quite get a hold of it. It was something Lithwick had said to Taggar, but Duncan had been weak and almost unconscious when it had been said, and he couldn't quite bring up the words.

Then Taggar and his guards emerged from their tents, standing together in the center of their camp, and his attention snapped to them.

They'd been packing. Duncan could see sacks on their backs.

"I need to hear them or take them. This far back, we can do neither." Luc slid down the slope, and Duncan kept level with him, easing both their way.

Luc sent him a startled look, then gave a nod of thanks, concentrating on trying to catch the conversation up ahead.

But it was too late.

Taggar had moved toward the river, and Duncan was just in time to see all four of them dive in and swim across.

"What are they up to?" Britta, the Skäddar warrior, asked, slithering to a stop beside them.

"They said they wanted another chance to try to kill Ava when we passed them earlier," Duncan said. "Maybe they're going back to the Gathering."

"And they've crossed to the Skäddar side because they're afraid we're coming along the Grimwalt side, looking for them after their attack." Luc turned to look up the hill, gave a quick hand signal.

Everyone moved toward them.

"What's happening?" Dak asked when he skidded to a halt.

"We're hunting the hunters."

"ANOTHER REASON THEY CROSSED THE RIVER IS THAT THEY'RE likely afraid of running into Lithwick on the Grimwalt side." Massi squeezed water out of her hair, and sat to put on her boots.

There had been some ribbing amongst the Rising Wave unit that Ava had gotten just as wet as everyone else this time, and Massi gathered the crossing at the Skäddar camp had been shallower than here.

Ava sat beside her, wringing water from her shirt.

"That point didn't escape me, either." Dragir sounded relieved. "It would have been my first choice to cross into Skäddar for our return trip, even if they hadn't gone over."

Duncan's hands flexed as he stood beside her, and Massi glanced up at him. He was obviously frustrated at the way Lithwick had them all so frightened.

"The roots didn't even do much damage," he said. "It was unexpected, but no one was seriously hurt."

That was probably because Massi had noticed tiny, jewel-like embroidery on sleeves, on collars, on the edge of cloaks on every single person in the group. Including the two Skäddar warriors, who

Dak had mentioned had traveled with them for a few days to lead them to the Gathering.

Ava had extended her protection to everyone.

It might have been a lot worse.

"It was like that with the skovva, as well," Dak said. "It wasn't able to get in any good blows. It looked worse than it was."

"And the gilla, that dramatic appearance and then a fox. That's the sum of it. Nothing dangerous happened, it was just disconcerting," Lucilla agreed.

"What would have happened if you hadn't stopped the roots?" Britta asked Duncan.

He blinked. "Lithwick sent them to harm you, but something prevented them . . ." He suddenly looked over at Ava, who was carefully looking down, pulling on a boot.

"Perhaps it knows you're the one it listens to, not Lithwick," Massi suggested, trying to deflect Britta's question. "It was fighting Lithwick's order as much as it could."

"I'm just thinking of the village that was attacked a few months ago," Britta said. "There were roots growing in a lot of the bodies. And it looked as if the forest had attacked them."

"Oh." Massi stood, stomping out the last of the water. "That was Lithwick. Duncan heard him admit it to Taggar."

Everyone turned to Duncan, and Massi winced at having put him on the spot.

"It's true," he acknowledged. "Taggar accused him of it, and Lithwick said the Speaker told him to give the spy he had on the Skäddar Collective a solid reason to question the alliance with the Rising Wave. To do something no one could ignore."

Dragir drew in a breath. "What happened there *was* impossible to ignore. It was brutal. The whole village died."

"So if he was able to kill an entire village, how did we get off so easily?" Dak asked.

There was a moment of silence.

"Luc." Ava got to her feet.

She was going to reveal herself.

Massi could see she was afraid they were underestimating their enemy, because it was very likely Ava's spell work had saved them. And if Lithwick were to come in contact with someone without her protection, they might not fare so well.

Massi could see the dread and determination in Ava's eyes.

"No." Luc caught her gaze, held it.

"I am going to deal with Lithwick." Duncan stepped between them, his gaze on Ava. "I once thought of him as a friend, when friends were rare for me, and that has been holding me back from doing what I have to do. After we get hold of Taggar, I'll find him. It needs to end."

Not everyone understood what was going on, but Massi did.

Her heart jumped in her chest, and she couldn't have spoken if her life depended on it.

Duncan was letting Ava know she didn't have to expose herself.

He would make sure her silence led to no harm.

Luc reached out and put a hand on Duncan's shoulder. He gave a tiny nod of thanks. "Let's go. I'm more in a hurry than ever to catch up with Taggar." He turned to the two Skäddar. "Do you know the way?"

They both shook their heads.

"I've never done guard duty along here," Britta admitted.

"I know the way." Duncan was the only one with no weapon, standing in his loose shirt and trousers. And yet, Massi knew, he was one of the most dangerous people here.

And he was hers.

She felt it suddenly, keenly——she wanted to stay with him for as long as it worked between them. She wanted more of the peace and quiet and the burning heat of passion he ignited in her.

The revelation, the certainty she felt, stunned her.

"How do you know the way?" Dragir was asking Duncan, a bite to his voice. "This is Skäddar territory."

"The forest doesn't care whose territory it is," Duncan said, and there was a challenge in his eyes. "And the forest is mine."

CHAPTER 34

Massi's friend was more than a little interesting.

Luc watched him move through the trees, charting a path for them. He did not make a single sound as he jogged ahead.

Not a leaf, not a twig, had crackled under his boots.

He was at one with the forest.

More than once, he'd noticed a branch seem to reach down to brush Duncan's cheek or touch his arm.

Like they were welcoming a dear friend.

Massi had been keeping in step with Dak, talking to him in a low voice, but now she moved forward, drawing level to him.

"He helped Ava," Luc said, nodding toward Duncan. He would give the forest man all kinds of leeway for that.

He owed him.

She said nothing for a long while. Then touched his arm. "I think I'm staying here. At least for a while."

That shocked him.

Massi had always been part of his life. Since the Chosen camps, she had been the glue that kept him, Dak and Revek together.

"That's a big change for such a short acquaintance."

She gave a snort. "How long did you know Ava for before you wanted to move the heavens for her?"

She had him there.

"It's like that?"

"I think so. If it isn't, I can come home. But I think it is."

"I wish the fates had found you someone closer to Cervantes."

She shrugged. "They didn't." Then she blew out a breath. "But that doesn't mean I won't miss you."

"He couldn't . . .?" Luc was going to suggest Duncan follow her, but then a branch reached down and Duncan stepped on it, and it raised him up. He leaped from it to the branch above, and in moments, reached almost the top of the tree.

Then he jumped straight down, and the leaves on the forest floor spun up in a whirlwind, met him halfway, and lowered him lightly to the ground.

Everyone stared at him, shocked into silence.

Massi shot a look at Luc and he swallowed his words.

"No. I can see he couldn't."

This man was the master of his domain. In a way Luc had never seen before.

Ava's magic was hidden, it went unnoticed and was all the more deadly for it.

But this magic was physical. Overt. And utterly astonishing.

"They're just up ahead." Duncan pointed, ignoring the stares. "Looks like they're meeting someone."

"The Skäddar spy." Britta swallowed her awe, suddenly more interested in the traitor in their midst, and Luc saw her eyes were narrowed. "I'd like to join that meeting."

Dragir gave a grim nod.

Luc did, too.

He checked to see Dak was covering Ava, and then he moved, running in the direction Duncan had pointed.

The forest man kept up with him easily, and Luc guessed he was using his magic to help silence all of their footsteps, because when they burst into the clearing where Taggar and his crew were standing with a fifth man, Luc could see the surprise and astonishment on their faces.

And the fear.

"Taggar." He addressed the man who'd set up Ava's abduction with a cool tone. This was the man who'd provided the rope that had leeched Ava's magic and strength to almost nothing and had endangered her life.

Luc had thought about this moment for months, and he had to exert more control over his rage than he'd ever had to do before at the sight of the bastard.

He was big, lean. And it looked like he had an injury to his right shoulder.

The three guards who'd come with Taggar looked frightened, and the fifth man was staring at Britta and Dragir in horror.

"You're part of the Furla," Britta said. "You're Jens's aide, aren't you?"

The man turned away from them, as if hiding his face could make a difference now. He looked around wildly for an escape, but the rest of the unit had reached the clearing and had encircled the group.

Dragir moved with him, blocking his way. "I heard the Furla didn't want the alliance with the Rising Wave, but how could you justify killing a whole village to further your aims?"

The man was shaking his head. "We didn't know they were going to do that! We didn't agree to it!" He covered his face with his hands. "Our agreement with Grimwalt was an incident to call the alliance into question. How could we have known they would do that?"

"How could you have known?" Britta took a step back in disgust. She glanced over at Luc. "We're taking him back to the Gathering."

He gave a nod. "We'll be along in a bit."

"See you later, then." Dragir grabbed the man's arm, and Britta took his other side.

They disappeared between the trees, heading east toward the Gathering.

For a moment, silence reigned, and Luc let it stretch out.

"We were just watching the border. I don't know about a massacre. I don't know anything." One of the guards, thin and unkempt, cracked under the strain.

"I believe you. You can go. Pack up your tent and get out of the forest." Duncan spoke calmly. "Don't come back, there is no welcome for you here."

"No fear." The man bolted, and the other two began to sidle in the same direction.

"You, too." Duncan waved at them and they ran after their friend.

Luc could hear them crashing through the undergrowth.

"No free pass for me?" Taggar asked. His gaze had swept their group, but Ava had been hidden by Dak and Lucilla, and now they both stepped aside.

Taggar saw her, and went very still.

"Do you see why that could never be?" Luc asked.

"I saved her life," Taggar said, pointing at Ava. "Sirna would have killed her with that rope if I hadn't taken it off her."

"You gave it to him in the first place," Ava said. "You were the reason he took me. And you left the rope with him, even though you knew he was inclined to take the easy way out."

"You look none the worse for wear."

There was a sudden silence, and Taggar looked around, eyes widening as he realized his mistake.

"Now I do." Ava smiled. "And only because I saved myself. That rope came close to ending me."

"I take offense at the harm done to my heart's choice." Luc stared at Taggar, and wondered what he was going to do with him.

He had wanted him dead, but death suddenly seemed too easy.

"Perhaps he could answer some questions the Skäddar might have about the Speaker's interference in their country?" Dak, ever the intelligence gatherer, suggested. "Because he obviously knows enough to be meeting with a spy, and I'm sure the Skäddar will be interested in what both sides saw as a benefit to their deal."

Taggar did not look happy with that suggestion.

Luc gave a smile. "Let's go." He took a step forward, and then gave a shake of his head. "Someone else will have to escort him. I can't trust myself."

Taggar looked away, and Luc wondered if the tables had ever been turned on him in this way before.

He would be used to control. And power.

Now he had neither. And Luc would make sure he never had either again.

LUC RANGED AHEAD OF THEM, UNABLE TO STAY IN THE GROUP.

Ava decided it was better to let him go. She was much slower, anyway, as she used the walk to the Gathering to work a spell for Taggar.

Luc had wanted to kill Taggar since the moment Ava had managed to get free of her abductors and had found Luc on the Jatan border, a month ago.

She could see in the way he powered ahead that now he had Taggar at his mercy, he had come to the realization that he wasn't going to be able to kill him, after all.

Between the Skäddar and the Grimwaldians, Taggar would be a vital witness to what the Speaker had done.

And she would be able to get him to tell the truth about that.

She lifted the fine linen square she was working on, and stitched another chicken onto the branch of a tree.

This working needed to be something that would be safe for Taggar to keep, that would inspire him to be frank with his questioners until the full truth came out.

In a way, this was the better revenge, and Luc would see it that way, when he was able to get over his need to pound Taggar into dust.

She caught him glancing back to check on her, and she lifted her fabric to show him. To remind him there were other ways to get vengeance.

He gave a tiny nod, and she thought his gait was a little smoother after that.

He waited for Massi and Duncan to catch up with him, and bent his head to talk to them.

Massi always seemed alert to her surroundings, even when she was walking easily in friendly territory.

Luc called her his arrow, and she was the finest archer in the Rising Wave.

Ava would have to ask her if the spell she'd worked into the collar of Massi's shirt, which had included accuracy, had made a difference, or if she was as good a shot already as she could get.

Duncan and Luc both shortened their strides so that Massi could easily match their pace, and Ava noticed the way Duncan brushed against her, touching her in subtle ways.

He'd understood Ava's dilemma, and had put himself between her and the secrets she kept.

Any debt he thought he owed her for the rope was now truly wiped away.

Lithwick would need to be dealt with, and Ava would assist Duncan any way she could.

She studied his clothing, which was nothing more than a shirt and trousers, with sturdy boots, and wondered if he didn't feel the cold, or whether he had nothing else.

She put the finished work she had sewn for Taggar back in her pocket and pulled out another square of linen, speeding up her pace as she worked on embroidering a forest on the soft fabric.

She made her way through the unit, focused on catching up to Luc and the others, and as if he could feel her moving closer, he turned back to look at her, murmured something to Massi and Duncan, and then waited for her to join them.

"We have to be close to the Gathering by now," she said, not even slightly out of breath after her exertion, she was pleased to note. She tucked a braid that had come loose behind her ear and held out the cloth to Duncan. "Perhaps you would accept this gift from me."

He took it——no one she had ever offered a spell-worked item to had ever not taken it. She was becoming convinced that was part of the magic, started before they even touched what she had made for them.

He looked down at it, rubbing it between his fingers.

"Protection," he said. "From Lithwick?"

"From anyone who means you harm."

He looked across at her, thoughtful. "Anyone?"

She met his gaze. "Even me."

He sent her a smile, and his serious, almost stern, features blossomed into a face so handsome, she blinked.

"Wear it against your skin for maximum effect." She slid her hand into Luc's.

Duncan nodded, tucking the cloth into the waistband of his pants.

Massi cleared her throat, and flashed Ava a quick look of approval.

"How's your aim these days?" Ava asked her.

Massi grinned. "Even when they've got a protection spell on them, I still manage to hit the target."

That was interesting. "Who?"

"Taggar."

"So if he runs, only you can bring him down," Luc said.

"And you," Massi reminded him.

He gave her a startled look, then inclined his head. "I'm so used to it, I forget."

"Let's try not to give him a chance to run." Ava didn't think any of them wanted the headache of that.

"Agreed." Although Luc sounded like he might not mind that much.

Ava glanced back at where Lucilla and Dak were walking on either side of Taggar, and wondered whether it would be worth letting him know he was safer staying their prisoner than trying to make a run for it.

He wouldn't believe her, anyway.

"Do you hear that?" Luc asked, stopping, head tilted, and Massi gave a nod.

They had such good hearing, it always amazed Ava.

A moment later Duncan gripped Massi's arm, face tight with concentration. "Fighting. Shouting." He took a step back. "Lithwick."

He accelerated away from them, disappearing from one blink of the eye to the next.

Luc turned to the rest of the unit and whistled, and then he and Massi ran, as well.

Ava didn't run, but she moved fast after them as the others streamed around her, weapons drawn.

While she could fight as well as anyone, her other skills might be more useful.

She crested the rise just as Dak and Lucilla caught up with her, gripping Taggar on either side.

Through the trees she caught glimpses of carnage in the Gathering camp.

The Skäddar were fighting roots and vines, and she could see at least two lay dead.

These people were not protected by spell work. Except Tuva, she recalled. She hoped the leader of the Collective was wearing the scarf Ava had given her earlier.

"What is it?" Lucilla sounded out of breath.

"Lithwick," Ava said. She tried to think of a good way to combat this.

Below, Luc roared out as he swung his sword, and she saw Massi standing, knife in hand, as Duncan crouched beside her. She hacked at whatever came close to them, protecting Duncan while he tried to concentrate, but then he suddenly stood, shook his head, and took a running dive into the river.

Massi stared after him, then turned back to the fight.

The Rising Wave unit was making headway, but there were over a hundred Skäddar here, and even with the Rising Wave soldiers they'd left behind, things were bad.

She noticed Dak and Lucilla were still beside her, and when she turned to look, she could see Dak had tied Taggar's hands behind his back.

"Better than nothing," he said, and then he ran, Lucilla on his heels, both drawing their swords as they went, leaving Taggar standing beside her.

She glanced at him, lifted her shoulders, and followed them down the hill.

Taggar was wearing a protection spell too, according to Massi. He'd be fine, and if he ran, Luc would get his wish to chase him down.

There were more important things to deal with now.

As she got to the bottom of the slope, a root snaked out, trying to curl around her ankle. It couldn't get a hold, but it managed to trip her.

She somersaulted onto her back, struggled to get her breath, and then sat up, staring at the carnage around her.

A Skäddar woman lying close to her was staring, blank-eyed, up at the sky.

A root was growing out of her stomach.

Duncan had asked them not to slice the roots in retaliation during the attack earlier, but that was when he was actively trying to counter Lithwick's command.

Ava guessed he'd seen Lithwick on the other side of the river and had swum across to deal with this attack at the source.

It looked as if they had to cut the roots this time. It was the only way to save the Skäddar, at least until Duncan caught up with Lithwick.

She scrambled to her feet, long knife in her hand, and dove into the fight.

CHAPTER 35

He'd caught a glimpse of Lithwick watching the chaos he'd unleashed from the Grimwalt side, and Duncan was determined to chase him down.

Lithwick was hooded, hiding in the shadows, out of the afternoon light, just like the dark force he was.

Duncan had had to leave Massi behind, still fighting the attack Lithwick had engineered, and that only made him angrier. More focused on getting Lithwick to stop.

He barely felt the icy water streaming off him as he hauled himself out on the far bank. He'd crossed the river quickly, ran straight for the treeline, but Lithwick was gone.

Coward.

At least the further he chased Lithwick from the Gathering, the weaker the pull would be on the roots and trees to do his bidding.

It would only help Luc and Massi in their efforts to protect the Skäddar.

Duncan ran into the trees, but before he went deeper, he looked back at the fighting in the camp.

The Rising Wave soldiers were making a difference, and Massi was still fighting, unharmed, standing back to back with Luc.

He needed to trust she could take care of herself, and concentrate on doing what only he could.

Put an end to Lithwick.

He turned back, reaching out to the trees, hunting his quarry.

Lithwick stepped out from behind a tree far up ahead, both hands gripping the trunk.

That tree would be dead, Duncan guessed.

Lithwick's only method was to take.

As Duncan ran toward him, he scooped up a stick, threw it straight at Lithwick's chest, willing the end to sharpen.

It hit him dead center, but though Duncan thought it had pierced him, and he cried out in pain, when he pulled it out, Duncan could see it hadn't gone deep, and the wound hardly bled.

It infuriated him that Lithwick was using the forest to heal himself.

He would need to wait, make sure when he finally struck, he made it count.

Lithwick would kill as many trees as it took to keep himself alive, and Duncan didn't want to harm his forest any more than necessary.

Lithwick disappeared again, and when he reappeared, standing beside a tree even further away, he stood with both palms flat against it, challenging Duncan. Taunting him.

Duncan didn't know if it was his imagination, but he could swear he felt the pull as Lithwick sucked up the tree's life force.

A breeze rose up, tugged back the hood of Lithwick's cloak, and Duncan saw for the first time that the forest had indeed taken its due.

He stumbled to a halt in shock.

Massi had only caught a glimpse of Lithwick before, and hadn't been sure of what she'd seen. Duncan took in the mushrooms she'd described growing on his face, the gray-green skin, but it was his eyes that were the most frightening.

They were completely brown, with no whites, no iris.

"Shocked?" Lithwick called out, and there it was, the taunting in his tone.

Duncan said nothing, he started moving forward again, slowly this time, his gaze fixed on what Lithwick had become.

"I *am* the forest now," Lithwick hissed at him. "It is me, and I am it."

Duncan rejected that outright.

Lithwick was only part of the forest in that he was a leech, sucking its lifeblood.

"It still obeys me," he called back. "Not you."

"Does it?" Lithwick disappeared, and above Duncan a branch cracked, sheered off the tree, and fell.

Duncan leaped to the side to avoid it and stared up. Reached out and put a hand on the tree.

There was something wrong here.

He hadn't been to this section of the forest since his return——he hadn't had time——but now he realized he was being drawn deeper and deeper into a place that had changed.

He touched trunks as he walked.

So many dead, or rotting from the inside.

So much decay.

This is where Lithwick had been hiding.

He should have gone looking, but the ancients had to be saved, and as he'd admitted to Ava, he'd hesitated to confront his former friend.

Because there was only one way this could end.

It was with a sense of inevitability that he followed the path Lithwick had made into a wide clearing.

Here was Lithwick's citadel.

It looked so much like his own.

"Why did you copy it, if you hate everything about me?"

He couldn't see Lithwick, but he knew he was close enough to hear.

"I didn't hate everything about you. I wanted everything you had." Lithwick came around the side of the stand of trees he'd styled into his home, although Duncan could already see the rot had sheared off the bark on three of them.

"Why? Why do you leech the forest this way?" He couldn't understand it.

"It becomes an addiction, after you do it a few too many times." Lithwick sounded wistful, as if thinking back to better days. "When you can take without giving, it changes you."

"You lied about being chased out of your old forest." Duncan was sure now that Lithwick had destroyed it, had come here because he needed a new place to cannibalize.

"No, the villagers from four different villages did actually chase me out. And I had no power left to fight them, because all my trees were dead."

"Where was this?" Duncan had kept to himself for a long time, but he was surprised the story of a whole forest dying hadn't reached him.

"North of Kassia. In a valley in the Jatan mountains. The Jatan leaders thought it had been ruined by the old Kassian queen's mines, which were in the mountains above. They were partly right. The soil was poisoned by the run-off from the mines, and the trees were struggling. I ended up taking too much from them, and that seemed to tip the balance. The villagers knew I was responsible for killing it off completely."

"So you went to the Speaker of Grimwalt looking for a new forest. Why?"

Lithwick shrugged. "I'd heard rumors from the Jatan soldiers who came through my woods that he was corrupt. I thought he might be interested in my services. I was surprised when he told me about you. About your forest. I thought I was unique."

"He knew about me?" That Duncan hadn't known.

"You were hardly hiding." Lithwick lifted a hand. "But the word was you were a fierce protector of the forest and the Speaker had his eye on logging this place, making some money. I might have been a little too willing to do as he asked in exchange for perma-nent residence here, even if I was going to have to lose parts of it to the Speaker's greed. I should have waited until he proved he could keep you under control, but I did have the run of it for a time, enough to have made it mine."

"You should have waited before you killed the Skäddar villagers?" Duncan asked lightly.

Lithwick disappeared in a flash, but not before Duncan saw his face twist in fury.

"I've paid him back for making me do that." His voice came from behind the citadel. "I made sure the Skäddar Collective saw me start the attack on them and their precious Gathering. They know it was someone from Grimwalt, and they'll blame the Speaker."

"He didn't make you do it." Duncan didn't try to hide his disgust. "Your welcome is rescinded, Lithwick."

He'd reached out for the power he needed as soon as he'd stepped into the forest, but it was so slow in coming. It had to travel so far to get to him, through the blighted wood.

And he would not strike until he had enough to make it count.

"You have no power here, not in this part of the forest," Lithwick laughed. It sounded just like his laughter when he'd first met Duncan.

Without seeing him, Duncan could almost imagine it was the old Lithwick he was hearing.

A skovva suddenly lumbered into the clearing, bigger than Duncan expected.

It threw something at him, and as the projectile brushed past his shoulder, he saw it was the same stick he had thrown at Lithwick earlier.

Then suddenly he was barraged with wood and stones and bark, and despite Ava's protection, tucked into his waistband, some of it hit home.

He danced back, aware of the slow build up of his own power. He forced himself to accept the delay, to give the forest time to send him what he needed.

He refused to take what wasn't offered.

The skovva collapsed, as if Lithwick couldn't hold it any longer. He must have expended too much energy today already. The attack on Luc and Ava, and then the Gathering.

Suddenly, another branch snapped above him, and plunged down.

Duncan stepped to the side and it slammed into the ground beside him. A root shot out of the ground, twisted around Duncan's leg, holding him in place, and then clamped him around the chest.

And squeezed.

Duncan curled his hands around it, tried to take control, keeping his breathing shallow.

But there was no controlling something he could not find.

His probing came up with nothing——a vast emptiness.

He looked up and understood with horror that while the trees that lined this clearing looked alive, they no longer were.

No wonder the strength he needed was taking so long to reach him.

That it was reaching him at all was cause for hope. There was a way to save this.

But first, Lithwick had to go.

The root tried to tighten a little more——Duncan could feel it shiver—— but it didn't clamp down any harder.

Ava. He could think of no other reason.

"Why are you not suffocating?" Lithwick finally stepped out, walking through the debris of the collapsed skovva.

"Because nothing in this forest can truly harm me." He had once thought that, but Lithwick had managed to corrupt part of the place he considered an extension of himself.

Lithwick didn't like that. He stopped, face working, and then he lost his temper, picking up a slim branch that had been dropped when the skovva disintegrated, and running at Duncan, swinging the branch as he went.

There was obviously only so much Ava's spell work could do, Duncan thought, turning so that the branch slammed into his shoulder, not his face.

At least he was still able to draw breath, but he could not move.

He bent down, picked up a stick and lashed out as he straightened, catching Lithwick on the upper arm.

Lithwick danced back, lips thin, and then took hold of his branch two-handed. "You can't go anywhere. How long do you think you'll hold out?"

Duncan shrugged. "As long as it takes."

The power he needed was coming faster now, the pathways open, but it was not the quick, instant flood he was used to.

"Takes to do what?" Lithwick swung the branch again, and Duncan felt his ribs take the brunt.

He took a careful breath, found it difficult. "To kill you."

Lithwick laughed. "Do you see where you are and where I am? Who is going to kill who, do you think?" He swung again, this time at Duncan's head.

Duncan blocked, leaning sideways, and swung his own stick in counter-strike, but it was shorter, and he missed.

"You can't block forever," Lithwick said. He spun, branch in both hands, and this time, Duncan's block wasn't enough.

His arm deflected the hit, but part of the branch still made contact, and pain exploded in his temple.

He saw lights dance in front of his eyes, and had the feeling the only reason he was still upright was because the root was holding him in place.

"It's over now," Lithwick said, and from the corner of his eye Duncan saw him spin again, almost like he was in a dance, arms raised, branch held two-handed.

And then he stumbled.

The shriek of rage that came out of his mouth was inhuman. It reverberated around the clearing, and Lithwick dropped the branch.

An arrow stuck out of his chest.

He pulled it out, screaming again in pain, and threw it down.

"It won't kill me." Lithwick was looking toward the path

Duncan had taken into the clearing, and Duncan forced himself to twist around, to see who was there.

Massi was standing between the trees, bow drawn with another arrow.

She let it loose and it hit Lithwick in the neck this time.

He gurgled, yanking it out, and Duncan saw dark, viscous fluid pour out, slow and sluggish, before the wound closed up.

"How many arrows have you got, archer?" Lithwick's voice was raw.

"Enough." She moved into the clearing, and shot again.

She was giving him time.

Duncan hung from the waist, letting Lithwick think he was barely conscious, and sipped up power.

He had until Massi ran out of arrows. She was forcing Lithwick to keep healing himself, but the moment she stopped shooting, he'd attack her.

And no matter how much strength he had when that happened, his hand would be forced.

Because he would not let Lithwick so much as touch her.

Not a hair on her head.

CHAPTER 36

S he had reached him just in time.

Massi had fought for another few minutes after Duncan had gone after Lithwick, working to protect Luc's back, and then she'd followed, using the pine cone scale to lead the way.

Taking in the scene now, she was sorry she hadn't left the fight at the Gathering sooner.

She stepped to her right, keeping the horror that was Lithwick in sight, forcing herself to keep her focus where it was needed, rather than check Duncan was all right.

She thought she'd glimpsed him turning her way, before he seemed to collapse.

He might be pretending to be more seriously hurt than he was. And that meant he was buying time.

She had seen him gather strength from the forest before. If that's what he was doing now, then she would give him as long as she could.

If not, she would face the consequences when they came.

She shot Lithwick again, in the gut this time.

He grabbed the arrow and pulled it out with a shriek that hurt her ears.

"Who are you?" he shouted.

"The person shooting you." She shot him again, aware her quiver was getting lighter and lighter.

Another six arrows, and then she was out.

She followed him, moving as he moved, always keeping him directly in front of her, forcing all his focus on her, on healing the wounds she was inflicting.

She shot him again and in a temper, he threw the arrow back at her.

She caught it, laughed, and notched it back into her bow.

"Thank you."

He screamed as the arrow pierced him a second time, where his right arm joined his shoulder.

This time, when he pulled it out, he snapped it in two.

But she was already shooting him again, aiming for his eye, and she didn't miss.

This time, his shriek of rage and pain caused birds to lift off in flight.

He pulled the arrow out, and the dark fluid that seeped out dried almost immediately on his cheekbone, filling in the hole in his eye as if it had never been pierced.

She shook off the weirdness of it, shot again, and her hand reached back to notch one of the three remaining arrows.

"You are running out of time," he hissed.

Massi refused to look over at Duncan, refused to remind Lithwick he was there. "Your time is already up," she said. "The Speaker is gone. Your deal is finished."

He faltered, surprised. "Gone?"

"Locked away." Massi shot him in the neck again, and he pulled it out without a sound this time, as if he'd mastered his fury at her attack.

Two more arrows to go.

She pulled them both out together, shot them one straight after the other, and while he was busy with them, darted forward to scoop up an earlier arrow he'd thrown to the ground.

She notched it.

He stood with an arrow in each hand, knuckles white.

"That's your last one." He cracked the arrows one-handed, threw them down. Slapped his chest. "Go on. Last time. Then it's your turn."

She took a step back, as if intimidated, and she saw he liked that. He moved forward after her, eager, and she shifted a little more, so that he stood with his back to Duncan.

"Finally worked out you're in trouble?" he jeered.

"No." She shot him a final time. Took the tiniest of moments to glance over his shoulder as he yanked the arrow from where his heart should have been.

Duncan was motioning for her to run.

She stood her ground. Lithwick would only turn back to Duncan if she did.

"Now it's my turn," he said, and when he smiled, she felt her stomach heave.

He no longer had teeth. She didn't care to guess what she'd seen in his mouth instead.

"I think it's mine," Duncan called, and as if suddenly remembering him, Lithwick spun to face him.

Massi looked around wildly as soon as his back was turned, found a stone, and hurled it at Lithwick's head.

He staggered to the side as it hit him, thrusting his hand backward, and a root ripped out of the ground and grabbed her, held her in place.

"I'll deal with you in a moment," he said, glancing back over his shoulder.

Then with a roar, he ran at Duncan, scooping up the branch he'd dropped, lifting it over his head as he ran, ready to hammer it down.

The ground grumbled and shuddered as he crossed the clearing, and Massi reached out to steady herself against the closest tree.

Suddenly, the center of the open space collapsed, taking the tree home Lithwick had built to mirror Duncan's, and both men, with it.

Dust and soil boiled up, creating a brown fog over the hole, and Massi glimpsed roots criss-crossing just below the surface.

Duncan was down there.

She struggled against the root, but while it had stopped tightening around her, it didn't let her go, either.

With a grimace, she pulled her knife from its sheath, and began to hack.

DUNCAN CARVED OUT A SPACE IN THE SINKHOLE FOR THE confrontation with such ease, he worried he was using too much power.

But he didn't feel a pull on his strength.

Lithwick rolled to his feet and stood as if stunned, looking at him with those fathomless eyes.

"The archer was buying you time," he said, in sudden revelation. "You know her."

"I do." Duncan smiled. He understood Lithwick's amazement. Massi *was* amazing.

"Who is she?"

"Fate's arrow," he said. "Inevitable. Unstoppable."

Lithwick blinked. The roots he had been coaxing out of the ground around them slithered toward Duncan, slowed, and then withered.

Lithwick stared down at them in surprise.

Green vines——thin, elastic——exploded from the sides of the hole and spun Lithwick into a cocoon, tightly bound as any spider's prey.

But they died, too, withering to gray, limp stems, and Lithwick shook himself loose.

Duncan walked forward. "It took some time to draw the full power of my domain to me, but the forest's inclination is for growth, not decay and death. It will always choose me over you, even if I hadn't been its friend for years before you came here."

Lithwick stood, head bowed, communing with the forest, and Duncan stopped, allowing him to hear it.

His head snapped up, strange eyes gleaming. "It rejects me."

He leaped up, grabbing roots and rocks on the walls of the hole, and stood above Duncan, looking down. "But if you are dead, it will turn to me."

He bent down, and when he straightened, he had a rock in his hand. "You can't recover from rock."

Duncan shook his head. "I agonized over how to deal with you. Tried to consider every way to not kill you but still keep you from destroying everything around you."

In answer, Lithwick heaved the rock at him and he dodged it, jumped up high himself, and at the top of his leap, threw the stone he'd had in his hand since he'd wrapped Lithwick in vines.

It hit Lithwick in the head, and he crumpled to the ground just as a flaming arrow struck him in the back.

He went up like dried wood, burning quick and hot.

Duncan pulled himself out of the hole and looked over at Massi, slowly lowering her bow.

She moved forward with a limp, favoring her right leg.

"I think I'd killed him, anyway," he said.

"Never hurts to be sure," she said. She studied Lithwick's body, which looked like a burned out log. "He was going to kill you."

"And this whole forest, in the end," Duncan agreed.

Massi sighed. Held out her hand. "Let's see if Luc's got the attack on the Gathering under control, shall we?"

It would have died with Lithwick, Duncan guessed. He just hoped too many hadn't died with him.

CHAPTER 37

"I never knew you were a healer." Tuva crouched beside Ava as she stitched closed a deep gash on one of the Skäddar warrior's legs. "What are you chanting under your breath?"

Ava looked up, trying to hide her annoyance. "I'm not a trained healer, but I am good with a needle. So I help when wounds need stitching."

"Hmm." The head of the Collective rocked back on her heels.

"What is going to happen to the man who was passing information to the Grimwaldians?" Ava asked, deliberately choosing to change the conversation to a topic Tuva would not like.

Tuva scowled. "Death." She glanced back at the main tent. "Same for Jens, his leader. The Furla live in the part of Skäddar that has the least natural resources. They wanted rights to the trade route that serviced Jatan and Grimwalt, which is where the village that was attacked was located, but it fell under the Huyst's control.

"I should have understood how deep the bad feeling went, how abandoned the Furla felt, but I also cannot forgive what they did in response."

"If it's any consolation, it didn't seem as if they understood the villagers would be killed. It was a shock to them when they were."

Tuva sighed. "It makes it even harder to deal with them. The trial will have to be public. Everyone needs to understand what happened, including what happened here. They're partly responsible for this attack, too. And we lost twelve people."

"What about Taggar? Will you use him in the trial?"

The Speaker's thug sat, trussed up and under watch, close to one of the fire pits. He hadn't got far with his hands tied behind his back, and the Skäddar wanted him to testify about the pact between Jens and the Speaker.

"We will. I'll contact the Grimwaldian Council when we get home and let them know we have him. If they need him for their own pursuit of justice, we'll hand him over when we're done."

Ava didn't want to be so crass as to bring up the implications for the alliance, so she turned back to the work at hand, finishing off the stitching on the wound, and then lifting a blanket over the unconscious warrior's form.

She straightened, arching her stiff back, and looked around for anyone else in need of her help.

The soldier she'd just stitched up seemed to be the last.

"Is he safe?" Tuva asked, straightening up beside her and nodding to Duncan, who was sitting beside Massi, drying himself out by the fire. Luc and Dak sat with them, and Massi was drying her hair with a towel, her boots off and close to the flames.

"He is safe in the sense that he has no wish to harm anyone. The forest stretches on both sides of the valley, and he is the master of the forest. My understanding is he is as much a part of the Skäddar side as the Grimwalt side."

Tuva stared at her. "We have never seen him. We didn't know about him before."

"Now you do." Ava shrugged. "He can command the forest, Tuva. Is he dangerous? Yes, to those who threaten his trees. Is he a good ally to have? Also, yes."

Tuva shook her head. "I thought the garanda was a myth, and here I am, looking at one."

"I would put that thinking away," Ava advised. "He is himself.

You risk confusing the myth with the man. And he is very real. Learn what he is or isn't from him. Not by using a mythical creature as your way of describing him."

As she said it, Massi made a joke, and leaned over to sling an arm around Duncan, and he tilted his body toward her, rested his cheek on the top of her head.

Tuva sighed. "Point taken. It seems we have an apology to make to you, calling you up here to be answerable to us, when it was our own internal problems that caused our troubles. I see no reason why our alliance can't be honored. We'll abide by the terms."

"It is never a waste to meet allies face to face," Ava said, and meant it. "I would have liked to meet you, anyway, and I'm only sorry its under such sorry circumstances."

Tuva gave a low chuckle. "You are a good queen, Ava Yngstra. A very good representative of your people."

Ava didn't tell her she hoped to shed that responsibility in time. The days of her believing she could hand the running of Kassia over to a representative council in a few months were over.

The handover would take time, and it would need to be done thoughtfully.

She would not risk Kassia going backward and undoing everything Luc had worked for for so long.

"We'll leave first thing in the morning," Ava said. "You've got enough to deal with, and we should get home. I think Grimwalt may well have had a change of Speaker, and I'll need to be ready to start talks with the new leaders."

"I'll have to send someone to Taunen, as well. Will you let Grimwalt join our alliance?"

"That's a decision for all of us to make. But personally, I think it will make us stronger."

Tuva gave a slow nod. "I'll need to consult the Collective, but I agree. We will be in touch."

They said their goodbyes, and Ava moved over to join the others by the fire.

"That was a long conversation," Luc said, making room for her beside him.

"I let her know we'll pack up and go early tomorrow. I don't think they need us underfoot after everything that's happened today, and I know General Ru is probably counting the hours until our return."

Luc relaxed, and Ava realized he was done here, too.

It was time to go home.

EPILOGUE

The unit had begun to pack up, ready to go first thing tomorrow, and Massi realized she was nervous.

Now was the time to speak, or let her dream slip away.

She took Duncan's hand, led him toward the river bank, giving them a little distance from the Skäddar and the curious eyes of her own people.

"Your things are in my house," Duncan said to her. "Will you come with me to get them?"

She pursed her lips. "I wondered if you would be happy for me to stay a little while."

"Stay?" He took her other hand, his grip tightening.

"I have no reason to, other than I like being with you. I like your forest, and I like the calm I feel." She forced herself to meet his gaze.

"I was about to beg you to return as soon as possible." Duncan's voice was quiet. Deep. "I didn't want you to go but I thought you might be obligated . . ."

"I've earned the right to some peace," she said.

"And you find peace with me?" He lifted a hand, gently cupping it over her cheek, sliding his fingers into her hair.

"I find a lot of things with you, Forest Man." She suddenly grinned at him. "Peace is only one of them."

"How long will I have you?" he asked.

She lifted her shoulders. "Luc knows where to find me. I'm sure I'll have to get involved again eventually, maybe run interference in Taunen. But not for a while."

"Say your goodbyes, then." He stepped back, and there was a coiled energy about him, as if he was drawing power.

She put her fingers to her mouth, gave a whistle, and the Rising Wave soldiers turned toward her from the hill above.

She waved an arm in goodbye, and then glanced at Duncan. "Done."

A spiral of roots burst out of the bank at their feet, twisting and weaving themselves into a bridge that arched delicately over the river.

Duncan stepped onto it, took her hand, and with a smile, she walked over with him.

As they touched down on the other side, the roots withdrew, unwinding and disappearing into the dark earth of the river bank.

She turned back, saw the slack faces of both the Skäddar and the Rising Wave soldiers who'd stopped to watch.

She caught sight of Ava, and the queen of Kassia lifted her hand to her lips and blew Massi a kiss. Luc stood beside her and his fist came up to tap his chest.

Massi tapped hers in return, and then Duncan scooped her up and with a laugh of joy, she was being carried through the forest ——silent and fast and free.

The fourth and final book in the Rising Wave series will be out early in 2024. The story will center on Melodie, the little girl

Ava befriended in The Threadbare Queen, now all grown up, and navigating the world of the Rising Wave fifteen years on from when Fate's Arrow ends. To get notification of when the new book is released, as well as have access to exclusive, subscriber-only content, sign up for Michelle's New Release Notification List at michellediener.com.

ALSO BY MICHELLE DIENER

FANTASY NOVELS BY MICHELLE DIENER

The Rising Wave series:

The Rising Wave (Prequel novella to THE TURNCOAT KING)

The Turncoat King

The Threadbare Queen

Fate's Arrow

Mistress of the Wind

The Dark Forest series:

The Golden Apple

The Silver Pear

SCIENCE FICTION NOVELS

Verdant String series:

Interference & Insurgency Box Set

Breakaway

Breakeven

Trailblazer

High Flyer

Wave Rider

Peace Maker

Sky Raiders series:

Intended (Short Story Prequel Available Free to Newsletter Subscribers)

Sky Raiders

Calling the Change

Shadow Warrior

Class 5 series:

Dark Horse

Dark Deeds

Dark Minds

Dark Matters

Dark Ambitions: A Class 5 Novella

Dark Class

Dark Class Epilogue: Free on newsletter signup

HISTORICAL FICTION NOVELS

Regency London series:

The Emperor's Conspiracy

Banquet of Lies

A Dangerous Madness

Other historical novels:

Daughter of the Sky

SHORT PARANORMAL FICTION

Breaking Out: Part I (Short story)

Breaking Out: Part II (Novella)

To receive notification when a new book is released, as well as get exclusive, subscriber-only content, sign up at michellediener.com.

ABOUT THE AUTHOR

Michelle Diener is an award winning author of historical fiction, science fiction and fantasy.

Michelle was born in London and currently lives in Australia with her husband and children.

You can contact Michelle through her website or sign up to receive notification when she has a new book out on her New Release Notification page.

Connect with Michelle
www.michellediener.com

ACKNOWLEDGMENTS

A huge thank you to Claire and Jo, who help me make my stories the best they can be. Thank you to Megan D., Michelle C., Tania H., Barbara E., James McR., Christine B., Lynn S., Traci, B. & Jess W. from my reader team for their eagle eyes. Thank you also to Creative Paramita for the amazing cover.